ROKKA:
Braves of the Six Flowers

2

ISHIO YAMAGATA

ILLUSTRATION BY
MIYAGI

ROKKA: Braves of the Six Flowers 2

ISHIO YAMAGATA

Translation by Jennifer Ward
Cover art by Miyagi

This book is a work of fiction. Names, characters, places, and incidents are the product of the author's imagination or are used fictitiously. Any resemblance to actual events, locales, or persons, living or dead, is coincidental.

ROKKA NO YUSHA
© 2011 by Ishio Yamagata, Miyagi
All rights reserved. First published in Japan in 2011 by SHUEISHA, Inc.
English translation rights arranged with SHUEISHA, Inc.
through Tuttle-Mori Agency, Inc., Tokyo.

English translation © 2017 by Yen Press, LLC

Yen On
1290 Avenue of the Americas
New York, NY 10104

Visit us at yenpress.com
facebook.com/yenpress
twitter.com/yenpress
yenpress.tumblr.com
instagram.com/yenpress

First Yen On Edition: August 2017

Yen On is an imprint of Yen Press, LLC.
The Yen On name and logo are trademarks of Yen Press, LLC.

The publisher is not responsible for websites (or their content) that are not owned by the publisher.

Library of Congress Cataloging-in-Publication Data
Names: Yamagata, Ishio, author. | Miyagi, illustrator. | Ward, Jennifer (Jennifer J.), translator.
Title: Rokka : braves of the six flowers / Ishio Yamagata ; illustration by Miyagi ;
translation by Jennifer Ward.
Description: First Yen On edition. | New York, NY : Yen On, 2017—
Identifiers: LCCN 2017000469 | ISBN 9780316501415 (v. 1 : paperback) |
ISBN 9780316556194 (v. 2 : paperback)
Subjects: | CYAC: Heroes—Fiction. | Fantasy. | BISAC: FICTION / Fantasy / General.
Classification: LCC PZ7.1.Y35 Ro 2017 | DDC [Fic]—dc23
LC record available at https://lccn.loc.gov/2017000469

ISBN: 978-0-316-55619-4

10 9 8 7 6 5 4 3 2 1

LSC-C

Printed in the United States of America

ROKKA:
Braves of the Six Flowers

2

Illustration / MIYAGI

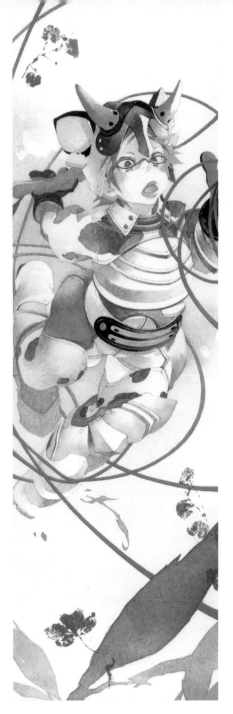

Rolonia

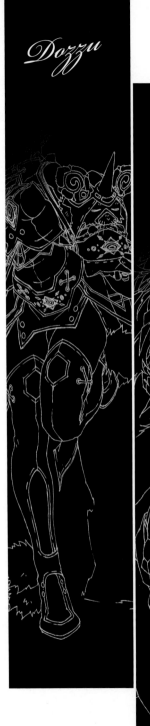

Dozzu

Cargikk

Tgurneu

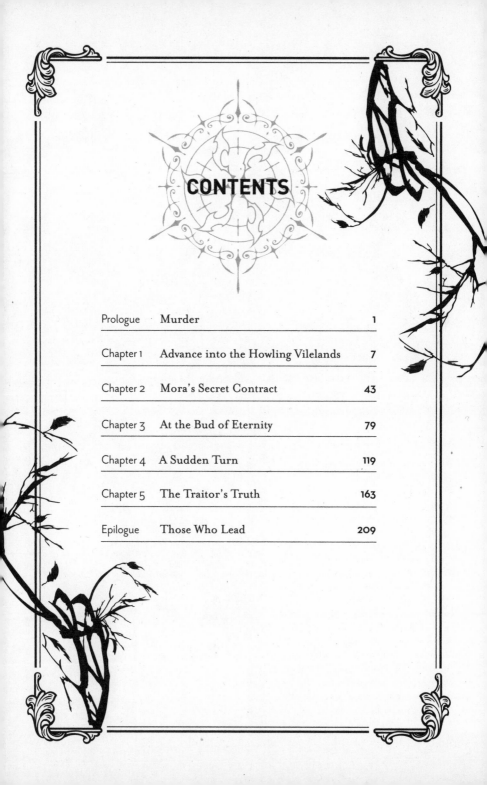

CONTENTS

Adlet

Fremy

THE EVENTS THUS FAR

When the Evil God awakened from the depths of darkness, the Spirit of Fate chose six Braves and bestowed upon them the power to save humanity. The self-proclaimed "strongest man in the world," a boy named Adlet, was chosen as one of these Braves of the Six Flowers and headed out to battle to prevent the resurrection of the Evil God.

But when the Braves gathered to meet at the designated location, they found that, for some reason, there were seven of them. The Braves, realizing that one among them was the enemy, fell prey to suspicion and paranoia. Thanks to Adlet's ingenuity, however, they managed to discover that the seventh was Nashetania. Until a girl named Rolonia showed up...

Mora

Goldof

Nashetania

Chamo

Hans

Prologue
Murder

Adlet sprinted as fast as he could over the parched earth, which was lined with angular rocks, flattening the sparse, withered grass underfoot. He was in the Ravine of Spitten Blood at the eastern edge of the Howling Vilelands, the peninsula that jutted out from the western edge of the continent and where the Evil God and its fiends resided. It was night. He made his way under the moon with only a luminous jewel affixed to his chest-plate to light his path.

"Hurry!" he shouted to the three lights behind him: Fremy, Chamo, and Goldof.

The boy breathed heavily. His heart pounded, his lips trembled, and his feet wouldn't move as he willed them—and not from exhaustion. It was because of the nightmare unfolding before him.

"Hans! Rolonia! Where are you?!" he called.

There was no reply from the darkness.

"Are you dead?! Hans! Rolonia! Answer me!" He leaped onto the rock face before him, wedged his hands and feet into the minute crevices in the wall, and clambered up the cliff in a flash.

As he ascended, he glanced inadvertently at the back of his hand. There, the Crest of the Six Flowers—the proof that he was one of the Braves destined to save the world—glowed faintly.

One of the flower's six petals was missing. One of the Braves was dead.

"Hans!" Adlet kicked off the cliff and sprang up to land at the top of the precipice, drawing his sword and taking a defensive stance. What he saw next, illuminated by the light of his jewel, left him speechless.

Hans Humpty—the strange assassin who fought like a cat, who bore the Crest of the Six Flowers—lay faceup on the ground. The carotid artery in his neck was slashed open, his blood splattered on the dry earth in a grotesque constellation. All color had drained from his face.

"Hans…" The sword began slipping from Adlet's hands. He couldn't believe what he was seeing. Adlet's confidence in Hans's amazing physical abilities and the sharpness of his wits had been absolute.

"You're too late, Adlet." The remark came from a woman who stood a little ways away from Hans. Her back turned, Mora Chester spoke quietly.

"Hans…it couldn't be…," whispered Adlet.

Fremy and Goldof clambered up the cliff after their comrade. The three aimed their weapons at Mora.

"There's no need to explain the situation, I'm sure. I've just killed Hans," Mora said, turning. Her face, chest, and iron-gauntleted hands were drenched in blood. Her armor was cracked open in various places. An ordinary human would already have been dead with such wounds.

"Mora…you…," Adlet began.

"Exactly so. I am the seventh." Dispirited and exhausted, she raised both her hands in the air and then quietly dropped to her knees, weakly hanging her head. No one said a thing after that, and silence alone reigned.

Mora was on her knees. Adlet stood mutely with Fremy, Chamo, and Goldof behind him. The last person among them who bore the Crest of the Six Flowers was sitting by Hans.

"…Rolonia."

Adlet called out to her—Rolonia Manchetta, the Saint of Spilled Blood. Her power was manipulating blood, and she was also the eighth person to have appeared bearing the Crest of the Six Flowers. She had a round face and wore glasses. Her expression was timid, her body petite, and her appearance made no suggestion that she was a powerful warrior. Had she not been wearing a full set of heavy armor and carrying a long whip at her waist, she could have been mistaken for some village girl.

Rolonia's palms, pressed to Hans's chest and throat, glowed faintly.

"Why did Hans lose?" Adlet asked.

The girl did not reply. Her attention was focused only on Hans.

"Answer me, Rolonia! Why is Hans dead? What happened?!"

Adlet realized that Rolonia was muttering to herself. He leaned in to hear the stream of words falling from her lips with every breath. "I won't let you die…I won't let you die…I *will*…save you…"

As the Saint of Spilled Blood, Rolonia could control blood to treat wounds. Adlet decided not to interrupt and instead touched Hans's wrist. He felt no pulse under the cooling skin. *It's no use, Rolonia*, he thought. There was hardly any blood left in the man's body. His heart had stopped. He was already dead.

"What's the meaning of this, Rolonia? Hans is dead, and you're not even scratched," accused Adlet. Why hadn't Rolonia fought Mora, the seventh? And the even greater question was why the traitor hadn't attacked Rolonia while she was defenseless.

Rolonia was desperately intent on trying to save Hans—blind to what was going on around her.

"You were with him. What were you doing?" Fremy asked her.

But the healer wasn't listening to her, either. "I'll save you… I will save you. If I don't…" Only her muttering reached Adlet's ears.

Chamo ambled toward Mora at her usual lazy, seemingly apathetic pace, wearing a carefree smile, as if she wasn't the slightest bit concerned that Hans was gone. "Aw, so the catboy's dead now? That's too bad." Chamo looked down at where Mora knelt and said, "Chamo really liked him. He was cute, and strong, and he talked funny. At first, Chamo hated him after he won that fight, though. But then traveling with him got kinda fun." Chamo clenched a fist and whacked Mora in the face. Mora's head rocked only slightly in response to the tiny blow. "You're not gonna get away with this. You're gonna die. And it won't be pretty!"

Mora averted her eyes from the enraged Chamo. "It matters not to me if you kill me. I am prepared."

"Ohh? So you're all ready, huh, Auntie? That's a big disappointment."

"But first," said Mora, "allow me the time to tell you the truth."

Chamo raised her fist once more, but Fremy grabbed her hand. "Talk, Mora. And make it as brief as possible. Once you're done, you die." Fremy's eyes also radiated quiet anger.

Still hanging her head, Mora began. "This was not my desire. I did not wish to kill Hans. Not him, not anyone."

"What did you say?"

"There was nothing for it but to kill him. Every avenue aside from his murder was closed to me." A single teardrop fell from her eye. "I wanted to protect the world. I wanted to defeat the fiends alongside you, to stop the revival of the Evil God."

"Who could believe that?" spat Chamo.

Adlet disagreed. Mora wasn't lying. He was convinced she was sincere.

"Up until just yesterday—no, up until one hour ago—I had every intention of doing just that."

Chapter 1

Advance into
the Howling
Vilelands

Mora Chester was the Saint of Mountains and the current Elder of the venerable All Heavens Temple, impeccably skilled and well regarded by the Saints. She had a reputation for being both impartial and strict in her governance, with a serious talent for educating the younger Saints. People said that, at this time—the eve of the revival of the Evil God, it was amazingly fortunate for humanity to have a Temple Elder such as her.

So why did Mora kill Hans Humpty? Part of the answer lay in the life she'd led.

Mora had been fortunate in life. Born in the Land of Silver Peaks, the youngest daughter of a wealthy lumber merchant, she had grown up beloved by her parents, her older brother, and their employees. Mora's father had deep connections with the Temple of Mountains, since the Spirit of Mountains was the protector of their family's industry, and it was through those connections that Mora had been initiated into that temple as an acolyte at thirteen.

Life at the temple had been busy and strict, but this did not trouble Mora. She had a serious personality, excelled at her studies, and possessed superior self-discipline compared to other girls her age. When she was nineteen, the previous Saint of Mountains retired, and Mora was chosen from among the acolytes to be the next Saint. As she was the most exceptional of their number, all agreed that she was the correct choice.

Following her selection, Mora's uncommon aptitude blossomed. In just three years, she became one of the most powerful fighters among the Saints. She also proved herself highly capable when it came to managing the temple's territory and other tasks. At the age of twenty-six, she assumed the office of the Elder of the All Heavens Temple. When she accepted the designation from the previous Elder, Leura, three-quarters of the eighty Saints endorsed her.

Mora had just about everything a person could want: favor, renown, status, power, wealth, and the talent to wield all of those resources appropriately. But to Mora, none of that mattered. She had accepted her position as the Elder of the All Heavens Temple simply by virtue of the fact that no one else had been suitably qualified. Her popularity and reputation were unimportant. As for wealth, getting by without struggling was enough for her. Even her great power as the Saint of Mountains was something she could easily cast aside once there was no longer a need for it.

Something else was more important to her.

Roughly three years before the awakening of the Evil God, Mora had attended the Tournament Before the Divine in Piena—the place where Adlet would later cause an uproar.

"Princess!" chided Mora. "How many times must I say this for you to understand?! You may manifest as many blades as you like, but there's no point if none of them hit!"

She was accompanying three young Saints who aspired to be Braves of the Six Flowers and whom she had been called upon to instruct. At the time, Mora considered it her most important duty.

"How about this, then!" said Nashetania, Saint of Blades, summoning her signature weapons from the ground in rapid succession and flinging them unrestrained at Mora. Impressive as the feat might have seemed, she was slow, and her accuracy was lacking.

Mora casually repelled the blades with her gauntlets and slipped under Nashetania's guard to give her a good, hard punch. "You have power in such excess, but you fail to control it! You may defeat weaklings like that, but never more powerful foes. Next!"

"Roger, boss! Today's the day I'm finally gonna beat you up!" The next to challenge Mora was the Saint of Salt, Willone. Her power turned anything she hit into a lump of salt. But even an instant-kill punch was pointless if it failed to connect. Mora dodged her monotonous swings with her upper body alone and swept the girl's legs out from under her at the first sign of an opening. Willone staggered, and Mora slammed her backward with a kick.

"Your attacks are dull and repetitive! And if you don't learn how to fight from a distance, you shall never grow! Next!"

"*Wahhh*, nooo! You're just too strong, Lady Mora!" Liennril, Saint of Fire, hurled flames at her mentor.

But with a mere wave of her hands, Mora dispersed the flames and deflected them back toward Liennril. "Is that your full power? Pray to the Spirit of Fire and strengthen yourself!" Mora was about to say *Next!* when she remembered that she only had three students, and Nashetania of Blades, Willone of Salt, and Liennril of Fire had been defeated. "You all lack discipline. All of you, come at me at once!"

The three struggled to their feet and attacked her. Their training continued until each of them was incapable of moving another muscle.

That evening, after training was over, Mora walked down the hallway of the coliseum that would host the Tournament Before the Divine. The three girls were headed out of the coliseum to the healer's room.

Nashetania's potential is frightening. She will likely surpass me within three years. Willone still has room for growth, too—but Liennril may have hit a plateau. Should I order her to retire and educate a new Saint of Fire, or would it be better to wait until Liennril matures a bit? How can I raise talented warriors and nurture their growth to the point where they are strong enough to defeat the Evil God? These were among the many ruminations swirling in Mora's mind as she walked.

But as she vacated the coliseum and continued through the lavish halls of Piena's royal palace, gradually, thoughts of battle faded from her mind, and she forgot about the looming confrontation with the Evil God.

"I'm home, Shenira. Have you been a good girl today?" Mora opened the door to the guest room in the corner of the palace, and a tottering girl leaped into her arms. In that moment, Mora changed from a warrior burdened with protecting the world to a simple mother. "What kind of games did you play today, Shenira?"

"I played snakes and ladders with Daddy," her daughter replied.

"Snakes and ladders, hmm? I'd love to play that with you, too. Oh, you cute little thing." Mora picked up her beloved only child. *She's gotten rather heavy.* The mother's face relaxed into a smile. "Up we go!" she cried, raising the girl high into the air.

"You're a pampered child indeed, Shenira," came a voice, and as Mora played with her daughter, an older man with strands of white in his hair appeared out of the guest room. "Good grief, Mora, you become an entirely different person when she's around." Ganna Chester was Mora's husband and twenty years her elder.

Saints were not required to be single. Nearly half of the seventy-eight had families, and many of the Saint candidates had lovers or husbands. Mora had married Ganna before inheriting the power of the Saint of Mountains.

"Shenira, your mother is tired. Come." Ganna picked up the child.

"I don't mind at all, not something like this. Come, Shenira, play with Mother," Mora said, stealing her daughter back from Ganna's arms.

As the little girl enjoyed her elevator ride, Ganna watched and shrugged. "Good grief. It's your fault that Shenira is growing up spoiled."

"What are you talking about? What's wrong with a bit of coddling? Come, Shenira, time for the swing!" Mora leaned over and swung her gently from side to side. She felt bad for her husband, but at that moment, she wanted to be with her daughter. Only Shenira could make her forget the weight of her role as Temple Elder.

Mora and Ganna had been married for over ten years. They had thought perhaps they couldn't have children, but just as they were about to give up trying, they had been blessed with a treasure. Shenira had grown soundly, with no illnesses or issues. Mora's daughter was well. Those without children would surely be incapable of imagining how much encouragement and resolve that fact gave the Saint.

Ganna was a good husband. He had no special abilities, and his knowledge and courage were average. But he was faithful and tenderly affectionate. He, instead of Mora, managed the household, occasionally assisting Mora in her role as Temple Elder. Without him, she most likely could not have withstood such exhausting work.

"Mommy, swing me more! Swing me more!"

Mora swung her daughter high, and Shenira shrieked her delight. The looming battle with the Evil God had completely vanished from Mora's mind.

Only one thing was irreplaceable to the Saint of Mountains, and it was not status or power: It was her beloved daughter and husband. They were all that was important to her.

That day had been three years earlier, when the world had yet been at peace.

Adlet Mayer stood in front of the tiny shrine that controlled the Phantasmal Barrier, speechless. Like him, the others were all silent. They stared at the girl, Rolonia Manchetta, before them.

"Um, why are there seven of us?" Rolonia didn't know what was going on, and it showed clearly on her face.

"It can't be. I didn't expect this," muttered Fremy.

"This is impossible. What is the meaning of this? Why is there yet another?" Mora put her head in her hands.

"U-um...another what?" Rolonia regarded Mora and Adlet timidly. Finally, she noticed Adlet was wounded. "Addy, how did you get those injuries? Was there a fight? Hold on, I'll heal you up." Rolonia tried to put her hands on the young man, but he stopped her. This wasn't the time.

Adlet scanned the group. Some were shocked silent, while others regarded Rolonia in exasperation—no two reactions were the same. No expression betrayed one as the seventh, however. "So, everyone, what do you think?" he asked.

Fremy sounded upset. "What do I think? We're back where we started, that's what."

Mora spoke next. "Yet another delay? When will we ever be able to leave this forest?"

Rolonia, unable to grasp what was going on, was simply bewildered. Her head swiveled between Adlet and Mora, then suddenly bowed. "U-um…I-I'm sorry!"

"Rolonia, what are you apologizing for?" asked Mora.

"Um…I think I've caused trouble for you all…because I was late… I'm sorry, I really am!" She dipped her head again and again.

Same as ever, Adlet thought. "It's not your fault. Probably. Raise your head."

Rolonia, cringing still, scanned the group.

"So who's this lady then, *meow*?" queried Hans.

Mora spoke in Rolonia's place. "'It's just as she said herself. This is Rolonia Manchetta, Saint of Spilled Blood. For the past two and a half years, she has lived with me at All Heavens Temple. She may look helpless, but I assure you, she is capable."

"Th-thank you very much." Rolonia conscientiously showed her gratitude for the compliment.

"She looks pretty weak, though." Hans scratched his head.

"*Capable?* No way. Everyone knows Rolonia is a useless dunce," announced Chamo, and Rolonia withered.

"Her strength or lack thereof is irrelevant. The issue is whether she's friend or foe." Fremy already had her finger on the trigger of her gun, and she wore the penetrating gaze of a warrior confronting a new enemy.

"Um…I-I'm sorry. This was my fault, and I do regret my actions, so p-please forgive me!" Rolonia bowed earnestly.

Adlet sighed. "Anyway, you should all introduce yourselves," he said to his bloodthirsty comrades.

Each Brave told Rolonia his or her name and displayed their crests. Rolonia already knew Adlet, Mora, and Chamo. She had not met Goldof before, but they had heard of each other. Fremy didn't mention that she was the daughter of a fiend, or that she was the Brave-killer, giving only her name and status as the Saint of Gunpowder. When Hans introduced himself as an assassin, the timid girl reacted with shock.

Once Rolonia had heard their names and seen their crests, she finally understood what was going on. "Th-there are seven Braves? What is happening here?"

Vexed, Fremy complained, "Must we explain?"

"I'm sorry…"

"One gathered here is an impostor. I think it has to be you." The bloodthirsty aura Fremy was giving off made Rolonia squeak like a mouse, and she shrank away.

Adlet stepped between the two of them. "Wait, Fremy. We don't know that yet."

"You're right, we don't," Fremy replied. "But I can't imagine any other answer. If she's not the seventh, then who do you think it is?"

Adlet didn't know what to say. Still shielding Rolonia, he recalled the group's fight with Nashetania. The seventh couldn't be Fremy. Without her help, Adlet would have died. The same went for Hans and Chamo. They had ultimately pinned down Nashetania. Mora had incited the others to kill Adlet, but he was positive Nashetania had simply deceived her. Goldof had been Nashetania's vassal. Perhaps that *was* cause for suspicion, but as far as Adlet could tell, he had been deceived, too.

"No one else could be the seventh," Fremy asserted firmly. Hans and Chamo seemed to agree.

"Wait," said Adlet. "Something doesn't add up. If Rolonia is the seventh, then why didn't she arrive with Nashetania? What would be the point in leaving Nashetania by herself?"

"Nashetania? It couldn't be—did something happen to the princess?" asked Rolonia. Unfortunately, there was no time to explain.

"Meowbe the plan was fer them to come together," suggested Hans, "but then somethin' happened, and they couldn't meet up."

"Something happened? Like what?" asked Adlet.

"Heck if I kneow what the enemy's thinkin'." Smiling, Hans shrugged.

"Adlet, move. You're in danger." Fremy leveled her gun at Rolonia, but Adlet still shielded the newcomer.

"Fremy, holster your weapon. Rolonia is not the seventh," said Mora. Fremy's gaze flicked to her. "As I said previously—I spent considerable time with her at All Heavens Temple. She's incapable of deceit."

"That's what you thought about Nashetania, too," countered Fremy.

"Rolonia did nothing at all suspicious. Neither could she have come in contact with any fiends or their pawns." Mora stepped in Fremy's line of fire. It was as if she was challenging her to shoot.

"Hey, Mora, do you get the position yer in, here? Yer the next meowst suspicious person here after Rolonia," Hans pointed out.

Mora frowned. "Your suspicions are warranted. But I'm quite certain Rolonia is a Brave in truth."

Still protecting Rolonia, Adlet ground his teeth. "Just stop it. This is the same thing all over again."

"Someone here is the enemy. We're not getting anywhere unless we figure this out," snapped Fremy, directing a fierce glare at Adlet.

Then something nearby caught Chamo's attention. "Someone's here," she said. The rhythm of horses' hooves approaching from the direction of the continent heralded the arrival of a cavalry unit all clad in magnificent black armor.

"Are they enemies?" Fremy turned the barrel of her gun to them.

"*Meow*, no. That's the king of Gwenvaella," Hans said. Gwenvaella was the country that neighbored the Howling Vilelands.

"Good Rolonia! Grave news! Are all the Braves of the Six Flowers present?" The cry came from the middle-aged man who rode at the head of the group—he had to be the king of Gwenvaella. He was also the one who had organized the creation of the Phantasmal Barrier. The king and his party of knights approached the temple, immediately dismounted, removed their helmets, and gave their respectful salutations. "Hearing of abnormalities in the Phantasmal Barrier, we, Daultom the Third, king of Gwenvaella, hastened to this temple with our royal guard, and we shall do our utmost to aid your party in your efforts." His manner was stately, maintaining his majesty without forsaking politeness.

No doubt a great ruler, thought Adlet.

"I am Mora Chester, Brave of the Six Flowers and Saint of Mountains.

We are greatly obliged to receive your aid. What is this urgent matter Your Majesty speaks of?" Mora addressed the king as the group's representative.

"We received report that fiends scattered about our nation are converging upon this forest. It is our belief that within a few hours, they will assault this area." A thrill of tension ran through the whole group at the king's report. The number of fiends on the continent was unknown, but probably two thousand at the very least. If all of them were to attack at once, every one of the Braves could very well fall.

We were careless, thought Adlet, grinding his teeth. The original purpose of the Phantasmal Barrier had been to hold back the fiends on the continent. Now that the barrier had been removed, their enemies would come surging back into the Howling Vilelands.

"Maybe we should withdraw for the time being," suggested Fremy.

"Aww, running away is so lame. Chamo's not scared of the seventh."

"B-but…we still don't know who our enemy is. We can't fight fiends like this…," said Rolonia.

"'Tis as Chamo says, Rolonia. There is nothing to be gained from retreat." Mora chided the frightened Rolonia.

"I'd have meowr fun if we just kept goin'," said Hans.

"What do you mean, 'more fun'?" asked Mora.

"Meowr danger means meowr fun, right?" Hans grinned.

The king of Gwenvaella and his retainers were baffled by the group's clashing opinions, and the fact that there were seven only compounded their confusion.

"Going in farther would be dangerous," said Fremy. "I just bet the seventh is preparing their next trap for us." The Braves continued their debate, ignoring the king and his party.

"Who's to say, *meow*? Could be even riskier to back off."

"What do you mean?"

"Meowbe Rolonia guessed we were goin' to retreat and set a trap for us, ya know? Well, that'd be funner, though."

Mora interrupted Hans and Fremy's dispute. "As I said before, Rolonia is *not* our enemy."

"Be quiet, Mora," said Fremy. "Sorry, but I can't really trust you, either."

"Wait. Who could trust *you*, though? Like, you're a fiend," Chamo pointed out, and Fremy let her anger show, albeit slightly.

Adlet raised his voice to rein them in. "Enough! Talking about this is pointless!" All eyes turned toward him. "We can't trust one another. The way things are now, nothing is gonna get settled, no matter how much we talk."

"Then what do you suggest we do, Adlet?" inquired Mora.

"I'll decide everything. All of you, just do what I say, and no complaints." Under normal circumstances, this outrageous suggestion would have invited opposition, but Adlet figured at this point, they had no other choice. "Right now, there's only one among us we can say for sure isn't the seventh: me. So the most rational choice would be follow me, right?"

Hans, Chamo, and Fremy clearly weren't thrilled with the idea. "Meowbe that's the best choice, but I'm still feelin' uneasy about it."

"Did you forget?" asked Adlet. "I'm the strongest man in the world. Don't you trust my judgment?"

"No, I don't."

"Nope."

Fremy and Chamo answered together.

"I believe that, as things stand, we have no other options. Adlet is right. At this rate, we will decide nothing," said Mora. Rolonia gave no opinion, but she didn't seem opposed.

"Well, what can ya do, then? He's an idiot, but he ain't a hopeless idiot," muttered Hans.

"You can trust me a little more than that. I'm the strongest man in the world."

"*Meow*, yeah, yeah," Hans responded off-handedly.

Despite the reluctance, the decision was now Adlet's. To proceed, or to retreat? "Mora, first I want to ask you something. Is there a Saint with an ability that could discover the seventh?"

The one who replied wasn't Mora, but Fremy. "I've heard the name

Marmanna, Saint of Words. They say she has the power to detect lies and make people tell the truth." Such an ability would indeed allow them to root out the seventh.

But Mora shook her head. "No, Marmanna is at All Heavens Temple. Even with the greatest haste, 'twould be a journey of seven days."

That wouldn't work, then. If they used up fourteen days on the round trip, they wouldn't have the time they needed to defeat the Evil God. There was also no guarantee that this Saint was still even safe. They had no choice but to accept their fate. Adlet turned to the king of Gwenvaella and said, "I am Adlet Mayer, the strongest man in the world. Your Majesty, you may not understand what's going on right now, but please don't argue and just do as I say. If you head out right now, how long will it take for you to reactivate the Phantasmal Barrier?"

"We have already prepared the water and rations necessary for a barricade. It can be done immediately."

"Okay," said Adlet, "then in half an hour, activate the barrier. We want you to keep on protecting it until we defeat the Evil God. Can you do that?"

"The barrier is made such that it will automatically dissipate once the Evil God has fallen. Until then, we shall not deactivate it, whatever may come," the king replied.

Adlet nodded and then looked at his companions. "We're heading into the Howling Vilelands. All right?"

Fremy didn't seem happy about it, but she didn't protest. Neither did Rolonia.

"The enemy may have concentrated their forces near the border of the Howling Vilelands," he continued. "Don't let your guard down. Let's go!" On Adlet's command, the seven raced off.

Rolonia ran up to his side. "Addy, grab on to my shoulder."

"I'm okay. I can manage," he insisted.

She rested her hand on his shoulder, and it glowed faintly as Adlet's body heated. "I'll treat you while we run. I'm the Saint of Spilled Blood. I'm good at healing wounds."

"All right. Thanks."

"Addy, what on earth is happening? I don't understand this at all."

Me neither, thought Adlet.

The group cut through the forest and out the other side to follow the coast, finally setting foot on the faintly noxious-smelling earth of the Howling Vilelands. After some time had passed, a giant ball of mist manifested behind them. Now there was no going back, and they would be unable to leave the Howling Vilelands until they defeated the Evil God. But Adlet was fine with that. They couldn't afford to lose this battle. It was better to cut off any path of return.

The Howling Vilelands was a peninsula that stretched up to the northwest, its eastern edge adjacent to the continent. At the pace of a regular human being, it would take about five days to traverse the length of it. The topography of the peninsula was extremely complex, and the full particulars were a mystery. All they knew about the interior was based on records left by the Saint of the Single Flower and the incomplete maps drawn by past Braves. It was said that it was no longer possible to land a boat on the shores of the Howling Vilelands, because the vast coastline was completely encircled by a complex array of shallows and cliffs studded with blades of rock. Over a long period of time, the fiends had turned the entire peninsula into a huge fortress accessible only by land or wing.

The Six Braves' destination was the northwestern tip of the Howling Vilelands, where the Evil God slept. The Saint of the Single Flower had named that land the Weeping Hearth. It would take about thirty days from the Evil God's awakening for it to be fully revived. If the Braves of the Six Flowers failed to reach the Weeping Hearth by then, the world would end.

Half a day had passed since they had embarked into the Howling Vilelands. Adlet was leaning on Rolonia's shoulder to stand. He could feel blood oozing from his stomach—the stab wound he'd gotten from Nashetania had begun hurting again.

"Addy, I'll treat your stomach. Let your muscles relax." Rolonia touched his stomach. Her power to control blood amplified his natural ability to recover. Before long, the bleeding stopped.

Adlet's party was in a ravine on the eastern side of the Howling Vilelands, known as the Ravine of Spitten Blood. Apparently, it was so named because once, when the Saint of the Single Flower had fought the Evil God, she had been so exhausted that she vomited blood in this place.

The party had made it to the ravine without any fights. Encountering none of the ambushes the seven had expected by the coast, they'd arrived in no time at all. They proceeded cautiously through the intricate network of the ravines, alert for danger, and as they readied themselves for attacks from the outside, they probed one another for possible signs of treachery or deceit. Progress was slow, and the landscape was eerily quiet. Fremy sniped a few fiend lookouts, but after that, they saw no signs of their enemies.

Fremy and Mora were currently ahead of the group, scouting. The other five awaited their return.

"Are you okay, Rolonia?" asked Adlet. "You're white as a sheet."

"I'm...o-okay..." Rolonia stuttered.

Earlier, as they'd advanced into the Howling Vilelands, Adlet had brought her up to speed on their battle with Nashetania. At first, Rolonia hadn't believed the story of the princess's betrayal.

He'd also informed her that Fremy was both the daughter of a fiend and the Brave-killer. Face pale, Rolonia had replied that one of the Brave candidates Fremy had killed—Athlay, Saint of Ice—had been an acquaintance of hers.

"I know you have mixed feelings about partnering with Fremy," said Adlet, "But leave that aside for now. There's no point in any further infighting."

"Y-yeah..."

"Adlet." Fremy had returned from her reconnaissance.

"Eeep!" Rolonia shrieked.

Fremy, who'd been about to give her report, was even more startled. "What's wrong, Rolonia?"

"Nothing! Nothing at all. I'm fine." Rolonia was afraid of her—and not just her. She was also terrified of the assassin, Hans; the violent Chamo; and Goldof, who had been Nashetania's retainer. The only ones the girl could manage a proper conversation with were those she'd known for a long time: Adlet and Mora. The boy understood the terror of a traitor in their midst, but Rolonia being too scared would cause problems.

"I couldn't see any fiends. We should be okay for the time being. Mora went on ahead. Let's catch up with her and regroup." Fremy brought him up to speed, then turned away from Adlet. The group picked up the pace after her.

Suddenly, they heard a cry from the top of the ravine, and Rolonia flinched with her whole body. When Adlet raised his head, he saw a deer crossing the valley.

The fauna in the Howling Vilelands was surprisingly populous. The toxin produced by the Evil God had no effect on creatures other than humans. It was also said that fiends only attacked animals for food.

"Aw, a deer! So cute. Chamo's pets are cuter, though." Chamo beamed.

Rolonia was the only one among them who'd been startled. Seeing her jump at a deer made Adlet uneasy. He wondered if she could handle what was ahead of them.

"Hey, cow lady. If you're such a weakling, how can you be a Brave?" Chamo demanded, waving her foxtail back and forth.

"Huh? Um..." Rolonia trailed off.

"Chamo knows all about you. You're a washout Saint. The Spirit choosing you was just some kinda mistake. Nobody'd believe someone like *you* could actually be one of the Braves of the Six Flowers."

"Um..." Rolonia simply hung her head. "I think...maybe...I might actually...not be."

What's she talking about? wondered Adlet.

"This is getting *really* annoying," complained Chamo. "If you're the seventh, come on and fess up already. If you say sorry now, you won't get hurt."

"Hey. Stop it," ordered Adlet.

"When the crest appeared, I just couldn't believe that I was one of the Braves of the Six Flowers... I thought, maybe...I was somehow chosen by mistake."

"Well, there you have it, then," said Chamo.

Just as Adlet prepared to reprimand her, a voice called out ahead of them. "I think Rolonia is strong."

It was Fremy.

"I heard that Mora was so charmed by her talents, she gave her special one-on-one training. The reason I didn't go after Mora was because Rolonia was at All Heavens Temple."

Chamo huffed. "*Hmph.* Then maybe she's sorta strong."

"Th-thank you very much, Fremy," stuttered Rolonia.

"You don't have to thank me. I still suspect you."

"...*Ulp.*" Rolonia winced.

"But that aside, I want to hear more about you. All I know about you is that you're the Saint of Spilled Blood and that you're supposed to be quite powerful."

"Oh, yeah, Rolonia. You should tell her," prompted Adlet.

"I became a Saint two and a half years ago," Rolonia began. "Before that, I was a servant. I was really supposed to have resigned right away, but Lady Mora ordered me to train to be one of the Braves of the Six Flowers. At the All Heavens Temple, Lady Mora and Willone, Saint of Salt, taught me to fight."

"Describe what happened between the Evil God's awakening and when you came to us," Fremy demanded.

"O-okay. Um, when the Evil God awoke and I received the Crest of the Six Flowers, I was in the Temple of Fire, in the Land of Golden Fruit. I was training with Liennril and...oh, Liennril is the Saint of Fire."

"And then?"

"I was supposed to have arrived earlier, but on the way, I met some people who'd been attacked by fiends. They were injured and asked me to help treat them...and I thought, 'But what if I'm late?' But I couldn't say no...and then I actually was late. I'm sorry."

"And when you arrived at the Phantasmal Barrier?" asked Adlet.

"I reached the forest late last night. The barrier had already been activated by then. The king of Gwenvaella was at the fort, and he told me about the barrier. According to His Majesty, some rogue soldiers had commandeered the fort, and the barrier was active for some reason. They had no idea what was going on."

"And then in the morning, the barrier lifted, and you met up with us," Adlet finished.

Rolonia nodded.

"Do any of you think there's anything suspicious about her story?" Adlet asked.

Hans was the one to reply. "Was she *really* at the Temple of Fire?"

"Let's check that with Mora later. I don't think there's any other part of her story that's particularly suspicious," said Adlet.

"True, *meow*."

Then Chamo, who'd been silently listening, interjected. "Hey, Adlet, how do you know her?"

Rolonia looked at Adlet, and their eyes met. He nodded with an expression that said she could tell them. "I met Addy two years ago," she said. "Do you know of Atreau Spiker?"

As Adlet listened to her tale, he remembered the past. At the time, he'd never have dreamed he'd see her again. When they first met, that Rolonia would grow to become one of the Braves of the Six Flowers seemed inconceivable.

When Adlet was ten years old, he'd apprenticed himself to Atreau Spiker, a hermit warrior who lived deep in the mountains. Over the course of eight years, he'd absorbed all of his master's fighting techniques and knowledge, as well as the skills to make every one of Atreau's inventions.

Adlet hadn't been Atreau Spiker's only student. Atreau had taken on a number of hopefuls aspiring to be Braves of the Six Flowers. Every single one of them, unable to handle his eccentric methods, had ultimately left the mountain—all except Adlet. But aside from those students, the master had also received requests to teach combat skills to elite and famous mercenaries, Saints, and others. They would appear with letters of introduction from ministers or mercenary captains and become short-term apprentices to acquire knowledge and new combat techniques. Atreau had lived like a hermit, but he hadn't cut off all contact with the world.

It was just over two years earlier that Rolonia Manchetta had approached Atreau with a letter of introduction in hand. At the time, she had been as cowardly and timid as she was now—no, even more so.

"Adlet."

Adlet had been throwing needles in the mountains day and night when, suddenly, his master came to speak to him. The boy ignored his master, continuing his practice as the man stood next to him. The blisters on his fingers had broken to expose raw, bleeding flesh, but still he kept throwing needles.

"This is Rolonia Manchetta. She's the Saint of Spilled Blood. For the next two months or so, I'll be instructing her on fiend ecology and how to handle them. Do not interfere," explained Atreau, indicating the girl beside him.

Adlet did not greet her or reply. Back then, he'd been different—darker, and hungrier. He cursed everything in the world, his own weakness most of all.

"Tell her your name, at least," prompted Atreau. Rolonia hid in Atreau's shadow, watching Adlet with frightened eyes.

"Adlet Mayer," he said to Rolonia. "Eventually, I'll be the strongest man in the world. But not yet. Don't talk to me."

"O-okay. I'm sorry," she responded.

"Let's go, Rolonia," said Atreau, and the moment he did, Adlet made his move. He hurled a needle at his master and simultaneously pulled out a knife and took a swipe at him.

"Eeek!" Rolonia screamed and sank to the ground beside Atreau.

Atreau flicked aside the needle with one finger and grabbed Adlet by the wrist before flinging him away. The boy didn't pause for an instant, slashing at Atreau's ankles. Right before it connected, the warrior sidestepped and kicked Adlet in the face. Blood spurted from his nose.

"A-are you okay, Adlet?" asked Rolonia.

"I told you not to talk to me." He tried to stand, but his feet got tangled up, and he couldn't move.

"Don't concern yourself with him, Saint of Spilled Blood," said Atreau. "That boy will be gone from here soon enough."

"Um...er...," Rolonia stammered.

"I ordered him to do that. He may also use whatever means he pleases. And if he fails to defeat me by his sixteenth birthday, he is expelled from this mountain. One month remains until he must go."

"*Ugh...*," Adlet moaned.

The warrior stepped on Adlet's face. "Smile."

Adlet tried to move his lips but was no longer capable of smiling. Hunger and powerlessness had stolen that from him.

Atreau spat upon his student where he lay on the ground. "Trash." He left him there and walked away, taking Rolonia with him. Adlet punched the ground and screamed.

Rolonia was living in a guest cottage Atreau had built. It was the only place on that mountain fit for human habitation. Atreau and Adlet lived in a cave, like animals. Atreau was constantly by Rolonia's side, teaching her about fiends and seeing to her meals and necessities. During that time, he ignored Adlet.

Every day Adlet challenged Atreau, and every day he lost. Wounded, fighting back the pain of his injuries by force of will alone, he stood up again and again. Adlet knew his teacher was not a lenient man. If he failed to defeat him in the next month, he really would be out for good. And he still hadn't learned all of Atreau's tricks. If he was kicked out, he'd lose his only means of becoming one of the Braves of the Six Flowers.

A certain fiend constantly lurked in the back of Adlet's mind. A fiend that walked on two legs, three wings growing from its back, with a narrow lizard's face smiling warmly in greeting. The monster that had destroyed his village and taken his sister and best friend away from him. He couldn't forget that creature, not even for an instant. Hatred alone reigned in

Adlet's heart. He couldn't live until he brought the beast down, until he watched his enemy die. No corner of his heart had any room for Rolonia.

One night, having lost to Atreau, as usual, Adlet collapsed in his cave and slept like the dead. He felt something touch his back and leaped away. Rolonia was sitting beside him, holding a lamp. "Why are you in here?!" he yelped.

The girl jumped back into a corner of the cave and began trembling violently. "M-M-Master Atreau told me to treat your wounds..."

"He did?"

"I'm, um, the Saint of Spilled Blood... I can heal wounds."

"...Please." Adlet prostrated himself on the ground.

Rolonia prayed to the Spirit of Spilled Blood, borrowing its power. When she put her hands on him, his wounds closed before his eyes. "Human blood naturally contains the power to heal," she explained. "By amplifying that, I can heal wounds, too."

"The Saints' power really is something," remarked Adlet. Flattered, Rolonia blushed faintly. "Are you training to be a Brave?" he asked.

"Huh?"

"I guess I didn't have to ask. That's what every warrior wants."

Rolonia shook her head. "Um, you might think I'm strange to say something like this, but..."

"What?"

"I'm thinking I'll leave this mountain."

"Did something happen with Atreau?"

"No...um, I think I will give up trying to be a Brave. I think I should also resign from Sainthood."

Adlet was shocked. He lived for the sake of becoming a warrior. He'd thrown away everything for power. To him, letting go of that newfound strength was unthinkable.

"I-I mean," she continued, "there's no way I can...can become one of the Braves of the Six Flowers. And then, if I were chosen by some accident, I'd be a burden to everyone. So that's why I think perhaps I should just resign as the Saint of Spilled Blood..."

"Why are you here? Don't you want to get stronger?"

"I…"

"Explain." Adlet's anger was audible.

Hesitantly, Rolonia related her story. She'd never studied to become a Saint. She'd been a servant at the Temple of Spilled Blood—washed the acolytes' clothes and such. About five months earlier, the previous Saint of Spilled Blood had retired, and they'd held the ceremony to select a successor. The choice hadn't been one of the acolytes taking part in the ceremony, but rather Rolonia, who'd been hanging laundry outside.

"Is that even possible?" marveled Adlet.

"The Spirit chooses the Saint… No one knows what they're thinking."

Rolonia had immediately tried to resign. The previous Saint and the acolytes had all believed that to be the obvious response. But then the order came down from the Temple Elder, who governed all the Saints. Rolonia was to continue as the Saint of Spilled Blood, and furthermore, she was to study combat and train to be a Brave of the Six Flowers. She was also ordered to move to All Heavens Temple to undergo the intensive education necessary to excel as a Saint.

"The Temple Elder says that I'll be a very powerful Saint," said Rolonia, "but that's never going to happen. I've been training for years, but I'm still so weak. I'm just a burden…"

As Adlet listened to her speak, hatred simmered in his chest. "I wish I were a girl," he groused. "If I'd been born a girl, I could've become a Saint."

"Huh?"

"If I were a Saint, I could get stronger. I could get the power to defeat that thing. But I was born a boy." Adlet slammed his fists on the ground. "This is bullshit! Why'd someone like you get that gift? Why you and not me?" He grabbed Rolonia by the collar and shook her. "I want power. I want power! I want the power to defeat that monster! I'll give anything for it—I just wanna be strong enough!" Every day, hacking up blood and bile had made him viscerally aware of the reality that he had no talent. Every night, he cursed his own helplessness as he fell into a dead sleep, in his head repeating, *I want power, I want power.* And the very thing that Adlet yearned for so badly, Rolonia was about to throw away. He deeply resented her for it. "Give it. Give your powers to me."

"I-I…can't do that," she said. "Transferring it to another person is an incredibly difficult technique—"

"Shut up! Just give it to me! Give me your powers!"

"I can't do that. The Temple Elder—even Lady Leura—couldn't do it… Someone like me couldn't possibly—"

"Why not?! Give it to me! Someone, give me power! I wanna be stronger!" Adlet released her, collapsed on the ground, and sobbed.

"I-I'm sorry, I didn't mean to…" Sitting beside him as he wept, Rolonia began crying, too.

Inside that cave, a girl who'd inadvertently been granted power and a boy who couldn't get it wept and wept.

Around daybreak, Adlet apologized to Rolonia. He wasn't the only one in the world who'd had it rough—which was obvious, but he'd forgotten it for a long time. She apologized to Adlet again, too, for having spoken unkindly without consideration for his feelings. After that, the two of them became friends. The connection lasted only a brief two months. It was the kind of relationship that would fade with the passage of time. But still, she was one of the very few friends Adlet had ever made.

"…And that's how we met," Rolonia finished. She had abridged Adlet's past substantially. Privately, Adlet was grateful. Remembering how he'd been back then was both embarrassing and depressing.

"So it was Mora who had you study with Atreau. I didn't know she knew him," mused Adlet.

"I don't think she knew him personally. But he is famous," said Rolonia.

In an odd way, we were already connected, Adlet thought.

"Meow-hee-hee-hee," laughed Hans. "Ya sure got real close in just two months. You act like a chump, but you actually got game, doncha?"

"Shut up," Adlet sniped, shooting Hans down. Fremy regarded the exchange with cold eyes.

That was when Mora returned. "How'd it go, Mora?" asked Adlet.

"There are no fiends to be found. The ravine is utterly deserted."

Adlet wasn't in the least suspicious of her. And there were, in fact, no fiends to be found in the ravine. But he failed to notice what those words obscured.

About ten minutes earlier, Mora had been walking through the ravine alone, alert to her surroundings. The complex terrain of the ravine couldn't conceal a large contingent of fiends, but it was the perfect spot for a small ambush. She pushed forward, an eye out for attacks from behind and above.

"!" That was when it happened. She noticed a fiend atop the cliff—a fairly small one that looked like a monkey. When Mora clenched her fists and adopted a fighting stance, the fiend jumped down to land directly in front of her, then bowed its head in submission, groveling on all fours.

"What?" Mora muttered when she saw its back and the message written upon it in black ink.

A warning for you, Mora: You have no time.

For a moment, she gazed at the submissive fiend. Then she stomped on its back as hard as she could. It was dead in a single strike, just like any other worthless, low-level fiend.

"…" She brought her foot down again and again until the writing was no longer visible. "I have no time? That…can't be…," she muttered. Then, abandoning the fiend's body, she left.

"So you didn't run into any fiends at all? That's actually even scarier," said Adlet.

"The seventh hasn't done anything, either. This kinda feels like a letdown," whined Chamo.

It really was. Adlet had expected to encounter another trap the moment they stepped into the Howling Vilelands—or maybe the seventh to attack at the first the opportunity. But things were too quiet.

"Meowbe it ain't that they're not doin' nothin'—it's that they *can't* do nothin'," speculated Hans.

"What do you mean?" asked Adlet.

"Ever since we set foot in the Howlin' Vilelands, Fremy's been itchin' to kill somethin'. If any of us steps out of line, she's gonna shoot 'em dead right there." Adlet looked at Fremy. She didn't deny it. "I've been feelin' twitchy since we got here," Hans continued. "She's one scary lady." He grinned like he was having a good time.

"Mora, what's up ahead?" asked Adlet.

"About fifteen minutes farther on, I saw a hill," replied Mora. "And beyond that, a mountain. I'm certain that's the mountain where the Bud of Eternity is located."

Adlet compared Mora's report with his mental map. It sounded like they were moving along down the route they'd planned and hadn't gotten lost. If his navigational sense was right, that mountain was where the Saint of the Single Flower had left a relic. It was a barrier known as the Bud of Eternity, an important safe zone. Adlet planned to spend the afternoon resting at the Bud of Eternity before pushing on.

"I have a proposal. The next open area we get to, we should take a break," said Fremy.

"We don't need to yet. I want to get to the mountains right away, and then to the Bud of Eternity," insisted Adlet.

Fremy shook her head. "There's something I want to talk to you about as soon as possible. It'll take a while, and it's important, so I'd like to settle down and take my time."

"What do you want to talk about?"

"Internal fiend politics," Fremy said, and tension ran through the group.

"I seem to remember before, you said the fiends had three commanders," recalled Mora. Adlet had forgotten about that, what with the battle with Nashetania and Rolonia's sudden arrival. But Fremy was right. This was very important.

"Why not discuss it at the Bud of Eternity?" advised Mora. "It's not far from the hill."

"If I were the enemy," Fremy replied, "I would deploy forces near the Bud of Eternity. I doubt we'd be able to talk long there."

"That may be so," Mora agreed. "And we needn't worry about surprise attacks in such an open space. Let's talk once we get to that hill, then."

"Now that that's settled, let's get going," said Adlet.

Hans set off first, and Chamo and Mora followed him. Goldof trailed behind them with a sluggish stride. Just as Adlet prepared to set out, Fremy tugged his sleeve. "What is it?" he asked.

"Can you feel it?"

"Feel what?"

"Someone's here," Fremy said, looking up at the sky.

For a moment, the shadow of the fiend that Adlet would never forget crossed his mind. An ominous smile on its face while soothing the villagers with gentle words, it had destroyed his home. It had taken his sister, his friend, *everything* from him.

"......"

Adlet's heart pounded. Shivers of exhilaration ran down his spine. He hadn't sensed anyone trying to kill them or picked up on any danger. But sweat still beaded his forehead. Something indescribable and irrational put him on edge.

"I feel something," said Fremy. "I don't know where, but *it's* here. I could never forget that presence. It feels like it's slowly coiling around my skin."

Adlet remembered what had happened two nights earlier. Fremy had told him about the fiend that had ordered her birth and about how it was one of three commanders. She'd said that fiend was the very one that had destroyed Adlet's home. His soul was telling him it was close.

"Let's go. As I said before, this talk will take some time," said Fremy.

"Can I just ask one thing?" Adlet paused. "What's its name?"

Fremy looked up at the sky and quietly replied, "......Tgurneu."

"Hey, what do you think is the most powerful force in the world?" As Adlet was learning Tgurneu's name, a particular creature was murmuring,

"If you think it through, *really* think it through, all the way to the end, you know it must be love."

In a certain place, there was a fiend. A fiend with two legs and two arms that stood just over two meters tall. Relatively speaking, it would probably be considered small. Green and tan scales formed a speckled pattern on its torso, and white feathers grew from its limbs. But the skin of its palms was moist, like that of an amphibian. On its back were great black birds' wings, and strangely enough, between them sprouted a single, swan-like wing. Its chest featured a large, amphibian mouth. The bizarre creature looked like a jumbled mix of a number of different animals. Its face was incredibly long and thin, just like that of a lizard. It sat on a tiny wooden chair.

"I don't quite understand," said the other present.

"You don't?" The fiend held a book in its hands. The plain, cloth-bound tome, a collection of plays by a celebrated playwright, was decorated with gold thread. The creature turned a page with a finger. "*Oh, Prince Wiesel, curse them! Curse those beautiful blue eyes! Curse the mother and father who gave them to you, and all of me, as I am reflected in them!*" In the script, a spy had infiltrated the palace in order to poison the king of a hostile nation, only to fall in love with the prince.

"I wonder why the protagonist yells that?" the fiend pondered. "Only moments before, she had been speaking of love. This is nothing more than a string of letters, yet it raises endless mysteries for me. The power of love is fearsome indeed."

"With all due respect, perhaps this is not the time for such pastimes. The Braves of the Six Flowers draw near."

"*Heh-heh-heh*, fair enough. I'll part with this fantastical love story for now and head out to face *true* love." The fiend put the book down and plucked a large fig from the table. "Once, the Evil God lost, due to the Saint of the Single Flower's love." The creature bit into the fig, chewed, and swallowed. "We were defeated twice by the Braves of the Six Flowers, by the power of love that supported them. But for this third battle, I think things will be different. Oh, third generation of the Braves, love will be your downfall."

Rising from the table, the fiend—Tgurneu—looked up and quietly smiled.

*   *   *

Fifteen minutes later, Adlet's party reached the top of the hill. Just as Mora had said, from this spot, they wouldn't have to worry about a surprise attack. Even if enemies did show up, the party could ready a counteroffensive while their attackers were busy climbing the hill. Presently, there was no sign of any fiends in the valley around them or in the sky above.

Adlet breathed a sigh of relief, lowered the iron box from his back, removed his leather armor, and checked his wounds. Between Mora's medicine and Rolonia's treatment, the wounds were mostly closed. By nightfall, he would probably be fully recovered.

"Ya kneow, we ain't even done nothin', but I'm still beat," said Hans.

Adlet felt the same. It wasn't just the anticipation of an attack that set him on edge. Various anxieties weighed on him.

The fiends had yet to show themselves, and the seventh wasn't revealing his or her identity, but it was more than that. Fremy was emitting a dangerously bloodthirsty aura, Chamo could go out of control at any time, Rolonia was endlessly confused and scared—his own allies gave him plenty to be uneasy about. And most of all, Adlet was worried about a particular member of the group.

"Are you okay, Goldof?" he asked the other man. Goldof didn't answer. He just sat there, eyes hollow, lips pressed in a thin line, his expression stiff. The knight hadn't said a single word, neither when Rolonia had appeared, nor as they made their way through the Howling Vilelands. All he did was watch the sky as if his mind was elsewhere.

It was understandable. The princess he loved had betrayed him—not only ridiculing, but discarded him. It wasn't difficult to surmise how he must have felt. And not even a day had passed since the revelation of her treachery, so it would be unreasonable to simply tell him to get over it. Though Goldof was a lauded, gifted knight, he was still just sixteen years old.

"Goldof, maybe it's pointless to tell you this, but c'mon, snap out of it," said Adlet. Of course Goldof didn't reply. It was like he hadn't even heard.

"Just go on and forget about her," said Hans. "Just think ameowt what it'll be like once we get back. You can just sit on your handsome, blue-blooded ass, and the ladies'll flock right to ya."

Goldof didn't even react.

"You were that in love with Nashetania?"

"Probably 'cause she had a pretty face, personality aside. And from the glimpse I got, her rack is pretty *meeeow*, too."

"...I don't think that's the issue here." Adlet sighed, then quietly pulled a needle from a pouch at his waist. Without making a sound, he threw it at Goldof's face.

"!" Goldof grabbed the projectile between two fingers and hurled it back at Adlet. Still looking at the ground, he hadn't so much as glanced up.

"Looks like even with a broken heart, he hasn't lost the strength to fight. He's quite the guy." Adlet smiled, but Goldof was still expressionless.

Then Mora beckoned to Adlet. He approached to hear what she had to say. "Adlet," she began, "the seventh is most likely Goldof. Should we not do something?"

"I'm suspicious of him, but we don't know for sure."

"At this point, I cannot imagine it could be anyone but. It's not me, not Rolonia, not you. Hans and Chamo brought down Nashetania, so it couldn't be them. If Fremy were the seventh, there would be no reason for her to have saved you. There is no possibility other than Goldof."

"Mora, stop it," Adlet insisted quietly, but firmly. "Right now, what I'm scared of most isn't the seventh. It's falsely accusing an innocent ally. Don't make these accusations when you're just guessing."

"Bu—"

"May I? I'd like to talk." Fremy interrupted the exchange.

"Don't worry. I'll find the seventh. You just relax and wait for it. I'm the strongest man in the world," Adlet assured her, smiling.

"I'm apprehensive, but...all right. I did decide to trust you." Mora acquiesced.

"Good. Just keep your mouth shut and follow me."

The group circled Fremy and sat down. They were all on the ready for a surprise attack, weapons in their hands. For perhaps the first time in history, humans would hear about the fiends' internal affairs. They'd been unable to even investigate for a very long time, much less actually acquire information. Fremy could turn out to be the Braves' greatest advantage. Knowing their enemy would significantly impact the tides of the battle.

"Like I've said a few times now, the fiends operate under three commanders. Their names are Cargikk, Tgurneu, and Dozzu," Fremy commenced quietly. Her manner was matter-of-fact. "About seventy percent of all fiends are lower life-forms, their intellect on par with animals'. Most of the other thirty percent have some degree of intelligence, but no complex feelings, and all they can think about is killing humans. But these three are different. They possess will, feelings, ideology, and aesthetic sense. They're also strong enough to control all the other fiends. Every one of them aside from myself has sworn absolute allegiance to one of these three. They're so loyal that if one of these commanders ordered it, they would not hesitate to give their own lives."

"How strong are they?" asked Adlet.

"I can't be certain. But don't think you would have a chance against any of them one-on-one." The prospect of three enemies they could never defeat alone. The Six Braves now had a good idea of just how disadvantaged they were. "But if we can defeat these three, we've basically won. There are no others capable of leading the fiends. Without their command structure, they would turn into a disorderly mob. We could pick them off one by one until they're gone, or we could just ignore them all and head for the Weeping Hearth. Whatever we want."

"I see."

"But the most important part is this—the three of them do not cooperate. In fact, I'd even go so far as to say that they're intensely antagonistic toward one another." This information about fiend affairs was startling. Before Adlet could make any sound of acknowledgment, Fremy continued. "Supposedly, the most powerful one is Cargikk. He looks like a lion and manipulates poison flames—he can easily roast a human, and the smoke from his flames contains a powerful toxin. He's an opponent to be feared."

"Who's stronger, Chamo or Cargikk?" probed Chamo.

"I don't know. I don't stand a chance with either of you," replied

Fremy. "Cargikk commands about sixty percent of all fiends. The majority are concentrated around the Weeping Hearth, where the Evil God sleeps, in position for a counterattack. I doubt Cargikk will move from that position. I think he plans to focus on defense."

"That's the type that'll give us the most trouble," observed Adlet. It was a simple tactic, but the most effective. Since the Braves of the Six Flowers were vastly outnumbered, they'd want to scatter the blockade somehow.

"Next…Tgurneu. It's a little difficult to talk about him." Fremy, who had been speaking dispassionately thus far, suddenly faltered. The mention of the name sent Adlet's heart pounding. "Up until six months ago, Tgurneu was the most important thing in the world to me."

"And now?" asked Mora.

"…The thing I hate most. Let me continue. Tgurneu commands around forty percent of the fiends. He's the one responsible for my creation and the one who ordered me to kill potential Braves." There was something that bothered Adlet, but he kept silent and let Fremy speak. "Tgurneu is a mixed-type fiend. He gained his powers through fusing with numerous different fiends. His combat style is simple—he crushes his enemies with overwhelming physical strength, speed, and resilience. It's safe to assume there is nothing he can't smash with his fists. But what's even more terrifying about him is his ingenuity."

"What do you mean?" pressed Adlet.

"My existence was just a tiny part of his plan. Frankly speaking, I can't even guess at the full scope of his machinations. I'm positive Tgurneu was the one who sent both Nashetania and our current seventh Brave."

"So the princess of a nation fell into the clutches of the fiends… I still cannot believe it," Mora murmured.

"It's absolutely probable," said Fremy. "Tgurneu had influence in the human world all the way back when I was born. The fiends who gather intelligence and do his bidding have skills related to shape-shifting, espionage, and hypnosis. I don't know just how far his reach into the human world extends, but he did easily determine things he could not have known unless he had penetrated to the center of a nation."

"..."

"Tgurneu was the one who made and raised me. On his orders, I gained my powers and killed Brave candidates. I respected him deeply, but at the same time, I also feared him. He seemed warm, but at times, cold. I could never see deeply into him, never understand him." Then Fremy seemed to realize the phrasing she'd been using. "No...I could never understand *it*," she quickly corrected herself.

"Goodness," Tgurneu muttered from a certain location as Fremy explained. "So that was what you thought of me, Fremy? You can't understand me? That's rather a sad way to put it. Even after I spoiled you rotten." The fiend chuckled.

The half-fiend continued. "Cargikk and Tgurneu are hostile toward each other. And just as their masters are divided, those under their command are also split. When Tgurneu's underlings and Cargikk's run into one another, they don't talk. Their rivalry is so intense that even lower-tier fiends incapable of speech of different factions will bare their fangs at one another and make threatening displays."

"Why, *meow*?" asked Hans.

"A number of reasons. Tgurneu is a schemer, while Cargikk prefers to fight head-to-head. So their philosophies have always been in conflict. But the greatest divide between them is their approach to humans. According to Tgurneu's ideology, humans are to be used. But Cargikk has an intense hatred of and deep contempt for them. It believes any involvement with humans is unclean. I heard that when Tgurneu came up with the plan to arrange my birth, they were one step away from killing each other. Cargikk apparently said it would not allow the intermingling of human blood with the proud blood of fiends."

"Hold on a second, please." Rolonia, who had been listening silently, raised her hand. "Um, so these commanders who lead the fiends...weren't there three?"

That was the thing that had been bothering Adlet. Fremy hadn't mentioned the other fiend at all. She'd said Cargikk led sixty percent of all fiends and that forty percent were under Tgurneu's command. So what did the third do?

"The third one...," Fremy began. "I don't know much about Dozzu. I've only heard that such a fiend exists."

"Who is this Dozzu?" asked Adlet.

"A traitor. They say that its powers are on par with those of Tgurneu and Cargikk. From what I've heard, two hundred years ago, Dozzu betrayed the Evil God and disappeared from the Howling Vilelands. I have no idea where it is or what it's doing. Maybe Tgurneu knew, but I wasn't told anything."

"Friend or foe?" inquired Mora.

"I don't know that, either. In any case, Tgurneu and Cargikk see Dozzu and its followers as enemies. And they say that some among both Tgurneu and Cargikk's factions have sworn loyalty to Dozzu. I personally know of two fiends that were suspected of belonging to Dozzu's faction and were purged for it."

"*Mya-meow*. Factions and purges! This is some pretty nasty stuff," Hans grumbled.

"Fremy, can you tell by looking which fiends are Cargikk's and which are Tgurneu's?" asked Adlet.

"To a degree. Like the fiends I ran into in the village where I first met you—those were probably Cargikk's. The one that tricked you in the Phantasmal Barrier and the one that ate Leura, Saint of Sun—those were Tgurneu's," she explained.

"So the princess is being controlled by Tgurneu, after all," mused Mora.

"It's very likely."

Fremy having finished the bulk of her explanation, the conversation paused for a moment.

"Then our concern is how to conquer them. We should see Tgurneu in particular as the most dangerous," Mora said, starting the discussion anew.

"I think Cargikk will be on the defensive, but Tgurneu will attack us. I don't know what kind of assault to expect, though," said Fremy.

"I think it's unlikely that Tgurneu will come attack in person," said Adlet.

"I agree. If their general went down, forty percent of the fiends would have their command structure collapse. I think some of them would submit themselves to Cargikk, but not many. It would be a massive blow. I doubt Tgurneu would risk that."

"I have one question," said Mora. "You said their command structure would collapse—but what specifically would happen were their commander to die?"

"The fiends and their masters are connected by invisible bonds. If Tgurneu dies, all of its fiends would know within moments. There would be immediate mass confusion. I think it would be total panic."

"Would you know, too, if Tgurneu fell?"

"...Probably," admitted Fremy, her eyes downcast.

"I see... Hmm. Tgurneu..." Mora trailed off.

Adlet noticed Mora seemed oddly concerned about Tgurneu—even though, unlike Fremy, she had no personal connection with the fiend.

"I bet it'll use the seventh to set a trap for us, *meow*," Hans said. He switched the topic so quickly that Adlet forgot about his doubts.

"Probably. The question is, what will they do?"

Chamo raised her hand. "Ohh, ohh! Chamo has an idea! How about this?"

"Nothing good, I'm sure," Fremy predicted coldly.

But Chamo ignored her. "Humans can't breathe in the Howling Vilelands unless they have the Crest of the Six Flowers, right?" The Crest nullified the toxin of the Howling Vilelands. This was common knowledge. "There are six humans here, and all of us can breathe properly, right? In other words, maybe that means that all six humans here have real crests. That means that the seventh is Fremy, since she's a fiend."

"I knew it. Nothing good." Fremy sighed. "It's possible for humans with no crest to survive within the Howling Vilelands. Some fiends of Tgurneu's faction can spawn a special parasite. If it enters a human body, it will nullify the toxin of the Howling Vilelands."

"Can you prove that?" demanded Chamo.

"In the central region of the Howling Vilelands, there's a place called the Plain of Cropped Ears. Human slaves live there." Saying that, Fremy glanced at Adlet. "Tgurneu has collected them. I don't know to what end, though. Adlet, the people of your village are probably there."

Without even thinking, Adlet stood. He recalled his vanished hometown and all the people who'd been taken away. "Those slaves...what's happening with them?"

"I don't know. I've never been there."

"You didn't hear anything? Anything at all?" Adlet pressed.

But Mora just chided him. "Those people are a concern, but we should concentrate on defeating the Evil God. We can neither save them nor return them to the human world unless we carry out our mission."

She's right, thought Adlet. But then, suddenly, every hair on his body stood on end.

Chamo tilted her head. "What's up, Adlet?" In the time it took her to ask, Adlet thrust Chamo back, Fremy rolled backward into an upright stance, drawing her gun, and Hans placed his hands and feet on the ground, arching his back like a cat.

The earth where Chamo had been just a moment before swelled up and exploded, and a fiend surged out of the cloud of dust. "Hello." Its voice was odd—high-pitched, yet hoarse. When Adlet heard it, his heart, which had quieted for a moment, began pounding again. "This won't do," declared the fiend. "What are you talking about? Who cares about some slaves, anyway?"

"Tgurneu!" Adlet cried. His blood boiled, and his heart filled with black rage. That shape perpetually lingering in his mind, that shape appearing again and again in his nightmares—Tgurneu was, at this moment, right in front of him.

"You should be more concerned about me." Tgurneu turned to Adlet and spread both arms. It was as if the fiend was saying, *Come get me.*

Hands moving faster than the eye could follow, Adlet hurled his needles. He aimed pain at Tgurneu's eyes and paralysis at its knees, bounding toward the beast: *I'll end this instantly*, he thought. *Eight years of nightmares over in a single moment.*

But the four barbs were ineffective against Tgurneu. The fiend stretched out its arms many times their original length to strike Adlet, and the boy had no way of dodging mid-leap. He just barely blocked the punch with his sword, but it still knocked him flat on his back.

"Watch out!" Mora swung a punch from the side. At the same time, Hans scampered on all fours along the ground, trying to get a slice at Tgurneu's feet as Fremy fired at its head. From behind, Goldof braced his spear against his side and charged in an attempt to skewer it.

"I've got ya neow!"

From where Adlet lay on the ground, he watched Tgurneu hug its forearm close to its body to block Mora's gauntlet. It raised a leg to avoid Hans's blades and, without giving him time to react, kicked back. Then it halted Goldof's charge with a punch to the chest courtesy of its free arm while catching Fremy's bullet in its teeth.

"That was really close," observed Tgurneu.

The party immediately backed off. *It can't be*, thought Adlet. Tgurneu had blocked four simultaneous attacks.

"Were you trying to predict what methods I'd use to kill you all? Such as assassinate you using the seventh, or have the seventh lead you into a trap? Well, I'm sure that's about all you managed to come up with." Tgurneu spread both arms but revealed no openings. Adlet got up, but only stood with his blade raised, not moving.

"Then how about this? I'll fight you all head-on, no tricks or schemes, and kill you all." Tgurneu smiled and then rushed at Adlet.

Chapter 2

Mora's
Secret
Contract

On a certain day three years earlier, an incident had occurred at All Heavens Temple that would lead Mora to kill Hans.

In a tiny annex in one corner of All Heavens Temple was the warm and humble abode where Mora, her husband, and their daughter Shenira lived. The time-worn interior of the building still contained the antique furnishings that had once belonged to the previous Temple Elder. The modestly built home was appropriate for a servant of the spirits.

Mora sat down on the sofa in the parlor, covering her face with trembling hands. One month had passed since she had begun coaching Nashetania and the other girls.

"Lady Mora...are you listening?"

There were three people in the parlor—Mora; her husband, Ganna; and the one who had spoken, a middle-aged woman in a plain white dress. Her name was Torleau Maynus, the Saint of Medicine. Her powers were only for healing wounds and curing illnesses—she essentially had no offensive capabilities. Reaching out indiscriminately to all who asked for her aid, the great Saint traveled around the world with the doctors under her command. She was one of the people who Mora respected most.

"Lady Mora...please, hold yourself together," Torleau said to the trembling Mora. The Temple Elder was incapable of any reply. It hurt to breathe, and her vision wavered. It was all she could do just to sit up straight.

"I apologize, Saint Torleau. My wife is not in a state for discussion. I shall speak with you instead." Ganna pulled Mora's hand and tried to escort her out of the room.

But she let go of his hand and sat down on the sofa again. "I'm sorry. Say that once more."

"Yes. Shenira's illness...is beyond my ability to treat."

Two weeks before, Shenira had complained of intense pain in her chest, and a strange, centipede-shaped mark had appeared on its left side. This condition had never been seen before. Her pain had worsened day by day, and eventually, it had gotten so bad that it had brought her to screams and cries. Her agony did not lessen one bit, and ten days after her illness had begun, she had ripped off her nails from clawing her chest so much.

Mora had done everything in her power. She had brought the doctors stationed at the temple to see Shenira, had summoned the most famous physicians in the nation, and had attempted to cure Shenira herself with the energy of the mountains. Finally, she had written a letter to Torleau, off in a faraway land, requesting that she come swiftly via horseback to All Heavens Temple.

"Tell me, Torleau. Please, tell me what is happening to her."

But three days earlier, the moment Torleau had arrived at All Heavens Temple, Shenira's pain had suddenly stopped. The centipede-like mark had remained, along with the scars on her chest and fingers, but otherwise, she seemed entirely fine. Though puzzled, Torleau had examined Shenira nonetheless. Mora had hoped that since the pain was gone, Shenira would be all right—but those hopes were dashed.

"A parasitic insect is nesting in her heart," said Torleau. "I've never seen or even heard of this thing before. I've tried every medicine I can think of, and I have no idea why they aren't working. I even pierced her chest with a needle to pour a solution directly onto the insect."

"What...what will happen to her now?" asked Mora.

"I don't know."

"Please. Just tell me it's not true."

The Saint of Medicine shook her head, then covered her face with her hands and cried. "This is awful, Mora. I'm sorry. Please forgive me."

Blaming Torleau had never occurred to Mora. The Saint of Medicine had done everything she could. If her daughter could not be cured, even after Torleau had tried everything, then...

A knock sounded on the parlor door. "Mommy, Daddy..." They could hear Shenira on the other side.

"Ganna, please," begged Mora. "Don't tell her."

"I won't. It's okay." Her husband must also have been grieving—in fact, this must have been an even greater shock to him. Only his sense of duty to support Mora allowed him to maintain a tenuous hold on his composure. He went to speak to his daughter on the other side of the door. "Shenira, your mother has to talk about something very important. This is a Saints' conversation, so you're not allowed to listen."

"Daddy, am I not gonna get better?" Shenira asked, sounding anxious.

"What are you talking about?" Ganna replied. "It doesn't hurt anymore, does it? Auntie Torleau says you're going to be okay."

"I'm better? But my chest is a funny color."

"That mark will disappear over time. It got better because you hung on. You're a good girl, Shenira." Father and daughter walked down the hallway. Left behind, Mora quietly sobbed as Torleau watched over her.

Torleau left some medicine with Mora and then departed All Heavens Temple. Mora tried to make her stay, but Ganna stopped her. Even if the Saint of Medicine remained with them, she still wouldn't be able to help, and she had a responsibility to save all those who suffered from illness around the world.

After that, Mora left her duties as Temple Elder to her husband and shut herself in her room. Shenira was anxious, worried that now her mother was the one who was ill. But three days later, Mora received a letter from Torleau, even though she was supposed to have been long gone.

Written on the front of the envelope was the word *Urgent*, along with a note that indicated the contents inside were not to be seen by anyone but Mora.

Alone in her private room, she read the letter. Her expression turned fearful, then angry.

"What the hell is this about, Mora?"

Five days had passed since receiving the letter from Torleau. Late at night, another Saint stood before her. The two of them were not in the parlor at All Heavens Temple but at an old fortress about two days' hurried travel by coach. There was no sign of other people inside the old fortress or its surroundings. Even the coachman had been sent away. The bastion was cold and utterly silent.

"*Agh*, this is such a chore. I want a drink. If you've got something to say, get it over with already," said the Saint, brushing back her dyed-red hair. Her decadent makeup did not befit a Saint, and her dress was lavish. The boozy smell of her hangover wafted all the way to Mora's nose. This was a beauty with the air of sloth. Her name was Marmanna Keynes, and she was the Saint of Words.

"I'm sorry for summoning you out here on such short notice. I apologize for my rudeness." Mora bowed her head.

"There's something I've been meaning to ask you for a while now," said Marmanna. "If you don't mind."

"What is it?"

"Why do you never age? How do you stay so young?"

"I eat my vegetables and don't stay up late."

"...That's not very useful to me."

I don't care, thought Mora.

Marmanna had received the power of the Spirit of Words. Among all the seventy-eight Saints, hers was the one that could be called heretical. She had no offensive capabilities, but her abilities were extremely useful. The power of the Saint of Words could prohibit lies and coerce people into keeping their oaths. Breaking any vow made to Marmanna was never

ISHIO YAMAGATA   49

forgiven—if you *did* break one, you would find yourself paying the appropriate, unavoidable price. This would continue to hold even after Marmanna's death. No Saint or fiend could nullify her abilities. The previous
Saints of Words had used their power to act as witness to transactions
between kings, nobles, and powerful merchants.

"Well, if this summons is for business, it can't be anything good,"
said Marmanna. "You want me to witness some backroom deal? Or make
sure some paramour of yours keeps quiet?"

"I suppose it is a backroom deal. I want to ask you to help me guarantee that a certain deal will be honored. It would cause difficulties for me
were the other party to renege on their word later."

Marmanna giggled. "Oh my, a hushed exchange behind closed doors.
And from the irreproachably moral Lady Mora! I'm dying to know what
kind of arrangement this is."

"My daughter has been taken hostage. I'm about to negotiate with her
abductor." The letter to Mora under Torleau's name had in fact been from
the one who had implanted the parasite within Shenira's body. The culprit
had designated a date and time for Mora to come to this old fortress. If
Mora refused, her daughter would die.

"Oh my, Shenira's been kidnapped? *Ah-ha-ha!*" Marmanna laughed
cruelly. Mora glared at her, but the Saint of Words was not perturbed. The
Elder beckoned, and they walked deeper into the old fortress. Within was
the party she would be negotiating with.

"Kids just aren't worth it," said Marmanna. "What's so great about them?"

"You'll understand if you have one. If you don't, you never will."

"Plenty of parents never understand even when they do have kids,
though."

Mora didn't reply to that. "I summoned Willone as well," she said
instead, "but she couldn't make it in time."

"Willone? What did you call that idiot for?"

Willone, the Saint of Salt, had been one of Mora's students about a
month earlier. She was skilled in close-quarters combat, wielding a purify-
ing power that could drive out poison and evil presences.

"I can trust her skills in battle, and I can trust her as a person, too."

"Hey…are you dealing with someone dangerous, here?" Marmanna's expression tensed.

The pair approached the location of Mora's appointment. Marmanna couldn't feel anything, but Mora sensed a presence ahead—that of a strong foe.

They reached the deepest part of the fortress, a place that looked like the king's quarters. A curious sound echoed from within. The sound of chewing. Not human chewing—the kind of sound that a beast or something even more fearsome would make. Something was enjoying a meal, violently and greedily.

On the ruins of the throne there sat a large shadow. Garbage was scattered about—the wings and feet of songbirds, a half-eaten fig, raw wheat, and frogs' legs. A fiend was sinking its teeth into a raw boar's head. As Mora and Marmanna watched, the whole head sank into the creature's mouth in the blink of an eye, bones and all. The being had the face of a lizard and the body of a beast, and on its back, three wings. Mora's instincts told her this was the one that had written the letter—Tgurneu.

"Hello," said the fiend.

"Tgurneu, was it? You're quite the vulgar creature," retorted Mora, looking up at the fiend as it licked off its palm.

"Pardon me. I'm such a horribly voracious eater. If I were to miss a meal, I'd be dead of starvation before you know it. I'll clean up. Hold on."

Were this creature's manners good or bad? Either way, Tgurneu gathered the fallen scraps into a bag before approaching the Saints. "It's nice to meet you, Mora. My name is Tgurneu. I'm the foremost retainer of the great Evil God." The fiend put its hand on its chest and bowed respectfully. Its body language was so human, but its form was not. It made for an unbearably eerie sight.

"…*Ah-ha, ah-ha-ha!* This really isn't what I expected, Mora!" Marmanna's voice trembled.

"Pardon me," said Tgurneu, "who is the beautiful lady here?"

"This is Marmanna, Saint of Words," said Mora. "I asked her to be witness to our negotiations."

"I thought I told you to come alone."

"I never said I would."

Tgurneu shrugged and then bowed to Marmanna as he had to Mora. "Well, whatever. You can never have too many opportunities to meet a lovely lady."

"*Ah-ha!* I got a compliment from a fiend." Marmanna laughed, and Tgurneu approached her, hand extended. Wondering what the creature could be thinking, she took its hand and gave it a proper bow.

"Now we will negotiate," declared Mora. "Marmanna, I must have you swear to me one thing: Do not speak of what we are about to discuss here today to anyone."

"Of course. If this story got out, it'd cause an uproar," said Marmanna. She used her power as the Saint of Words, manifesting a little ball of light from the tip of her index finger, and spoke to it. "This I swear to the Spirit of Words: I will speak to no one of what happens today in this place. May I die if I break this promise." The ball of light jumped into Marmanna's chest. Now the oath was complete. Not even Marmanna herself could release herself from this contract.

"Tgurneu, you will swear, too," instructed Mora. "Do not speak of this to any humans, fiends, or the Evil God. I take it you won't mind that?" If what was about to occur in this place were revealed to the world, Mora's life would be over. She would most likely be banished from All Heavens Temple and lose her qualifications as the Saint of Mountains. Her husband and daughter could also come under fire, as the family of the evildoer who had contracted with a fiend.

"Sure." Surprisingly enough, Tgurneu agreed readily. "I doubt you would strike a deal with me if I didn't. Then I would have come here for nothing."

Marmanna created a ball of light, and Tgurneu swore to it. The ball of light sank into its chest, and the contract was complete. The power of the

Saint of Words also worked on fiends. About two hundred years before, experiments on captive ones had confirmed that as fact.

"My, my, Mora. You're not going to swear?" asked the creature.

"Is it necessary?"

"...Well, whatever, then." Tgurneu shrugged. "Now then, let's begin the negotiations. As you know, one of my subordinates has created a parasite, and right now, it nests in your daughter's heart. The only way it can be removed is by my personal order for it to destroy itself. With a snap of my fingers, I could make your daughter suffer hellish agony and die. You've already had a taste of what that anguish could be like." The ten-day nightmare Shenira had endured—that had been a threat for Mora. Rage so intense it made her dizzy welled up inside her.

"But don't worry, Mora. I have no desire for your adorable little Shenira's death. If you hear my request, then I'll save her. If I order that parasite to destroy itself, it will vanish in an instant."

"What is your demand?"

"Do you really need ask? I have only one desire." Arms spread wide, Tgurneu gesticulated like a bad actor. "The Evil God's resurrection is nigh—our third encounter, with the life or death of mankind and fiendkind hanging in the balance—the final battle is at hand."

"Tell me your demand," Mora repeated.

"Mora, I want you to kill the Braves of the Six Flowers."

She replied without hesitation. "I refuse."

Tgurneu regarded her for a moment. "...Oh?"

"If the Braves of the Six Flowers are defeated, then the world will end. If the Evil God is fully revived, then my daughter and husband will both die. That would make any deal moot."

Marmanna looked at Mora with wide eyes. "Wait, are you serious? Didn't you come here to save Shenira?"

The Elder did not reply. She crossed her arms to hide her shaking hands. What she really wanted to do was throw herself at Tgurneu's feet and beg for mercy. She wanted to cry out that she would do anything to preserve her daughter's life. But that would not save Shenira. She couldn't keep her beloved daughter safe if she didn't keep the world safe, too.

Tgurneu pondered quietly, and then, for some reason, suddenly burst into applause. "That's a good answer, Mora. I thought you might say that." The fiend's hands stilled, and it continued with a smile. "Now then, let's continue our negotiation. The night is still long. We have plenty of time for discussion." Tgurneu carried over two chairs that had been beside the throne and offered them to Mora and Marmanna, then sat down on the rubble. "I understand, Mora. You've come here to save your daughter. You've come here to make a deal. We have some talking to do."

Mora hesitated for a moment, then took a seat on one of the chairs. Though confused, Marmanna sat down as well. "If you have other demands, I shall comply," said Mora. "If it's my life you want, I can offer it to you this instant. But under no circumstances will I take the Braves' lives."

"Is that so? But I don't want your life." Tgurneu smiled an uncanny smile. "I can say this with certainty, Mora: I will make you kill the Braves of the Six Flowers."

With Tgurneu rushing at him, Adlet realized that it hadn't even occurred to him that this might happen. The attack from underground had taken them all by surprise. But most shocking of all was that he hadn't even imagined that an enemy would ambush them alone.

"Whoops, I forgot." Tgurneu suddenly stopped.

After it had escaped their team attack, Adlet's allies had surrounded the fiend, readying their weapons. Not perturbed in the slightest, Tgurneu smiled and said, "Come now, don't be so impatient, Braves. There's something that must be done before we fight, now, isn't there?"

"What did you say?"

"We must greet one another. When you meet someone, you say *hello*. When you part ways, you say *good-bye*. Greetings are the first step toward living a bright life, right?"

Adlet didn't understand what Tgurneu was talking about. He got what the words meant, but he couldn't grasp the intentions behind them.

Beside him, Hans bobbed his head in a bow. "Hello, *meow*."

"That's it, Hans. Hello to you, too. All right, then, let's start this fight." Tgurneu opened its mouth and raised its face to the heavens. Adlet couldn't hear the sound, but it was yelling something. It had sent a message at a special frequency only fiends could hear.

"It's called for reinforcements," said Fremy. From just beyond the hill to the northwest sounded the faint voices of fiends. A tiny tremor rippled through the ground toward them. Adlet now realized that the reason there had been no sign of any fiends in the Ravine of Spitten Blood was because they had been gathering their forces for this surprise attack.

"This is bad, Adlet. What do we do?" Fremy asked him.

"Need you even ask?! We destroy this monster here and now! Attack, all at once!" Mora yelled and charged Tgurneu, who stood there with an obvious lack of concern. But none of the others followed. "Why do you hesitate?!" In a panic, she stopped and hopped back.

"Come here, Adlet. What's wrong? Let's enjoy a nice battle to the death." With a broad smirk, Tgurneu took one step toward him.

The boy hesitated. The hill would soon be surrounded, and Tgurneu might have engineered a trap. Furthermore, they had no idea what the seventh might do. Normally, he would not hesitate to flee from this sort of situation. You can't fight on the enemy's playing field—Atreau had taught him that.

But at this point, Adlet was not thinking calmly. "Chamo! Hans! Goldof! You hold back the reinforcements coming from the northwest!" he yelled, grasping his sword in his right hand. "You back us up from a distance, Fremy! Mora and Rolonia, stick with me!" He pulled a smoke bomb from the belt at his waist and threw it at the commander's feet, dashing into the smoke as he did. "We're taking Tgurneu down!"

They all moved simultaneously. Chamo stuffed her foxtail down her throat and vomited up the monsters known as slave-fiends from her stomach. Hans and Goldof ran together with them, heading northwest.

Fremy jumped backward, raised her gun, and aimed at Tgurneu. Her role was to hold the fiend still and cover the others. Mora circled around from behind and charged, joining Adlet in a pincer attack.

"That's it," said Tgurneu. "I thought you might do that." From the smoke, a single arm reached out to the redhead, who ducked to the ground to avoid it. Though Adlet had blocked the counterattack with his sword before, the impact had made his arms go numb. Tgurneu was far stronger and much faster. The smoke bomb hadn't worked, either.

Mora swung her iron gauntlet toward her foe's shoulder, but it dodged her without moving its lower body at all. The fiend's supple and efficient movements indicated clearly it had studied martial arts. Right, left, right, left—Mora fired off punch after punch, but she didn't even graze Tgurneu. "Get back, Adlet! You cannot match its power!" she yelled.

But Adlet knew that already. He could not hope to match Tgurneu in a head-on fight, no matter how much he struggled, but he had come this far with the intent of fighting such powerful enemies. He took the second strike with his pauldron, making sure to decrease the force of impact. It knocked the wind out of him, and his bones groaned—but in that moment he took the secret tool hidden in his left hand and slapped it onto Tgurneu's arm.

It was a cuff attached to a long chain. As the spike, fitted into the metal piece on the end of the chain, bit into the fiend's flesh, sturdy wire instantly wrapped itself around Tgurneu's arm.

"Hmm." Tgurneu's voice seemed to rumble.

Adlet sheathed his sword and grabbed the chain with both hands, pulling the fiend's restrained left arm as hard as he could. When it lost its balance, Mora hit it in the face.

"I see. So you're trying to hold me still," observed Tgurneu, jerking the chain with tremendous strength. Adlet judged he would not be able to stand his ground and quickly hopped forward. When Tgurneu raised its arm, the boy was flung into the air like a fish on a line.

"Watch out!" Fremy yelled. The fiend struck back at its airborne opponent, and Adlet just barely managed to block the attack with an iron plate in the heel of his boot. Agony shot through his ankle with a quiet, nasty sound. But he didn't let go.

Though the chain was firmly attached, it didn't hinder the fiend much. Still, Tgurneu was ever so slightly slower. Mora and Fremy took advantage of this sliver of an opportunity with their fists and bullets. Distracted by the tug-of-war with Adlet, Tgurneu was slow to dodge. Mora's fist skimmed its face, and Fremy's bullet pierced its shoulder.

"Don't let go, Adlet!" Fremy shouted as she loaded another bullet.

"I'll focus on keeping Tgurneu down! You guys finish it off!"

"Good, Adlet! Keep ahold of it!" called Mora as she blocked Tgurneu's fist with her iron gauntlets. She was about to strike back when a shrill, inhuman cry rang across the battlefield.

"Shutyourfaceyoumaggotyfilthyou'relowerthanarottenfiend'spileof crapandyou'renotgoinganywhere!"

As Adlet pulled on the chain, he scanned the area. *Is this a new enemy?* he wondered, readying himself. He saw Fremy reflexively point her gun in the direction of the voice. Even Tgurneu's eyes opened wide.

"I'llripoutyourorgansyoustinkingfiendI'lltearyoutopiecesshow-meyourguts!" The vicious and bloodthirsty string of abuse, delivered in one breath at unbelievable speed, was coming from Rolonia, who had been watching the fight from a distance. Taking up the whip at her waist, she lifted it high and swung it with both hands, undulating the thirty-meter-long iron rope, as if it was alive. The tip was hardly visible to the naked eye.

Tgurneu leaned over to avoid the whip, but the tip barely scraped its chest. Immediately, copious amounts of blood, the same red as a human's, gushed from the wound. "*Ngh!*" it grunted, exhibiting its first indication of pain.

Adlet knew about Rolonia's power. The core of the whip had been soaked in the Saint's own blood, which she manipulated within the whip to move it abnormally. Furthermore, it could draw blood from enemies' bodies upon contact. "That's pretty intense," Adlet murmured. Rolonia had grown—and in a manner far different from what Adlet had expected.

"Yourbloodisn'tenoughformeIwantyourgutsI'llsliceyouupshowmey-ourguts!" Rolonia kept thrashing the whip, an expression on her face that would inspire him to make a quick escape if she were not his ally.

Adlet focused everything on restraining Tgurneu. The fiend was far stronger than him—the boy couldn't compare. But still, by timing things perfectly, he kept the fiend in place. When his captive pulled on the chain, Adlet would stop, and when it relaxed, he would pull instead. This method of chain restraint was one of the techniques he'd learned through Atreau's instruction.

Tgurneu tried to remove the metal spike digging into its left arm, but Fremy stopped it with a shot from her gun. While it was distracted, Mora slammed it backward with a string of blows.

"*Ngh!*" Rolonia's whip skimmed Adlet's ear. But he couldn't let go of the chain. Even as Tgurneu swung him around and flung him to the ground, he continued to grapple with the chain, praying that Rolonia still retained enough of her senses to avoid friendly fire. Blood spurted from the creature's body, dying the earth red. But then, right when Adlet thought, *Maybe we can kill it now*, a single gunshot rang out through the battlefield, and Rolonia's whip stopped.

"!" Fremy had just shot at Rolonia. The bullet hadn't connected—it had merely skimmed right in front of the girl's nose.

"What are you doing, Fremy?!" Adlet yelled without thinking.

Fremy reloaded. "You were in danger."

Rolonia clenched her whip in both hands, glaring at Fremy. For a second, Adlet thought a fight might break out among their allies, but Rolonia immediately turned her bloodthirsty gaze upon Tgurneu.

"My, my, a falling-out? How unsettling. What on earth is going on here?" the fiend said innocently, taking the opportunity to attempt to remove the restraints before Fremy shot a bullet through its right arm.

"Don't let your guard down, Adlet. Anyone could be the enemy," she said, readying her gun. Adlet understood that although the barrel was aimed at Tgurneu, she also had an eye on Rolonia and Mora.

"I'm the strongest man in the world, so you don't have to protect me. Concentrate on Tgurneu."

"He's right, Fremy. Refrain from doing anything thoughtless," advised Mora. But she, too, could tell that the gunman was on guard.

Adlet ground his teeth. Fremy's paranoia about her own allies was dragging the whole group down, but if they weren't careful, the seventh might do something. They still didn't know who their enemy was. Once more, Adlet felt keenly just how precarious their situation was.

For a brief while, the battle was paused, having turned into a staring contest as they all tried to probe out one another's weaknesses. Adlet held Tgurneu down from the front, while Mora and Rolonia waited on the left and right. Fremy observed from behind.

"I'llkillyouI'llkillyouI'llkillyouI'llkillyouI'llkillyou!" Rolonia slowly pressed closer to her target.

Suddenly, Tgurneu said, "You got me. I made a mess of this one. I shouldn't have tried to catch you by surprise." None of them displayed any reaction. "I thought you'd all be surprised when I popped up out of the ground, but I didn't consider that you would then gang up on me." The fiend laughed. "So? Was that joke funny?"

"It was terrible," said Mora.

"I see. So it was a poor attempt. Human jokes are so difficult." Tgurneu put a hand to its chin, and immediately, Rolonia swung her whip with a shriek, while Fremy's bullet pierced the creature's back. The three Saints attacked all at once, and Adlet clung to the chain to keep Tgurneu in place, with no thought to his own life. The battle seemed to be in their favor, but their enemy still looked unconcerned.

Adlet turned his eyes to the area northwest of the hill. Chamo's slave-fiends had taken up position, meeting the fiends' assault. One approached from the air, but Hans flung a sword to bring it down. Goldof had rocketed straight into the center of a crowd of enemies, slicing up every one that attacked him. There was no sign that their defenses would be broken.

Tgurneu dodged Rolonia's whip and said, "That won't do, Rolonia. Vulgar words degrade the nobility of the heart." Tugging on the chain, the fiend addressed Adlet next. "This restraint is quite well made. Since you went to so much trouble to put it on me, will you give it to me?"

Large volumes of blood flowed from the gashes covering Tgurneu's body. But its blithe remarks did not stop. Adlet just couldn't understand—what was this monster's goal? At this rate, it was looking like Tgurneu had simply come their way to be killed.

Then Fremy approached Adlet from behind and said quietly, "If the fight continues like this, we can't win." Eyes still fixed on Tgurneu, the red-haired boy did not reply. "We need to hit Tgurneu with at least five times this much firepower if we want to kill it."

Adlet was shocked. He had thought they were at an advantage, but in fact, the odds in their favor were no better than fifty-fifty.

"If we can keep up the fight like this, we might be able to win," she continued. "But the seventh will strike before that happens. They'll take you by surprise and kill you, or they might attack you while pretending it was an accident." Fremy looked to the northwest. "Or they might go for Chamo or Hans." Mora and Rolonia were gradually nearing Tgurneu, but the fiend's smile did not falter as it prepared itself for their attacks.

"That's no problem. We're sticking to this fight," said Adlet.

"..."

"Relax. I've figured out a way to win." Adlet had a secret plan—hidden not only from Tgurneu, but also from Fremy, Mora, and Rolonia. He had a deadly weapon hidden within his left pauldron, the final tool that his master had passed down to him six months earlier. Atreau himself had called this weapon, which could kill a fiend in a single strike, his finest masterpiece.

Adlet's dedication to restraining Tgurneu was merely the first stage of that plan. He would divert Tgurneu's attention to the others, and then when the opportunity arose, he would unleash his deadly attack. He planned to seize the moment when Tgurneu began to slow down, when its focus was elsewhere. He desperately waited for that opportunity.

Mora and Rolonia inched closer and closer. Still gripping the chain, Adlet looked for the chance to strike—but then Tgurneu remarked, "Let me tell you something." Startled, all three attackers froze instinctively. "I know what you're thinking, Adlet. Fighting you on my own like this has to be some kind of trap. But it's not. I came here to defeat you all head-on."

"Don't listen to what it says," warned Fremy.

"It's time for me to get serious," said Tgurneu. "I suppose I'll use my trump card now."

What is Tgurneu trying to do? wondered Adlet. If the fiend really did intend to use its trump card, there would be no need to announce the fact verbally. Was there some purpose in that, or was Tgurneu just that unconcerned?

A strange change occurred in the fiend's chest. The flesh wriggled like a pulsing vein, forming something that looked like a large, amphibian mouth. Tgurneu plunged its right hand into the new orifice.

Adlet's party reacted immediately. Rolonia swept her whip in a sideways arc as Fremy shot the mouth in Tgurneu's chest. But even with the chain still attached to its left arm, it dodged the attacks as if dancing. "Behold, my trump card!" The creature pulled its free hand from the opening. In it was a large fig. Tgurneu took a bite and said, "Whoops, wrong one."

Fremy shot Tgurneu in the head. Still holding the fig, her target's whole upper body snapped backward. Mora swooped down from the left, swinging her fists into the fiend's flank. Rolonia whipped its shoulder, and blood spurted from the wound.

Tgurneu smiled as it fought back. "Wait, hold on there. Let me use my trump card."

As Adlet kept trying to hold Tgurneu still with the chain, an uncanny foreboding came over him. They couldn't allow the fiend to gain a sure advantage. If they didn't kill it before then, things would get bad. Adlet tried to find the right moment to unleash the secret tool hidden in his left pauldron.

"!"

But his own nervousness had distracted him. Tgurneu feigned relaxing its arm, then yanked as hard as possible. When the boy staggered, Tgurneu bit off the chain with far more strength than it had shown thus far. So, their enemy hadn't been playing seriously before.

"Damn it!"

Tgurneu vaulted over the four surrounding him and ran off toward its reinforcements to the northwest. It possessed frightening speed—as fast as Hans, or faster. Adlet threw a knife in an attempt to stop it, but Tgurneu didn't slow for even a moment.

"All right, *now* I can use this," said Tgurneu, and Adlet saw it shove a hand into its chest again. It withdrew a handful of grape-sized bombs and, still running, hurled them high into the sky.

On the edge of the hill, Hans, Goldof, and Chamo kept the reinforcements in check. There weren't that many—about three hundred, not even one-thirtieth of the fiend army. The fight was evenly matched. About seventy slave-fiends held back the enemy mass like it was nothing. However, if Tgurneu joined the fray, the balance would instantly collapse.

"Hans! Goldof! Go for Tgurneu!" yelled Adlet.

Then the bombs exploded over their heads. Sparkling silver powder mixed with the smoke and rained down upon the slave-fiends. Immediately, they heard a sizzling sound, and white smoke began to rise from the bodies of Chamo's servants.

"Huh?" Chamo muttered. Her slave-fiends screamed and fell to the ground, writhing.

"What the *meow* is this stuff? Hot, hot!" Hans covered his eyes.

The silver powder covered the fiends, the slave-fiends and Hans, but only the enemy seemed unharmed.

"What the heck?! Guys! What happened?! Pull yourselves together!" cried Chamo. She completely lost it, clinging to a nearby slave-fiend. The enemy army descended upon her in unison, and Tgurneu was about to join them.

"Hans! Goldof! Protect Chamo!" yelled Adlet. The two immediately rushed to her side to intercept the fiends about to attack her. A bullet pierced Tgurneu's leg from behind, halting its charge. Once they caught up, Mora and Rolonia attacked Tgurneu to protect Chamo.

All at once, the battle turned into a chaotic melee. Now that Chamo's slave-fiends could no longer fight, the assault began from all sides. Adlet and his allies frantically dodged the attacks while also defending against

Tgurneu. Only Chamo stood frozen as she watched her slave-fiends writhe in agony.

"Chamo! Snap out of it!" Adlet yelled as he protected the girl from the advancing creatures.

But Chamo couldn't hear him, senseless to everything going on around her. She clung to a giant slug slave-fiend, trying to wipe off the silver powder stuck to its body. "What the heck is this?! It's hot! Really hot!" Smoke rose from Chamo's hands as she brushed off the monster's body.

Instantly, Adlet understood. That silver powder was emitting heat. Atreau had taught him about a certain kind of metal that radiated an intense heat when it came in contact with water. The powder from Tgurneu's bombs was most likely that metal. Chamo's slave-fiends were all aquatic, and heat was fatal to them. The fiend commander's secret weapon could render their party's most powerful fighter useless.

Adlet scanned the area. Rolonia was under intense fire, surrounded by Tgurneu and its horde, while Mora and Fremy somehow managed to protect her.

"Chamo! Make your slave-fiends fight! At this rate, we'll all die!" he yelled.

"No! They're all hurt! If they don't get treated now, they'll die!" Bawling like a child, she opened her mouth wide and yelled, "*Nnngh!* Guys! Come back! Come back!"

All the swamp creatures, still covered in silver powder, disappeared into Chamo's mouth one after another. When she sucked them down, she moaned in pain, and then vomited up boiling white mucus. Inside the mire in her stomach, she was washing away the metal. "Come back, guys! At this rate, you'll all get torn to pieces!" One by one, the slave-fiends disappeared from the battlefield.

Without thinking, Adlet yelled, "Chamo! Don't call them back!"

"Shut up!" Chamo sucked up a few more and then vomited up another round of mucus.

"Think about our situation! They're going to kill us!"

"Shut up shut up shut up! I don't care!" Chamo stomped and yelled, and the attacking battalion flooded toward her. Adlet did all he could to hold them back. "Chamo's pets are wounded!" she cried. "All those cute little guys, they're crying, 'It hurts, it hurts!' Who cares about you?! They're in pain!" As the last of the slave-fiends vanished from the battlefield, three hundred fiends stormed at the Braves of the Six Flowers.

The party had completely lost control. It took everything they had just to hold their ground against the surrounding fiends. Tgurneu stopped fighting and withdrew from the crowd to observe the battle. "You made quiet the blunder, Adlet," it said. "You should have run. You should have known that you weren't ready to fight."

"Damn it!" Adlet cut down a fiend that was charging him and then pointed his sword and Tgurneu.

"Don't, Adlet! You'll die!" Fremy yelled. With her hands full fighting fiends, she couldn't back him up.

"Stop! You cannot hope to match such a foe!" Mora shouted. But Adlet did not lower his sword.

Tgurneu smiled. "You shouldn't be so reckless. I recommend you flee."

"GAAAAAHH!" Adlet howled and sprinted for Tgurneu. To any onlooker, it would surely look like he had lost it and was charging in head-long. No matter how Adlet might struggle, he could not hope to stand up to one of the three commanders. However, Atreau's former trainee had a plan. His seemingly reckless charge was an act to make the fiend drop its guard. Tgurneu would be sure to get careless. The greater its advantage, the less attention it would pay to what was going on—and if it thought that its opponent had lost his head, then all the more so.

"I'm disappointed," said Tgurneu as it reached out to strike with a knifehand. It easily blocked Adlet's charge, sending him rolling to the ground. The boy bounded right back to his feet and lunged again.

"*Meow!* What the hell're ya doin'?!" Hans darted over in an attempt to protect him.

Adlet shot him a look. Their eyes met for just an instant. Hans should be able to figure it out—Adlet was distracting Tgurneu, acting as bait. Hans would understand and do what Adlet needed him to do.

Tgurneu thrust Adlet backward and sent him sprawling to the ground. Three fiends closed in from behind, while two more fiends on his left and right blocked off his escape. Adlet stood in place, ignoring the fiends that surrounded him, and pointed his sword at Tgurneu.

"Watch meowt!" Hans yelled, vaulting into the circle of fiends. Anyone would think that Adlet had lost his head and that his companion was trying to save him. But Adlet caught him mid-leap, and Hans used the Brave's shoulders as a springboard to rocket toward Tgurneu.

"!"

The fiend was taken by surprise. It took a defensive stance in an attempt to block Hans's sword—but Hans wasn't trying to attack.

"Ya fell for it, *meow.*" He'd actually aimed for the cuff digging into Tgurneu's left arm and the torn end of the chain that hung off it. Midair, Hans sheathed his sword, grabbed the chain, and yanked it with all his might, restraining Tgurneu's left arm. At the same time, Adlet threw a smoke bomb at his feet. The fiends around him all froze, and in moments Adlet escaped from the circle.

Tgurneu tried to pry off Hans with its free hand, but Mora dashed in and restrained it to protect Hans. Now that both of Tgurneu's arms were pinned down, Adlet ran straight at the fiend, pulling out the secret tool hidden within his left pauldron—a spike about twenty centimeters long. It looked like just a big nail, nothing irregular about it. But fitted onto the tip of that spike was the blood of a certain Saint.

It was common knowledge that Saints' blood was poison to fiends, but up until this point, none save the Saint of Spilled Blood had made use of their blood as a weapon. To kill a high-order fiend like Tgurneu, she would have to pour about a whole cup of blood. But Atreau had successfully extracted the poisonous element of Saints' blood and concentrated it. That toxin coated the crystal tip of this spike, and if Adlet impaled a fiend with this, the poison would instantly spread through its entire body.

It would be absolutely impossible to counteract or eject from the body. Atreau had named this weapon the Saint's Spike—his finest masterpiece.

"!" Tgurneu sensed the impending danger and tried to intercept Adlet with a kick. He ducked to avoid it and, as he did, took one step forward. Clenching the Saint's Spike in his hands, he came within striking distance of the fiend.

Eight years ago, this monster had stolen Adlet's home. It had killed his sister, stolen his friend away, and robbed him of his life of peace. He would kill it. For that sake alone, Adlet had become a warrior. For eight years, he'd yearned for this moment.

Adlet plunged the Saint's Spike deep into Tgurneu's stomach.

"You did it!" cried Mora.

"Just what we were goin' for, Adlet!" Hans cheered, jumping away from Tgurneu along with the Temple Elder.

With an audible throb of pain, Tgurneu's body violently convulsed, evidence that the poison had begun its circulation.

The initial symptoms of this toxin were madness and intense pain all over the body. Next, the fiend would completely lose its sense of balance. After that came visual and auditory hallucinations, and then its memory would start to become impaired. Finally, it would be in agony for five to ten days, with inevitable death waiting in the end.

Adlet stood there, just gazing at Tgurneu as it shuddered. He felt incredibly calm and quiet. *Oh. That's anticlimactic*, he thought. But the moment he did, something happened.

"Duck!" Mora yelled, and that moment, a violent impact hit Adlet in the face. He didn't even have the time to think, *What was that?* He was instantly knocked out.

"Hey, Adlet, are you actually taking this seriously?" The last thing the boy saw as his vision grew dark was his mortal foe, the Saint's Spike still in its stomach, calmly swinging a fist.

Mora had thought they had finished the battle—that when Adlet had stabbed that nail-like object into Tgurneu's stomach, victory would be theirs. As Tgurneu had spasmed wildly, Adlet had stopped, watching it with pity, like he was sure they had won. But then Tgurneu had swung a punch like nothing had happened, throwing him backward.

"Duck!" she had yelled, but it was far too late. The Brave's body flew through the air, rolled about twenty meters, and then stopped moving.

"Adlet!" Fremy screamed.

"Huh? Addy?" Rolonia had been spewing profanities and scattering fiends, but now her eyes widened. In an instant, as if she had been replaced by another person, she was back to her old, timid self.

Fiends surged toward the fallen Adlet to finish him off. Mora bounded over to him and slung him over her shoulder. She touched his neck—it wasn't broken. He was breathing.

"Oh my, he's still alive?" The lizard-like creature approached leisurely, the spike still protruding from its stomach. The fiends massed around Tgurneu, protecting their leader.

This battle was now a lost cause. Chamo could no longer fight, and they had lost Adlet, too. Far from actually killing Tgurneu, the whole party could very well be annihilated. Still holding her companion, Mora thought, *I must use my secret weapon.*

"You still intend to fight, Mora? Well, that's no surprise."

Mora glared at the fiend and steeled herself. She could not back down now. She could not let this chance to kill Tgurneu slip through her fingers. There was a reason she had to do this.

But the moment she was ready, a shadow blocked her path. Hans grabbed Adlet's unconscious body away from her. "We have to run, Mora. Don't use it yet." There was no way that Hans could have known about her last resort. He had merely read her expression and understood that she was about to do something. Mora's secret weapon was to blow herself up and take Tgurneu with her.

"You hold back Tgurneu, Mora! Goldof, you carry all our packs! The rest of ya—run!" Hans yelled, and he wove through the stampede of fiends. He found Chamo where she lay curled up, spewing mucus, picked her up, and carried her and Adlet away at blinding speed.

"Let me go, you dummy! Dumb, dumb dummy! Chamo can still fight!" Chamo pummeled Hans's back, but he ignored her.

"You think I'll let you go?" Tgurneu tried to follow, but Mora realized what it was trying to do and punched the fiend from the side. Hans's words had brought her to her senses. This would not necessarily be her only chance to kill Tgurneu. For now, it would best to escape and regroup.

"I'll cover you, Mora." Fremy threw a bomb, scattering the troops protecting their leader.

"Run…run? How should I…?" Rolonia defended herself from the fiends as she nervously looked around the area.

"Rolonia! You go, too! Follow Hans!" Mora yelled at her, and the newest member of the group finally came to her senses and ran off after Hans. The hill was completely surrounded. Rolonia snapped her whip while Hans fought back with kicks, but they couldn't secure a way out.

"All of you, get down!" Fremy chucked her bombs indiscriminately, every which way. A number of fiends were blown to pieces, and the blast caught Hans and Rolonia, too. But still, she opened up the slimmest of escape routes. "Mora! You run, too!" She fired a bullet into Tgurneu, and Mora took the opportunity to turn her back to the enemy and escape.

"Head to the mountain! Flee to the Bud of Eternity!" cried Mora. The whole group broke out of the encirclement and ran down the hill to Goldof, who was carrying their packs. With the group reunited, they headed for the mountain rising in the distance.

"We're the rearguard, Fremy," declared Mora as they fled. Tgurneu was chasing after them with incredible speed. It would be Mora and Fremy's job to hold the fiend in check.

"Don't worry. I'm good at fighting in retreat," said Fremy, clenching her gun.

The party continued their retreat, traveling away from the hill and passing through the ravine. Their goal was not the east, where the continent lay. They were headed west, deeper into the Howling Vilelands. Their retreat turned into a battle even fiercer than regular combat. The one with the toughest role of all was Mora, who was at the group's tail, having to run while simultaneously defending the group from Tgurneu's attacks.

"*Ungh!*" Mora grunted. Tgurneu caught up to them again, and Mora dodged to the side to avoid its fist. The next blow she blocked with her gauntlets.

Fremy joined the fray to help her, firing at Tgurneu from behind Mora, the bullet skimming past the other woman's face. When Tgurneu leaned away to avoid it, Mora flung the fiend back with a kick to the stomach and ran. Fremy hurled a bomb at their pursuer to slow it down. Her claim that she was a skilled fighter while retreating had been no bluff, and her precise support fire enabled Mora to manage their escape, albeit narrowly.

The vanguard didn't have it easy, either. Though Hans, Goldof, and Rolonia encountered repeated ambushes and fiends that had circled ahead, it was the Saint among them who somehow succeeded in defending the group.

Once they emerged from the ravine, a smallish mountain came into view. The three in the lead were already running up the slope to the Bud of Eternity. If they could reach it, they would be safe for the time being. Their pursuers were slowly declining in number. The commander was still hot on their heels, but one by one they were shaking off the rest of the fiends.

"Watch out!" cried Fremy.

That was when it happened—Tgurneu sprung forward to grapple with Mora. She grabbed Tgurneu's wrists, restraining the fiend with both hands, and the two of them struggled against each other. Tgurneu was far stronger—even borrowing the power of the Spirit of Mountains, it was all Mora could do to hold on for a few seconds.

"Mora!" Fremy came to her aid with a bomb to Tgurneu's back. The blast caused Tgurneu to stagger, and during that brief window, Mora sent the fiend flying with a punch and escaped from its grasp. Tgurneu got to its feet and, for just a moment, grimaced. Rather than standing firmly, it swayed a little. Upon closer inspection, it was wounded after so many hits from Mora, Fremy, and Rolonia. Adlet's spike weapon was still impaled in its stomach—though it didn't seem like that had any effect.

"I think now's a good time to quit, Tgurneu," said Fremy, pointing her gun at the creature. The Bud of Eternity was likely only minutes away. The other fiends had pulled back, and most of their pursuers were gone.

Tgurneu smiled faintly and withdrew one big step. "It looks like you've grown a lot since you left six months ago. I'm glad." She didn't reply. "It's so lonesome, Fremy. There's so much we have to talk about now. Hey, why don't you come back? We betrayed you, but that couldn't be helped, and even now, I still—"

Fremy cut Tgurneu off with a bullet to its face. The fiend caught it in its teeth, spat it out, and shrugged. "Get lost," she sneered.

"I understand how you feel, Fremy. You're scared your heart might waver. You think that if this conversation continues, you'll allow me to convince you. Adorable as ever."

Fremy's jaw clenched as she ground her teeth. Mora watched her silently. The Saint of Gunpowder's position was complicated, and her feelings for Tgurneu had to be complicated, too.

As Mora watched the two glare at each other, she remembered what had happened about an hour ago—when, before Tgurneu had taken them by surprise, she had encountered that strange fiend in the Ravine of Spitten Blood. The message written on its back, that she had no time, had most certainly been from Tgurneu.

"..."

Mora wanted to ask what having *no time* meant. But she couldn't discuss that with Fremy present. She couldn't allow her allies to know about the secret agreement she had made with Tgurneu three years prior. She couldn't let them even suspect her of it.

"Let's go now, Mora. I'm worried about Adlet," said Fremy, and she slowly backed away. It seemed Tgurneu did not intend to give chase. It stood there idly, giving no sign it would move.

"Should you really be ending the battle now?" taunted Tgurneu. Fremy ignored it, but Mora froze. "This might be your last opportunity to defeat me—it might be your only chance. You have no time."

"What do you mean?" Mora asked, without thinking.

"You have two days left. If you fail to defeat me before that time is up, things will be bad for you. Very bad for you."

"Two more days?"

Fremy tugged Mora's shoulder. "Don't listen. It's a bluff. If there really were something happening in two days, Tgurneu wouldn't just warn you."

"But…" Mora hesitated, while Fremy urged her to go.

Watching the two, it waved and smiled. "As Fremy advises, I'll leave you for today. Good-bye, Braves of the Six Flowers. We'll see one another again." The fiend turned around and left. Mora couldn't follow—Tgurneu was too fast.

There was no sign of any enemies—apparently the fight really was over now. Breathing hard, Mora gazed after Tgurneu. "What a buffoon. *That* is a commander of the fiends?"

"Tgurneu has always been like that. It's so bad, it makes me want to gag," said Fremy, but this time, her gun was fixed on her comrade.

Mora wasn't really shocked. She didn't think Fremy was the seventh—if she were, then she would have attacked while Tgurneu was present. "What are you doing, Fremy?"

"I want to ask you one thing, Mora." The look in Fremy's eyes was not murderous, but rather suspicious. Fremy suspected Mora as the seventh. "Did something happen with you and Tgurneu?"

"What makes you think that?"

"When Tgurneu said, *You have no time*, you were acting odd."

Mora's heart hammered, though she desperately tried to stay calm. She feigned confusion, as if the suspicions Fremy had just voiced were utterly groundless. "'Acting odd'? If a gun were pointed at me every time I acted odd, I would be dead many times over."

"Don't dodge the question. Give me a straight answer."

"Nothing happened. Does that satisfy you?" Mora approached Fremy, grabbed the muzzle of her weapon, and forced it down. "Fremy, you are free to attempt to deduce who the seventh may be. But don't act so eager to kill."

Fremy didn't reply, her eyes locked with Mora's.

"You would only attract suspicion to yourself instead. You'd be accused of using a search for the seventh as a pretense to create the opportunity to kill one of us. If I said to the others, *The seventh is Fremy—she accused me of being the seventh and tried to kill me!* what would you do then?"

"Fine." Fremy holstered her gun and headed off to the Bud of Eternity.

Mora followed after her. Somehow, she'd managed to change the topic. *I wonder if I fooled her,* she thought. Mora had never been good at lying, and she rarely hid things. Honesty had been her principle throughout life. She had always believed that living an honest life, with no duplicity, was the true path to happiness.

"I think Tgurneu was bluffing," said Fremy, "but it bothers me that it brought up a specific date. What did it mean by *two days left?*"

"I don't know." Mora didn't think Tgurneu had been bluffing. In fact, she was certain its threat had been genuine—because Tgurneu could never lie to Mora.

Mora recalled what had happened three years prior and the secret, unforgivable agreement she had made with the fiend general.

Inside the old, empty fortress, Mora and Tgurneu glared at each other. Tgurneu rested on a mountain of rubble, while Marmanna sat beside Mora, watching her anxiously.

Mora hesitated. She had to save Shenira's life, whatever it took. Shenira was her purpose—her everything. But she would not kill the Braves of the Six Flowers. That would be a betrayal of every human alive. *How can I save my daughter?* she agonized.

Then Tgurneu made her an offer. "I'll compromise. You may kill one—just one of the six. Would you be able to accept that?" Mora didn't reply. "Oh, dear. You won't even take that? Such a cruel mother," said Tgurneu.

Mora trembled with rage. "Even if I fulfilled that promise, it's doubt-
ful you would actually release my daughter."

"I see."

"I'm sure you would think nothing of breaking an oath to a human.
With no guarantee you will be true to your word, no negotiations can be
made," said Mora.

Tgurneu grinned. "You're quite right."

"What did you say?"

"You're right. I have no problem with lying in order to win. I can't
recall ever keeping a promise to a human."

Did that mean that Tgurneu had had no intentions of freeing her
daughter?

"But this situation right now is different," the fiend continued. "I
need you to trust that I'll keep my promise. Kidnapping is a crime of trust.
You can't do it without good faith between the aggressor and the victim."

"Good faith, hmm?"

Tgurneu glanced at Marmanna, who sat beside Mora. "It's a good
thing you brought the Saint of Words. In the event that we come to an
agreement, why don't I make an oath to her? I can swear that if I break my
promise to you, I will offer my life in exchange."

Mora's heart wavered. After a few moments of thought, she replied,
"Impossible."

"Why?"

"Fiends see nothing of throwing their lives away for the sake of victory. Your life alone would guarantee nothing."

"I see. So that's how you're going to be." Tgurneu closed its eyes and
considered for a while. "What you point out is entirely true. But I'm no common fiend. Among the countless fiends, *I* am of the elite, the cornerstone, a
general in charge of forty percent of the whole army. If I were to die, the chain
of command would collapse. It would be a massive blow from which they
would never recover. They need me to defeat the Braves of the Six Flowers."

"A commander of fiends, hmm?" Mora could trust that. Just sitting
face-to-face with this being, she could tell that it possessed fearsome

power. She also sensed what it had said about commanding forty percent of the army might just be true.

"This is the life I'm offering to you as a guarantee. I believe this proposal should inspire trust."

"Marmanna, tell me if it speaks truth or lies," Mora directed her.

Using the power of the Spirit of Words, Marmanna manifested a tiny sphere of light that jumped into Tgurneu's mouth. "Repeat what you said just now," she said.

"I am a leader among fiends. I command forty percent of all the army. If I die, the chain of command will collapse, and that blow would be catastrophic for them. The fiends would most likely be unable to beat the Braves of the Six Flowers without me." If it were lying, the orb would be ejected from its mouth and return to Marmanna. The light remained in place.

"Tgurneu is telling the truth," said Marmanna. But even so, Mora couldn't believe the fiend.

"You still can't trust me? Then let's do this: I'll swear to the Saint of Words that I'll never lie to you. If I lie, then may this core be shattered. By the way, I promise that I'd release your daughter, too," said Tgurneu, indicating the place its heart would be if it were human.

The core of a fiend was like its brain. Though fiends boasted powerful vitality, they would always die if their core was broken. Every fiend had a core—a glossy, metallic sphere. The larger ones would be about five centimeters in diameter, and on the smaller side, they could be smaller than the tip of a pinky finger.

"I'll even show you." Tgurneu put a hand to its chest. The flesh cracked open, revealing its organs. Thanks to the fiend's construction, whatever it was, not a single drop of blood dripped out. And right there, in the place Tgurneu indicated, was its core. "Now then, will you trust me?"

"...Swear to the Saint of Words. Then I will trust you."

Marmanna nodded and borrowed the power of the Spirit of Words. The little sphere appeared and disappeared into Tgurneu's body.

"This I swear: I will not lie to Mora. If I do, then may the core in my chest shatter to pieces, while at the same time, I kill the parasite in She-nira's chest." Tgurneu's body sparkled. The covenant was made. "Is that enough for you? Good grief. Now we can finally start negotiating," said the fiend, shrugging. "Now then, I'll make my demand once more. I want you to kill one of the Braves of the Six Flowers."

"I will not accept that demand. I offer my life instead. You should be satisfied with that," Mora said resolutely.

But Tgurneu shook its head. "I refuse. If you die, someone else would simply be chosen as a Brave."

"I'll offer you the life of one Saint who will eventually be chosen as a Brave, in addition to my own: Athlay, Willone, or Nashetania. How about that?"

"What?!" Marmanna, who had been listening beside them, shrieked. "What are you thinking?! Do you intend to become a murderer?!"

"Did I not make that clear?" said Mora. "Yes, I do."

"You're not in your right mind."

You're absolutely correct, thought Mora. A mother whose daughter had been taken hostage could never be in her right mind.

"That won't work. The only life I want is that of a Brave of the Six Flowers. No matter how many candidates you kill, I won't release your daughter. My demand is for you to kill a Brave. That is all." Tgurneu rejected her offer.

Left with no choice, Mora made another concession. "I will be chosen as a Brave. When I receive the crest, I'll kill myself then. How about that?"

"No."

"What?!"

"If you aren't chosen, then taking a hostage as I have done will have entirely been a waste. And besides, do you think the Spirit of Fate would anoint someone who intends suicide as one of the Braves? My demand won't change. Kill one of the Braves of the Six Flowers. That is all." For a long while, Mora and Tgurneu glared at each other. There was no sign that

Tgurneu would give in. "Do you understand that if we fail to negotiate a deal, then there's no reason for me to let your daughter live?"

"..."

"Oh, well," said Tgurneu, beginning to stand up.

"Wait. I have one condition." If the negotiations broke down, then Shenira would die. Mora had no choice but to meet Tgurneu's demands. "If you die, you must release my daughter immediately, even if I haven't killed a Brave."

"Sorry, but I can't accept that condition. If I did accept it, you'd just use all your power to try to kill me." Tgurneu shook its head.

"Then let's set a time limit. I'll promise to kill a Brave of the Six Flowers before a certain deadline, but if you die before then, then that promise will be void. I will not under any circumstances withdraw this condition."

"I see." Tgurneu put a hand to its slim jaw and considered for a while. "And when is this deadline?"

"Twenty-two days after the Evil God has awakened. If you're alive, I promise I will kill one of the Braves of the Six Flowers by that date."

Hand still on its jaw, Tgurneu continued to ponder. "That sounds reasonable. Fine. I accept your condition." They had finally settled on something. Now Mora had found a way she could save Shenira. "Twenty-two days after the awakening of the Evil God. You will kill one of the Braves by then. But if I die before the deadline, the contract will be null and void, and I'll release your daughter. You're fine with that?"

Mora nodded. "And I'll add one more condition. Do not touch my daughter before then."

"Of course. I promise. And the fiends under my command will not touch your daughter until twenty-two days have passed after the Evil God's awakening. I will also not let any other fiends not under my command touch her." Somehow, they had managed to reach an agreement, and Mora had settled a way to save Shenira without killing any of the Braves of the Six Flowers. All she had to do was kill Tgurneu before the twenty-second day after the Evil God's revival.

"I'd like to add two more conditions of my own," said Tgurneu. "In the case that you are no longer capable of fulfilling your promise, I will take your daughter's life. In other words, if you die before you kill a Brave. My other condition is that if you kill yourself after being chosen, I will not accept that as a fulfillment of your promise."

The first condition made sense to Mora, but the latter half seemed to her an odd proposal. If Tgurneu's goal was to kill a Brave, then why would it care if Mora killed herself? Her intention had been to kill Tgurneu before the time limit defined in their agreement was up, and if she could not kill it by then, to end her own life to protect Shenira. But now that was not an option. She could attempt to stick to her guns, but if Tgurneu ended the negotiation, her daughter would die. "I accept your conditions," said Mora.

"Then I suppose the contract is made," said Tgurneu.

"Let me confirm one more thing. What will happen if we kill each other?"

"In that case, you win. Your daughter will be freed."

"Then fine." Mora prompted Marmanna. The contract could not be complete without the Saint of Words guaranteeing the contract. Marmanna's little ball of light vanished Tgurneu's body.

"Tgurneu so swears: If I should die, I will force the parasite in Shenira's chest to die with me, even in the case that Mora and I kill each other. If I break this oath, may all the fiends that serve me perish."

"Tgurneu," said Marmanna, "when the compensation you're offering is the life of someone else, you also need their consent."

"Oh? Then what do we do?"

"Through the Spirit of Words, I'll now ascertain the desires of your followers. I'll ask them if they're willing to give their lives on your command." Marmanna closed her eyes and fell silent for a while. Then she opened them and said, "All your followers have declared they would die if you ordered it. The contract is valid." Tgurneu's body glowed. The first agreement had been made.

"Tgurneu so swears: If Mora should kill a Brave of the Six Flowers, I will make the parasite in Shenira's chest die. May I die if I break this oath. But if Mora commits suicide, then this contract will become null and void."

"Do you agree to this contract, Mora?" asked Marmanna.

"I agree to the contract," Mora complied, and yet another deal was made.

"Tgurneu so swears: Until twenty-two days past the revival of the Evil God, no fiends will cause harm to Shenira. May I die if I break this oath. However, if Mora perishes before twenty-two days past the revival of the Evil God, this will become null and void."

"...I agree."

Tgurneu's body shone. Now all contracts were concluded. The discussion was over. Mora needed to kill Tgurneu within twenty-two days of the Evil God's revival. If she could not do so by then, she would be forced to murder one of the Braves of the Six Flowers. If she could do neither, then Shenira would die.

"Now then, I'm going back to the Howling Vilelands. Good-bye, and may we meet again." Tgurneu stood and walked to the door of the old bastion. Mora instantly kicked away her chair, stood, and swung a punch at the fiend. "Whoa, there." Tgurneu caught what would normally have been a fatal blow. Before she could unleash a second strike, her target turned around and jumped out the window. Mora tried to give chase, but the fiend immediately faded into the black of night and disappeared.

"This is totally crazy, Mora. Are you seriously going to kill one of the Braves of the Six Flowers?"

"Hardly. I'll kill that fiend and save my daughter. That is all." Gazing into the darkness of might, Mora thought, *I suppose I could say that negotiations ended well.* She had been able to secure Shenira's safety. If she could just defeat Tgurneu, she could go without killing any of the Braves. As a bonus, she'd even managed to prevent Tgurneu from ever lying to her. *But was this truly a good idea?* she wondered. She had the feeling her foe had further tricks planned for her.

As Mora climbed the mountain with Fremy, she mulled over Tgurneu's words. She was sure it had meant she had only two more days to save

Shenira. But how could that be? That day, Tgurneu had agreed that the deadline was twenty-two days after the Evil God's revival, and it had only been thirteen. There should still be nine days. An oath sworn before the Saint of Words could not be redacted, no matter what. Even if Marmanna had been conspiring with Tgurneu, that would not change the contract. There were still nine days. That was a sure thing.

"That fiend..." Tgurneu had sworn to Mora that it would die if it lied to her. It should be utterly incapable of attempting to deceive her. So what did it mean by only two more days? And how should she kill Tgurneu?

Chapter 3

At the
Bud of
Eternity

The Ravine of Spitten Blood was situated on the eastern edge of the Howling Vilelands. To the west, there was a small mountain—scraggy, steep, and dotted with numerous caves and cliffs. It had no particular name.

At the entrance to a cave halfway up the slope bloomed a strange flower. The six-petaled blossom was small enough to fit in the palm of one's hand. At first glance, it looked like just a normal flower, but there was none like it in the natural world. The bud looked as if it was opening, or closing, but never quite one or the other. Halfway between open and closed, this flower had been blooming for a thousand years. This was what the Saint of the Single Flower had once used as her weapon.

One thousand years ago, the Saint of the Single Flower and the Evil God had been locked in a mortal struggle. The Saint had exhausted her strength on this very mountain. Wounded all over and at the peak of exhaustion, she finally collapsed. The Saint of the Single Flower had not been almighty and invincible. She had been a human, and when wounded, she would suffer pain, and when exhausted, she would fall.

Before the Saint of the Single Flower had collapsed, she had thrust her weapon, her flower, into the earth, erecting a barrier to keep away the Evil God and its fiends as she healed her wounds over the course of three days before setting forth once more to do battle. Even once the struggle was over, her barrier remained in the earth and prevented any fiends from drawing near ever since.

This was the origin of the barrier known as the Bud of Eternity.

Mora and Fremy headed for the safe area halfway up the mountain. The circular barrier extended for a radius of about fifty meters around the cave, generating a repulsive force that would repel any fiends or the Evil God if they approached.

"Can you enter it, Fremy?" Mora asked when they entered.

Fremy was able to step into the barrier with no incident. "Looks like it's okay. I think it's because I have the Crest of the Six Flowers now. Before, I couldn't even come near it."

"That's some comfort. 'Twould be terrible if you were forced to stay out here all alone." Mora approached the rest of the group. The first to catch her eye was Chamo. The girl was leaning against a boulder near the edge of the barrier, moaning in pain. "Are you okay, Chamo?" she asked, approaching her.

She was heaving and retching with snot and tears running down her face. Her cloudy white vomit was speckled with silver powder. Apparently, she was washing out the silver powder that clung to the fiends inside her stomach. "The wounds...all the wounds won't heal... What should Chamo do? This is the first time this has ever happened... Guh..." Chamo vomited again. Mora felt bad for her, but she had no way to help. Chamo was the only one who could heal her slave-fiends.

"The strongest Saint alive is less reliable than I thought," muttered Fremy from behind Mora.

"What did you say?" Chamo asked, wiping her tears.

"It's true. If you don't do something about that silver powder, you don't have a chance with Tgurneu."

"*Nghh!*" Crying, Chamo smacked the boulder. "Shut up shut up! Chamo's the strongest! Once the little guys' wounds heal, that dummy'll be a pushover! Chamo'll tear that fiend to pieces and eat it! And then it'll stay alive, with no arms and no legs, inside Chamo's tummy!"

This is just what I feared, thought Mora. Chamo had tremendous power.

But her emotional maturity seemed inversely proportional to her strength. She was selfish, arrogant, and completely lacking in the ability to collaborate. When she had the advantage, she would let her guard down, and when she was outgunned, she would lose control of herself. Mora should have taught Chamo how to be emotionally prepared, how to behave as an adult warrior. The Elder's failure was her own fault, but at this point, it was too late for regrets.

"*If* you can do something about that silver powder," said Fremy.

"*Nggahh!*"

"You're being rather cruel, Fremy," said Mora.

Goldof was a little ways away, keeping his back to Chamo as he stood still, gazing vaguely into the distance. It seemed he had still not recovered. All this time, Mora had been convinced Goldof was the seventh. She had thought his dazed manner was an act. But during the battle with Tgurneu, the knight hadn't done anything but help Hans and Chamo hold back Tgurneu's reinforcements, and during the retreat, he'd run the whole way carrying all their packs. Was he really the seventh? Mora didn't know anymore.

"Goldof, where's Adlet?" asked Fremy. Goldof silently pointed into the cave. Side by side, Mora and Fremy headed into the cavern.

"Are you not suspicious of Goldof, Fremy?" Mora asked quietly.

"Of course I am. I'm suspicious of him, and you, and Rolonia, and Hans and Chamo, too."

"Hans and Chamo..."

"I don't trust anyone aside from Adlet," Fremy asserted quietly and flatly.

"Is Adlet all right?" Mora called into the cave.

Hans and Rolonia were beside Adlet where he lay on the ground with a wet cloth on his forehead. Rolonia was treating his wounds with her power as the Saint of Spilled Blood. Farther in the enclosure was a boulder of about waist height, and on top of it bloomed a tiny flower. That was the center of the barrier, the Bud of Eternity. Thankfully, there was a spring welling within the cave, so they would have plenty of water.

"So yer alive. I was goin' to go get ya," said Hans.

"We're fine," said Fremy. "What about Adlet?"

"He's alive, but there's a crack in his skull, and he won't wake up. I can't heal him with my power," said Rolonia. Her ability was to control blood. She could treat gashes and internal bleeding, but not bones.

"I'll take over. The power of mountains is the power of healing." Mora sat down beside Adlet, absorbed energy from the mountain and channeled it into the boy's skull, stimulating the natural healing abilities that every human has to repair the damage.

"Is it workin'?" asked Hans.

"Yes. No issues," said Mora.

Fremy stood behind Mora, observing her intently. She must have suspected that she might pretend to treat Adlet while she in fact killed him. If Mora did anything suspicious, Fremy would be sure to shoot her down before she could even react.

"He was hurt quite severely," noted Mora.

The atmosphere in the cave suddenly became heavier. They had lost a head-on battle, and to make it worse, the enemy had not even had their full army at their command. Did they even have a chance of winning in this sorry state?

"If there'd been six of us, we probably could've won," said Hans. Mora looked at him. "We're always suspicious of each other when we're fightin'. We don't know who might betray us, or when, or what the attack'll be or where it'll come from. We can't fight at full strength like this right neow. We're at sixty percent, maybe."

"You're right," said Fremy.

You're part of the reason we lost, Mora wanted to say.

Then suddenly, Hans burst out laughing. *"Meow-hee-hee!* We're in big trouble. This is fun. This is what I came meowt to the Howlin' Vilelands to get a taste of."

Unsurprisingly, Mora's response was sharp. "And just what do you find so amusing about this, Hans?"

"Meow? Ain't you havin' fun? Ya don't get in a pickle like this often. It's a waste if ya don't enjoy yerself."

Mora wanted to bury her face in her hands. She just couldn't understand Hans. "But what was Adlet attempting to do? He charged in recklessly, then all of a sudden left himself wide open while Tgurneu pummeled him. What was that about?"

Having treated Adlet as best she could, Rolonia said, "Um…Addy had this look on his face like he was sure he'd won."

"But Tgurneu was unharmed."

Hans explained to the puzzled Mora. "He seemed like he was aimin' for somethin' big. That's why I backed him up by grabbin' Tgurneu. I wasn't expectin' it to end up like this at all."

"Whatever the case, we'll ask him once he awakens," said Mora.

"When will he wake up?" Fremy asked her.

As Mora sent energy streaming into Adlet, she checked how he was doing. "Most likely, in a few hours. He's inhumanly tenacious."

"I'm so fed up with him," Fremy said suddenly. Not getting her meaning, the others looked at her. "This is the third time he's almost died. Just how much does he have to make us worry before he's satisfied?" She sighed.

"He's not goin' to neow that yer worried if ya don't tell him," said Hans.

"Even if I did tell him, that idiot wouldn't get it. Besides, I don't really want to talk right now."

As Mora treated Adlet, she remembered that she had almost killed the boy herself just a day before. At that time, she had sincerely believed he was the seventh. Now, in retrospect, there had been times when she'd had reason to doubt that verdict. But still, back then, she'd been unable to see Adlet as anything but the enemy—because when he had run, he had taken Fremy as his hostage. Mora had been enraged by his use of her as a shield. His convictions about doing what it took to win were not wrong. But even so, Mora believed there were some things that you simply couldn't do. The moment that Adlet had pressed a blade to Fremy's throat, Mora had seen Tgurneu in front of her.

Now, things were different. Mora was convinced that Adlet was the most trustworthy of all. "Let's wait for him to awaken. We can talk after that. He's bound to have a way out of this situation. I'm sure of it."

Rolonia nodded firmly. Hans shrugged. Fremy's expression was inscrutable as she simply watched Adlet.

Why? That was all Adlet's unconscious mind thought about. In a space that was neither dreams nor reality, Adlet fought Tgurneu. He hurled a smoke bomb in an attempt to distract the fiend, but his foe was undeterred. Adlet threw poison needles, but they didn't work at all. He lobbed a regular bomb at the thing's face. No good, either. Adlet leaped high and struck the fiend with his sword, using all the strength in his body. Tgurneu effortlessly sent Adlet flying. He stabbed Tgurneu with the Saint's Spike, but even Adlet's final, ultimate attack didn't work.

Why? he thought. No fiend could endure the Saint's Spike. There was no way. If the Saint's Spike didn't work, then he had no weapons left. There was no way to defeat Tgurneu.

"*Hey, Adlet,*" said Tgurneu, as if speaking to a friend. "*Are you actually taking this seriously?*"

Screaming, Adlet sprung awake.

He was in a cave. Noticing a faintly shining flower beside him, he immediately understood that it was the Bud of Eternity. Bandages were wrapped around him all over his body, and he pieced together what had happened—he was inside the mountain where the Bud of Eternity bloomed. The others had taken Adlet and run.

"Addy? Are you awake?" Rolonia approached him from the back of the cave with a damp cloth.

"Is everyone okay?"

"Yes. All seven of us are right here."

When Adlet heard that, he picked up his sword from where it lay on the ground and stood. His iron box with his tools was there, too, though he didn't know who had brought them. He refilled the pouches at his waist with his assortment of weapons.

"What are you doing?" asked Rolonia.

"I'm going out to fight Tgurneu one more time."

"Wait! You're injured!"

"That's nothing new." That dream was seared into his mind. His body burned with the compulsion to fight, to win. He couldn't sit still. He tried to leave the cave, but Fremy blocked his way.

"Where are you going, Adlet?" She watched him calmly. Meeting that gaze, Adlet finally pulled himself together. "If you're stupid enough to try to go fight now, then you *should* die," she said.

"You're right. That was wrong of me. Sorry," Adlet said, sheathing his sword. Rolonia breathed a sigh of relief, and he smiled. The more painful the times, the more he had to smile.

"We're all resting, eating, treating our wounds, and tending to our weapons and tools," said Fremy. "You should do the same."

"I can't. I have to think of a way to kill Tgurneu."

Exasperated, Fremy sighed. "You should leave the thinking for later, too. You're still not in your right mind. I doubt you'll come up with any decent ideas like this."

"*Urk.*" Adlet couldn't say anything to that.

"The strongest man in the world is quite the nuisance." Fremy walked past Adlet and into the depths of the cave and then removed her cloak and top.

"What're you doing?"

"I'm going to bathe. I haven't washed in days," said Fremy. Still holding her gun in one hand, she took off her clothes. Flustered, Adlet left the cave.

Just outside, Hans was having a meal. He was soaking some smoked meat and dried bread in water as he stuffed his face with food. "So yer awake. Meow're ya feelin'?"

"I feel good. So good, I wanna go out and kill Tgurneu right now."

"Drop the lame jokes. Just eat somethin'."

Adlet helped himself to a portion of Hans's smoked meat. When he picked it up, he noticed it was unusually soft. The fatty meat had good color, and it didn't smell. The oiled paper wrapped around it had a familiar brand on it. "Hans, wasn't this Nashetania's?"

"*Meow*. When she ran, she left her packs behind. That woman was carryin' some damn good eatin'."

"I'm impressed you're into eating the enemy's food."

"No one out there is dumb enough to poison their own food," said Hans, who heartily devoured his meal.

While Adlet hesitated over the food, Rolonia emerged from the cave. "If you're worried about poison, you don't have to be. Torleau—the Saint of Medicine—gave me an all-purpose antidote. My own powers can counteract poisons a little, too."

"Sorry, but I'm just not into it. The strongest man in the world is the careful type," said Adlet, and he pulled some travel rations from a pouch on his belt, a single small cube about four centimeters wide.

"What's that? Does it taste good?" asked Hans.

"This is a little something I've named 'the strongest rations in the world.'"

"I shoulda neown it'd be somethin' like that."

"Refined flour, the extract of an organ from a certain animal, and a powder from twelve kinds of medicinal herbs mixed with hardened beef fat. Since I'm the strongest man in the world, I can last all day on just this."

"I'm not sure strength has anything to do with that." Rolonia looked puzzled.

"So is it good?" asked Hans. Adlet eyed his rations for a moment and took a few deep breaths to calm his heart.

"What're ya doin'?"

"There's a trick to eating this. First, you banish from your mind all memory of every good thing you've ever eaten." Adlet pressed a finger against his forehead to aid the power of psychological suggestion on himself. "And then you make yourself believe that this is the most delicious thing in the world. If you manage to do a good job tricking yourself…"

He closed his eyes, shoved the whole cube into his mouth, chewed it up as fast as he could, and swallowed it down all at once. "If you slow down for even a second, hell awaits you. But if you can avoid that, this stuff really is the strongest rations in the world."

"And that's the only way you can eat it, *meow*?" Hans was flabbergasted.

"Anyway, has everyone else eaten?" Adlet asked, now that he was done with his meal. He and Hans were the only ones eating. Fremy was bathing, and Goldof and Mora were keeping watch by the edge of the barrier. Chamo was leaning against a boulder, her eyes closed.

"Goldof was off by himself havin' some kinda meal. All the ladies said they don't eat. I don't know why," said Hans.

"They don't?"

Rolonia explained to Hans and Adlet. "I don't need food. I can manipulate the nutrients within blood. Lady Mora can absorb the energy of the mountain to sustain herself, so she doesn't need food, either."

That's convenient, thought Adlet. "And Chamo?"

"Chamo... I wonder why she doesn't need food. Sorry, I don't know."

From a little ways away, the girl in question piped up. "Do you think Chamo'd need normal food?"

"I don't really get what you mean, but now I'm convinced you don't," said Adlet.

"Chamo's treating her pets right now, so go away," she said and closed her eyes again. Adlet could just faintly hear the moans of her slave-fiends from within her stomach. He remembered how the creatures had writhed, covered in silver dust. It was probably best to do as she said and not bother her.

"And Fremy... Oh, yeah. Because she's half-fiend." Atreau had taught Adlet about fiend biology—they didn't eat every day the way humans did. For them, one big meal about once every ten days at most was enough.

"...?"

That was when Adlet sensed something odd. He cocked his head in contemplation.

"Is somethin' up, *meow*?" asked Hans.

Fiends ate about once every ten days—but if that was true, why had Tgurneu been carrying around that fig? But in the end, Adlet's questions led him nowhere, so they faded from his mind.

Mora was standing at the edge of the barrier when she saw Adlet exit the cave and begin a leisurely meal. Seeing she didn't need to worry about him, she relaxed. She scanned the whole mountain, observing the fiends' movements. Only when she was on a mountain could she use her powers of clairvoyance—though she was only able to observe the mountain she occupied. Presently, there were around two hundred fiends near the Bud of Eternity. The ones that had followed them were scattered about the mountain in groups of five or so. There were a large number of superior fiends among them that she supposed had some degree of intellect.

We're trapped rats, she thought. Perhaps Tgurneu's goal was just to keep the Braves of the Six Flowers from leaving this spot.

Next, Mora probed for traps. The Bud of Eternity was an almost certain stop for the Braves, so the chances were high that there was a trap there. Mora searched the mountain and even underground for anything out of place. But as far as she could tell, there were no tricks on the mountain.

Tgurneu was not in the area, and there was no sign it was giving instructions to the other fiends that lurked on the mountain. Mora still didn't know what it had meant by *two more days*.

"..." She was indecisive. Had running really been the right choice? Maybe she should have done whatever she could to kill Tgurneu right then—even if it had meant her life.

No, that would have been unwise, she thought, reconsidering. Blowing herself up and taking Tgurneu with her should be a final resort, because if she erred, then Shenira would die as well.

"What's the situation, Mora?" Adlet, having finished his meal, had come to talk to her.

"We're completely surrounded but in no immediate danger." She suspended her observation for the moment and explained her powers of clairvoyance to Adlet.

"Why don't ya take a break for neow, too? Looks like it'll be a while before we get another chance," Hans suggested.

"You're right, I'll rest a spell. I want to bathe, too," Mora said, entering the cave. With her powers still active, she continued to observe the area vigilantly. Within the cavern, she found Fremy nude and wiping off the soot stuck in her hair. As the woman entered, Fremy picked up the gun she'd laid beside her.

"Don't be so antagonistic. I'll do nothing to you," Mora said, stripping off her armor and vestments before she dipped herself into the cold spring. Dust suddenly clouded the spring, but they had already secured enough drinking water, so it wasn't a problem. A comfortable coldness seeped into her body. Before the chill could reach her core, she got out of the spring and began to clean off the dirt with her nails and palms. "It's a blessing to have such an abundance of water. At the very least, it's good to not have to worry about grooming." Mora breathed a long sigh. It was always comfortable to spend time cleansing the body. Though even if she wanted to relax, Shenira never left her mind.

"Um, may I join you?" Rolonia came into the cave and spent some time taking off her armor.

"It's careless for all three of us to bathe at once. What if something happens?" said Fremy.

"It doesn't worry me. One can still battle nude. Being seen weakens nothing," Mora said as she scooped water in her hands to wash off the grime. "You must be surprised, Rolonia, to be suddenly thrust into such a situation."

"Y-yes. I really...don't know what I should do. I still can't believe that there's an impostor among the Braves of the Six Flowers."

"I feel the same. When you arrived, I thought my heart would stop," Mora said with a smile.

"I don't get you, either, Rolonia," Fremy said suddenly.

Rolonia, who had still been working on her armor, jumped in surprise. "Oh! Um! What?"

"At first, you were even scared of a deer, but then when we ran into the enemy, you were ranting and raving on some kind of rampage. Which one is the real you?"

Mora replied for Rolonia. "The timid and indecisive Rolonia is the 'real' one. All that howling is, well…a sort of ritual for her."

Fremy didn't seem to understand, tilting her head in puzzlement. "Let me ask you something, Rolonia. Who do you suspect?"

That made Rolonia wince. "I don't know. It doesn't seem like any of you are the enemy."

Fremy glared at her. "If I were you, the first person I'd doubt would be me. I'm the daughter of a fiend and the Brave-killer. I even killed someone you know—Athlay. And I'm a warrior raised by Tgurneu. How could you *not* suspect me, considering all of that?"

"I…"

"What are you scheming?" Fremy demanded.

Unable to stand it any longer, Mora interrupted. "Enough, Fremy. She has no schemes. Rolonia has never had the disposition for distrust."

"I'm sure."

"You might attempt to be less callous. Your attitude will only isolate you," said Mora.

Fremy looked away. "This is the only way I can deal with people."

"Fremy, I—" Rolonia began. "I did think that you might be the seventh. But Addy and Lady Mora both trust you, so I stopped doubting you."

"…I see."

"Are you close with Addy?"

Fremy did not reply; instead she began to get dressed. In moments, her slim figure was covered in black leather. "'Addy,' hmm? You two are pretty close, yourselves," she commented, and with her gun in hand, left the cave.

Mora thought Fremy was like a hedgehog: cautious of all that drew near and always afraid of something. The only way she could interact with people was by turning her weakness into hostility. Perhaps it was not Rolonia who was the truly cowardly and timid one, but Fremy.

Apparently more nervous than she'd seemed, Rolonia sighed in relief and resumed taking off her armor.

"You're in a rough position, Rolonia. It seems she's not at all fond of you."

"Yes, it looks like it." The girl seemed embarrassed as she smiled. "But I'm relieved, too. She seems to be a much better person than I first assumed."

What about our conversation just now could have made her think that? wondered Mora. "What you said reminds me—I wasn't aware you and Adlet knew each other. The world is small indeed."

"Oh, yes. I just never got the chance to talk about it."

"Hmm. Do you have feelings for him?"

Rolonia's hands paused in their task once more. "Um, well, uh, I don't know." Her reply was so funny, Mora couldn't help but smile. "I don't think so. Probably not, I suppose. I don't think it's that I like him."

"I think that is for the best. Adlet is a reliable man, but also a tremendous fool. I'm sure it would be endless trouble were you to fall for him."

"You think so? He doesn't really seem that way to me, but…hmm."

These youngsters are so carefree, thought Mora. Even in the direst of situations, they could still manage to think of romance. She found that charming. As for her, while she chatted of such trivial things, Shenira was never far from her thoughts—not for one instant.

Evening approached, and they had all finished bathing and doing maintenance on their weapons and tools. The seven sat down in a circle in front of the cave—it was time for a discussion.

"Have you calmed down, Adlet?" asked Mora.

Adlet, sitting in the center of the group, nodded. Mora was continually amazed at how tenacious he was. She could hardly believe he was flesh and blood.

"So anyway, what's the situation?" he asked. "Is Tgurneu nearby?"

With the help of the Spirit of Mountains, Mora determined there was no change in the situation around them. "There's no sign of Tgurneu," she said.

Adlet paused to think. "Two hundred, huh? That's odd. That's not really a full crowd. It's way too few to be trapping us here."

"There are likely more just outside the mountain. We'd probably lose in a head-on clash."

"Even if we couldn't win, we could still run. If Tgurneu wasn't here, those numbers wouldn't be scary at all," said Adlet.

"*If* Tgurneu wasn't here," Fremy emphasized.

"First, I want to ask you guys something. Do any of you have a clue as to who the seventh might be? Not just suspicion toward someone or something fishy one of you did—I need a definitive lead." Mora had nothing. None of them replied. "Could you describe to me in detail how you escaped Tgurneu? I was unconscious, so I don't know anything about it."

Mora and Hans took turns explaining how they'd fought to get here. Once they finished the story, Adlet's expression turned somber as he pressed one hand to his forehead. "I don't know. From what you've described, every single one of us had the chance to kill one another." Mora nodded. If Fremy was the traitor, Mora would be dead.

"If Goldof or Rolonia had backstabbed us, I might've been in a pickle," said Hans. "Even if I'd gotten away, I don't neow if I could've saved you and Chamo, too. And if the kid was the enemy, I would've gotten killed."

"Hmm…and if it was the catboy, Chamo'd be dead," Chamo added.

"Why isn't the seventh doing anything? What's their goal?" Adlet agonized over the quandary. Mora wondered, too. No matter how they approached it, it was clear that the seventh had let multiple opportunities slide.

Then Fremy spoke. "I planned to kill the seventh if I found out who they were, even if it meant my life."

"Huh?"

"I've been ready for it this whole time, and I've been trying to sound out who it is. Maybe the seventh knew that. Maybe it's not that they aren't doing anything, but that they're afraid of me and *can't* do anything."

"But I still think it's fishy they didn't do nothin' durin' that fight. If they'd played their cards right, all of us'd be dead," said Hans. Mora agreed.

"There's one more possibility," said Fremy. "Tgurneu may have ordered them not to act."

"Why?" asked Adlet.

"To mess with us."

"Huh?"

"Tgurneu often toys with people. It always says things that don't make sense and has no problem doing things that would put itself at a disadvantage. I don't know what Tgurneu is thinking—perhaps nothing at all."

She was right. Between that over-familiar tone, clownish attitude and inconsistent way of fighting, the only conclusion was that Tgurneu was merely fooling around.

"So in other words, Tgurneu is just having a few laughs, here?" said Adlet. "You're saying it's not seriously trying to kill us?"

"I don't know. It might be pretending to fool around while it's planning something, or it could be fooling around for real."

So that meant even trying to surmise what was on Tgurneu's mind was pointless. *Quite the bothersome opponent*, mused Mora. "On that hill, we were ambushed. What if the seventh led us there?" she suggested. Adlet folded his arms and considered.

"Yer the one who found it, though, Mora," said Hans.

"And I'm the one who suggested having a discussion there," said Fremy.

Then Rolonia timidly raised her hand. "Um...I-I'm sorry. May I say something?" When Adlet prompted her, she finally spoke. "Maybe...the seventh doesn't want to be found out."

"What do you mean?" he asked.

"I mean, the seventh doesn't want their identity revealed, right? So if they don't do anything, then we'll never find out. I'm sure they don't want to be suspected."

"But then why even be here? If they're just sitting here to avoid being discovered, then there's no point infiltrating the Braves in the first place," Fremy said, shooting down the suggestion.

"No, Rolonia might be on to something," said Adlet. All eyes gathered on him. "This is ultimately just my own deduction, but…I doubt the seventh has done anything. They didn't lead us to that hill, and they didn't tell Tgurneu we were going there."

"What makes you think that?"

"If the Braves planned to follow the safest route in an attempt to avoid a surprise attack, we'd be sure to pass over that hill, and Tgurneu predicted that. The fact that we took a break on that hill was simply coincidence. We wouldn't need to stop there to get caught. Tgurneu would just wait for the moment we passed through and attack us from behind."

"So why isn't the seventh doing anything?"

"That was the plan all along," Adlet explained. "They'd just stay with us and keep pretending to be one of us. That's the only reason they're here."

"What do you mean?"

"The traitor is waiting for the moment they're sure they can kill all of us. They could've attacked us during that last fight, but a few of us probably would've gotten away. I bet just killing one or two Braves isn't enough." The group was silent. "The seventh probably won't make their move until the perfect opportunity arises, because as long as they don't do anything, they won't be discovered. Well, that's just a hypothesis, though."

"If that's the case, then how can we expose the impostor?" said Mora. "As long as they do nothing, we'll have no clues as to their identity. But when the seventh does act, it will be when our situation is most desperate. What on earth can we do?"

Hans clapped his hands like he was amused by all of this. "*Ma-meow!* What a *cat*astrophe! Is this checkmate?"

"It's not just Tgurneu. There's a buffoon among us, too," commented Mora grumpily.

The assassin answered with an expression of deepest offense. "I'm serious! A game's no fun if ya don't play for keeps, right?"

Good grief.

Adlet continued. "From what Fremy's told us, I don't think it's possible to know what Tgurneu might do, because it doesn't follow logic in order to win. And, like with Tgurneu, we can't predict what the mole will do, either."

"But yer the strongest man in the world, ain't ya? Ya givin' up that easy?"

"We're completely surrounded, Adlet. How do we get out of here?" Mora inquired.

"Even if we do get away, it would just make our situation worse. We need a plan to solve the root problem," Fremy insisted.

As his allies pressed him for answers, Adlet concluded quietly, "There's only one way to get out of this situation."

"What?" Hans asked.

"We have to solve the mystery of Tgurneu."

The entire party went silent. Mora had no idea what he meant by *the mystery of Tgurneu*.

"Guys, look at this," Adlet said, pulling a twenty-centimeter-long spike out from under his jacket. It was identical to the one he had used in the previous battle.

"What is that thing?" Hans appeared quizzical.

Adlet explained to them the weapon he called the Saint's Spike, how it was poisoned with a crystal made from Saints' blood fitted at the tip, and how if a fiend was impaled with it, the poison would instantly circulate through its whole body.

As Mora listened to his explanation, she thought about Atreau Spiker. She had only been aware that he was a warrior knowledgeable about fiends, but it seemed she had incredibly underestimated him. She'd never considered using Saints' blood as a weapon at all, much less extracting the poison from that blood.

"And...you impaled Tgurneu with that? Are you sure?" Mora asked.

Adlet nodded vigorously. "I know I stabbed Tgurneu with that spike, and I even saw the toxin affect it—but it's still alive."

This is difficult to believe, thought Mora. Rolonia and Fremy had gone pale.

"Why didn't it work?" said Adlet. "If we can figure that out, we should find a breakthrough and defeat Tgurneu."

"*Meow.* Is this problem that important, though?" asked Hans. Chamo also seemed unconvinced. The two didn't fully understand how impossible it was for a Saint's blood not to harm a fiend. "I don't know everythin' about it, but there's a lot of different types of fiends, and they all have different powers, right? This just means Tgurneu's strong against poison."

"I guess you don't understand. I'll be a little more precise." Adlet sighed. "Fiends can choose how they develop—it's based on what they want. I think you've seen a lot of them in your life, but none of them looked exactly the same, right?"

"*Meow.*"

"If they want to grow fangs, they can grow fangs. If they want to get bigger, they can get bigger. It takes them decades or even centuries to evolve. And occasionally, the process fails. But fundamentally speaking, if fiends have the will, they can obtain whatever powers they want."

"Huh. So then couldn't Tgurneu just've evolved the power to nullify the poison in Saints' blood?"

"There are exceptions to the rule," said Adlet. "There are things they can't do no matter how much they want it. They can't evolve their own cores."

"What's that?"

Fremy explained. The core was like the fiend's brain. They always had one somewhere in their body, and it was their weakest point. "The core is the main body of the fiend. You could even say all flesh aside from it is simply auxiliary. Fiends can change their auxiliary bodies, but not the core itself. A Saint's blood is what destroys that core."

Hans and Chamo still didn't quite get it.

"The poison within Saints' blood originates from the power of the Spirit," she continued. "Its properties are completely different from those of other toxins. Once it enters the body, it reaches the core immediately. A fiend can't mutate their body to prevent this. And once the poison has penetrated, there is no way they can counteract it."

"In other words…"

"The poison works on all fiends without exception. That's what a Saint's blood does," she finished.

"Meow? It's that powerful?" Hans said, only now catching on.

"I have a technique I can use to get my blood into a fiend, too. Master Atreau told me this technique will always work on any fiend," said Rolonia.

"Just who is Atreau Spiker, Adlet?" asked Mora. "How did he acquire such techniques?"

Adlet tilted his head. "Sorry, but I don't know, either. He basically never talked about his past."

"Who cares about that weird weapon? Chamo doesn't care about that Atreau guy," she said, sounding bored. "Yeah, this weapon is supposed to be amazing or whatever, but it didn't work on Tgurneu, right? So we don't need it anymore. Chamo'll kill Tgurneu, slice it all into pieces and eat it up, and make it a toy for the pets in Chamo's tummy."

"Do you get what we're saying, Chamo? An attack that was supposed to *always* work *didn't*," Adlet insisted.

"So what?"

"If your slave-fiends tear Tgurneu limb from limb, will it die? If Rolonia drains all its blood, will it die? If Goldof and Hans cut it up, or Mora pounds it to a pulp, or Fremy shoots it, will it die? We don't know any of those things for sure." Adlet hammered Chamo with questions.

"Who cares? Chamo just has to beat it up."

"We need to be certain we can kill Tgurneu. In order to find a way to take it down for sure, we have to solve this mystery."

This is not good, Mora fretted. Chamo's mood was worsening. She might snap.

"…So what do we do, then?" Counter to the Elder's expectations, Chamo reluctantly backed down.

"I'll figure out the puzzle and find a way to kill that monster," said Adlet. "You think about how you could kill it—and how to counteract that silver powder, in particular."

"Okay. Chamo actually does have an idea to test out," she said.

Mora was more than a little bit surprised at how cooperative Chamo was being. She was growing. Her progress was slow, but it was sure.

"We still haven't solved anything, though," said Fremy. "We haven't solved the mystery of Tgurneu, and we still don't know who the seventh is."

"If we can corner Tgurneu, I think the traitor will reveal themselves," Adlet answered.

"What do you mean?"

"The seventh is most likely connected to Tgurneu. At the very least, they're our enemy, so we have no reason to doubt that they're allied with the fiends. If we kill a commander, the seventh would consider that as a massive blow. So if Tgurneu is about to lose, the seventh will try to protect it. That's what I think."

"I see. So we don't wait for the traitor to act—we create a situation in which they are forced to act," said Mora.

"What happens if we have Tgurneu cornered but the seventh doesn't do anything?" asked Fremy.

"Then we kill Tgurneu," said Adlet. "That's really the best option, since killing Tgurneu would be a far bigger victory than figuring out who the seventh is."

"*Meow.* And if we can do both, all the better." Hans nodded.

"I feel like this is too dangerous. We don't even know what Tgurneu or the seventh might do," Rolonia cautioned.

"My master taught me there's nothing worse than a risk-free plan that only goes halfway. Sometimes, jumping right into danger is the safest thing to do. Right now, the best choice is to devote everything we've got to taking out Tgurneu."

Rolonia looked even more anxious.

"Relax. I'm the strongest man in the world."

"Oh, *meow.* There he goes again," said Hans, looking exasperated.

"I understand. I'll trust in you. You're the strongest man in the world." Rolonia nodded. They all seemed to agree to Adlet's plan. They would focus all their resources on killing Tgurneu. For Mora, Adlet's decision was a welcome one. Defeating it was the only way she could save her daughter.

No matter what, she had to kill Tgurneu. "I have one suggestion." Mora raised her hand.

"What is it?" asked Adlet.

"I have a secret plan. A technique I've spent many years developing in preparation for this day. I believe now may be the time to use it."

"What does it do?"

"I would enclose this whole mountain within a barrier, instantly, to trap Tgurneu here. It would both cut off reinforcements and prevent Tgurneu's escape. I can only use this technique once, but I believe it's worth an attempt."

When Rolonia heard the plan, her eyes went wide. "Hold on, please, Lady Mora! That barrier is dangerous."

"I'm fully aware of that. But you heard what Adlet said." Unable to counter her, the Saint of Spilled Blood fell silent.

"Will the barrier last very long?" inquired their leader.

"No. Six hours, at most. But that should be enough time to kill Tgurneu."

"I understand. Then do it," he said without hesitation.

"When Tgurneu next appears, I'll let you know immediately," said Mora. "You decide whether or not I should activate the barrier, Adlet."

The boy nodded. "All right. Then we've decided our course of action. I'll work out what's happening with Tgurneu, starting with why the Saint's Spike didn't work, and figure out a way to kill it. You help me out with that, Fremy."

"…Fine," she acquiesced.

"Hans and Goldof, you clean up the fiends on the mountain. Get their numbers down, at least somewhat. Can you do that?"

"Of course. I could meownage that by myself." Hans smiled. Goldof didn't reply, but he seemed to accept the order at least.

"Mora, you use your powers to keep watch over the mountain. If anything odd happens, tell me right away. And give Hans and Goldof backup, too."

"Understood."

"Chamo, you figure out how to deal with that silver powder. If I can't solve the mystery, you'll be our main force. Don't blow this."

"Duh. Worry about yourself. You do your best, too."

"Um…what about me?" Rolonia raised her hand. Adlet hesitated for a moment.

"Rolonia is the Saint of Spilled Blood and an expert on the subject. I believe she'll be of use to you," said Mora. He nodded.

Thinking Adlet had concluded his instructions, the group was just about to move out when he stopped them. "I want to say one last thing—to the seventh among us." He scanned his allies and said, "If you wanna win, you'd better figure out how to kill me first. If you don't do it soon, you'll be too late."

No one said a word. Silence fell around them.

"Was that supposed to sound dramatic or something? 'Cause it was pretty lame," said Chamo.

She was quite right. Mora and Hans couldn't restrain their laughter. Rolonia lowered her eyes, covering her mouth, and Fremy had averted her gaze, too. Even Goldof had something resembling a faint smirk on his face. *This is the first time we've all smiled together,* thought Mora. Perhaps there was some solidarity growing in the group, if only very gradually. Adlet was quite the man, willing to play the clown to calm his allies.

Each of them went off to their separate tasks. Adlet returned to the cave, sitting with his back to the wall. His face was red. Chamo had humiliated him. *Damn it, I'm the strongest man in the world!* he cursed in his head.

Fremy and Rolonia came into the cave and sat down a little ways away. They didn't look at each other. The former was still expressionless, and the latter appeared extremely uncomfortable.

"I can't fault you for being wary, but try to get along. We can't solve the mystery of Tgurneu if we don't cooperate," said Adlet.

"Y-you're right," said Rolonia. "Let's work together, Fremy."

"Yeah, might as well." There was no sign that either of them would shift closer to the other. "I'm putting on some lights." Fremy placed a tiny gem on the ground in the dark cave. She recited an incantation, and it began to glow.

"What's this?" asked Adlet. "Is this your power, Fremy?"

"No. This is something Mora brought. She said Pipi, Saint of Light, made it. And she brought lots more, so I'll give you a few." Adlet accepted the gems, and Fremy told him the incantation. The three of them sat in a circle around the little jewel.

"I'm sorry, Adlet, but..." began Fremy, "...I frankly doubt you can solve this. We know too little about Tgurneu. We only fought for half an hour."

"What makes you say that? You should know Tgurneu better, Fremy," he said.

"Sorry, but you shouldn't count on me." She shook her head. "I don't know any of Tgurneu's weaknesses, and I have no idea why the Saint's Spike didn't work, either. Tgurneu planned to have me killed all along—obviously I wasn't going to be trusted with any important information."

She doesn't get it, he thought. "Did you feel that Tgurneu was hiding something?"

"...No."

"That's critical. Tgurneu planned to kill you, and so it didn't allow you to learn anything important. That's the key."

"What do you mean?" asked Fremy.

"It's pretty hard to hide something from someone who's familiar with you—and even harder to keep them from realizing that you're hiding something. You have to lie, keep them away from the truth, and act natural about all of it. That always leaves some kind of trace behind." Adlet looked Fremy in the eye and continued. "If we can figure out what Tgurneu lied about, it should be easy to figure out the truth."

"We still don't have enough information, though," she insisted.

Then, Rolonia hesitantly joined the conversation. "Um, Addy...can you lend me your sword?" Adlet didn't know what she wanted it for, but he handed it over, sheath and all. She drew it out and looked at the blade. "Oh, so you've already cleaned it. Do you have the cloth you wiped it with?" Adlet went to the trash pile by the cave entrance to pull out the rag he'd discarded there. She took it from him and put it in her mouth.

"Hey!" Adlet cried.

"That's disgusting," said Fremy.

The two of them grimaced. Though clearly embarrassed, Rolonia kept on sucking on the blood-soaked rag. "You cut six fiends with this blade." She removed the rag from her mouth and pulled out her whip, and then licked it like she had the rag. "And I hit nineteen fiends with this whip. There's only one type of blood among all of those that tastes the same as the blood on your sword, Addy—I've managed to identify Tgurneu's. If you'll give me a moment, I'll analyze it in detail." Rolonia licked the whip and the cloth in turn. Apparently, she was examining the remnants of Tgurneu's blood clinging to them both.

"You can learn stuff by doing that?" asked Fremy.

"Blood contains a wide variety of information, from what the creature ate to their physical attributes and their personal history. I can learn most things about them by licking their blood." Rolonia alternated between the whip and the cloth for a while and then closed her eyes and reflected. "I understand now."

"Understand what?"

"First of all, Tgurneu is a mixed-type fiend—one that absorbs other fiends in order to make itself stronger. The base of its body is a lizard-fiend, but that's just the foundation. It seems that its entire strength originates from the other fiends."

"That's quite impressive," said Fremy. "But I knew that, too."

"The base is fused together with seven other fiends," Rolonia continued. "First, it gained its physical strength by fusing with a giant ape-fiend. It also fused with an octopus-fiend in order to acquire the power to stretch and contract its arms. A crow-fiend gave it sharp sight, and a dog-fiend gave it powerful hearing and a sense of smell. And then a swan-fiend gave it agility…" Rolonia closed her eyes as she continued to analyze Tgurneu's blood. "This is amazing. Tgurneu has absorbed a primitive amphibian-fiend to gain incredible powers of regeneration. There's also a snake-fiend that contributed further endurance and strengthened its regenerative abilities. Those are all the different fiends in Tgurneu."

Adlet and Fremy met the stream of information pouring out of Rolonia with wide-eyed shock. "I didn't know that much—not which types of fiends Tgurneu has fused with," Fremy admitted.

"Where did you get the ability to do that?" asked Adlet, amazed.

Rolonia turned her gaze downward shyly. "Um…Lady Mora made me practice licking blood to analyze it. She said it was useful for a lot of things, like healing or counteracting poison. Master Atreau also taught me about fiends, so I thought maybe I could put that to use…"

Fremy asked Adlet, "Did you know she could do that?"

"No, this is news to me. Rolonia's done nothing but surprise me lately," said Adlet. She responded with a pleased smile.

Once Adlet, Fremy, and Rolonia entered the cave, Hans and Goldof left the Bud of Eternity to kill the swarming fiends. Mora observed the situation through the earth. The swarms of fiends rushed to attack Hans and Goldof, reacting to their presence immediately.

"*Mya-meow.* You clean up the small fry, Goldof. I'll kill the biggest critters," Mora heard Hans say. Her powers enabled her not only to see from a distance but also to hear.

The sun had fully set, and the red tint on the edge of the mountain was now gone. It was their first night in the Howling Vilelands. The light of the moon and stars illuminated Mora and her comrades. *This is bound to be a tumultuous night,* she considered. There was a large number of fiends in the area she could observe. Once the enemies learned it was time to fight, they began streaming toward Hans and Goldof.

"Hans, five approach from the east, and ten from the south." Mora modulated her echo ability so that the sound would only reverberate near Hans. This way, the fiends would not hear her.

"Goldof, once we're done cleanin' things up here, run straight north. It'll be a pain in the ass if we get surrounded," Hans instructed. The two of them quickly finished off the cluster of fiends and went on the move. At this rate, it looked like there was nothing to worry about as she continued tracking the battle from afar.

Then her gaze happened to shift to the side, where she saw Chamo plunging her foxtail down her throat, spewing up a few slave-fiends. "And what are you doing, Chamo?"

"You don't need to help, Auntie. Chamo can do this alone." The slave-fiends left the Bud of Eternity's barrier.

Mora observed them with her powers. For a moment, she thought they were heading out to fight the fiends, but then one dragged a pika from its hole. The others went on to capture squirrels, field mice, and more, carrying them back in their mouths.

"There, there. You're all such good little guys." When her creatures returned, Chamo petted their heads, then sank her teeth into the wild animals they had brought her. One after another she downed the kills, splattering her lips bright red.

"…That girl mystifies me." Mora didn't understand what the Saint of Swamps was trying to do, but surely, she had her own plan in mind. Mora decided to leave her be.

Meanwhile, it seemed all the fiends were now aware of Hans and Goldof's assault. The mountain was a flurry of activity, and she could hear the fiends that could talk speak to one another.

"They made their möve."

"Trying to rün?"

"No, just two attàcking."

Perhaps listening in on them could help her figure out their plan. Mora stayed alert, listening intently. There was much to do. She could not let her focus weaken for the whole night.

"But where is Tgurneu?" She scanned the mountain multiple times, but there was no sign of the commander anywhere and no sign of any fiends going to it to receive instruction. What was that fiend doing, and where was it?

"Don't let them éscape."

"Just two enémies. Just Hans and Goldof." The fiends didn't mention Tgurneu, either.

Tgurneu couldn't possibly continue to just do nothing. It *would* act. Perhaps it was already done setting the stage for an attack.

That was when Rolonia appeared beside Mora. "Pardon me, Lady Mora," she said. She grabbed her gauntlet, licking it again and again.

"What is this, all of a sudden?" the Elder asked, startled.

"I understand, now!" Rolonia cried, and she went back into the cave.

Mora was baffled. "What are they doing in there?"

"How'd it go?" Adlet greeted Rolonia when she returned to the cave.

"There wasn't much, but there *was* some of Tgurneu's blood on Lady Mora's gauntlet, too."

"Did you learn anything?" he asked her.

"There was a Saint's Blood in it. Enough that I could tell from just one lick."

"I see." So the poison had permeated Tgurneu's body, after all. That eliminated the possibility that the Saint's Spike had failed to hit its target. "Rolonia, can you determine the composition of Tgurneu's body from its blood, too?"

"Yes, generally."

"Is there a core inside its body?"

"There is. I could tell that quite clearly from the taste."

"How many?"

"Just one," she replied. Adlet made a sour look. "Unfortunately, I don't know why the Saint's blood didn't work. I'm sorry, Addy. I want to do a better job, but…" Rolonia's shoulders drooped.

"What the hell're you talking about? We're so close to solving the puzzle. How could the strongest man in the world get this much information and then *not* solve it?" Of course, this was all hot air. Adlet was worried. He was glad to have Rolonia's analysis—but it had only deepened the mystery.

Adlet had posited a few possible solutions to the riddle of Tgurneu. For example, there was a kind of fiend known as division-type, which could split its own body into pieces to make subsidiary units. It could be that Tgurneu was a division-type fiend that had split its body into two or more parts. It would hide the main unit—the one that contained the core—somewhere else, and then use the other part, which contained no core, to attack them. That hypothesis would explain why the Saint's poison hadn't worked. If there was no core inside the body, then the Saint's poison would have no effect.

But Rolonia's examination forced him to reject that possibility. There was a core within Tgurneu's body, so it was not a division-type fiend. The theory had been shaky to begin with, anyhow. The subsidiary units that division-type fiends could create were only lower-level animals or parasites. An auxiliary could not possibly be as powerful as Tgurneu.

Adlet had had one other hypothesis: Tgurneu could be a number of fiends merged into one that pretended to be a single being. The head, torso, arms, and legs were all different, independent fiends. Only one had been killed by the Saint's Spike, while the head and other parts had survived. But this, too, didn't hold water in light of Rolonia's analysis. Tgurneu was a single, mixed-type fiend, with only one core inside its body. Adlet was forced to discard this idea, as well.

So that left one final possibility—that Rolonia was mistaken. But she was such a timid and cautious person, he found it highly unlikely that she would bring forth anything if she wasn't sure about it. He could trust her analysis.

"So that disproves both your division-type theory and your fused fiends theory. Can you think of anything else, Adlet?" asked Fremy. Apparently she had been thinking the same thing he had. Adlet shook his head. "Now we understand the situation even less. If Rolonia's analysis is correct, that means Tgurneu has no hidden powers."

"I-I'm sorry."

No need for her to apologize, he thought.

"Rolonia, leave us alone for a minute," Fremy requested.

"Huh?" The sudden demand confused the other two.

"Now."

"O-okay. I'll go right now. Sorry," Rolonia said, rushing out of the cave. Fremy glanced outside, checking to see that there was no one listening.

"What's this about all of a sudden, Fremy?"

"Do you believe what she said?" She glared at him.

"Of course. She's got our only clue to figuring out what happened with Tgurneu."

"You're the one who deduced the seventh would try to protect Tgurneu, aren't you? Rolonia may be trying to lead you in the wrong direction."

"You don't know that."

"I'm saying it's a possibility."

"And I've taken that into account. But until we know for sure that she's the enemy, I'm gonna trust her."

"You're not being careful enough!" Her voice rose to a yell. Rolonia peered into the cave from the outside, and Fremy ordered her away with a gesture. "You need to be more cautious. Be on your guard with the others. At this rate, you're going to be deceived and end up dead."

"If the seventh comes for me, they're just playing into my hands. I'm the strongest man in the world."

Fremy's expression betrayed anger and the slightest hint of sadness, and Adlet couldn't tell what she was thinking. "You're not the strongest in the world."

"What did you say?"

"You're weaker than me. In fact, you're the weakest of all seven of us. Drop the ego and know your limits."

Adlet believed he was the strongest man in the world. He had conviction. If he were to stop believing in himself, then he wouldn't be Adlet anymore. "I'm the strongest man in the world. I *will* kill the Evil God. I'm not scared of the seventh. I'll protect you and the rest of us. Everyone."

Fremy didn't say anything. She just shook her head sadly. "I've got something to say to you, too. You need to trust your allies more. It's like you see everyone but me as your enemy."

"Because I do. As far as I'm concerned, they are. As long as we don't know who the impostor is, what else should I think?"

"You're going about this wrong. If we don't trust our own allies and cooperate with one another, then we can't beat the Evil God. The one who'll really benefit from that loss of solidarity is the seventh."

Fremy didn't move. She just stared at Adlet. "No. I've had enough of trying to trust these people."

"You're so—"

"If you would let me, I'd kill all of them but you. Then I wouldn't have to think about the seventh anymore."

"Fremy!" At the conclusion of their battle with Nashetania, Adlet had thought they had come to an understanding. But maybe that had all been in his head. He felt a gigantic rift between the two of them. Belief and trust in the other were beyond them, and it had always been like that. An ache stirred in his chest.

"Rolonia, you can come back. Let's think about Tgurneu." To distract himself from his irritation, Adlet called over the other girl.

"What happened?" asked Rolonia. "You two looked really serious."

"It wasn't that serious," said Adlet. "Just a pointless waste of time."

Fremy revealed no reaction. She looked away from Adlet and stared at the ground.

The three resumed their discussion, beginning with a question from Adlet. "Rolonia, does Tgurneu actually not have any hidden powers?"

"It does not. I can tell that quite clearly. Tgurneu is not hiding any abilities at all. If it did have any other powers, I should be able to tell by licking its blood."

"So in other words, Tgurneu's powers are…"

"Amazing physical strength, vitality, regenerative abilities, and a flexible and tough body. That's all," said Rolonia.

That meant Tgurneu did not have the power to counteract Saints' blood. "So then it wasn't Tgurneu's power that nullified the Saint's poison? Should we assume that someone else used some kind of power to protect it?" suggested Adlet.

"But Tgurneu was the only one there," countered Rolonia.

"We can't know that," said Fremy. "There could have been someone else hiding underground. Another fiend…or a Saint."

"A Saint?" Rolonia was shocked.

"That's obviously something we should consider," said Adlet. "Nashetania betrayed us, so it's surely plausible that another Saint could be a traitor."

"Maybe so, but…"

Fremy sighed. "Isn't it Mora's job to supervise the Saints? What was going on with her management?"

"L-Lady Mora couldn't be responsible for—"

"I'm not attacking Mora. I'm just whining," Fremy said coldly.

Rolonia's shoulders drooped. "Maybe it's my fault."

"Why would it be?" asked Adlet.

"Because Lady Mora spent all her time training me. And she was putting a lot of effort into her own training, too…so while she was busy teaching me to fight, she left the management of the Saints to others. If I were just better…"

"You really want to make everything your own fault, don't you?" Fremy complained. "It's obnoxious. Cut it out."

"I-I'm sorry." Rolonia wilted even further.

After that, the discussion continued for quite a while. The three Braves shared opinions on what kind of power might render Saints' blood ineffective. Adlet summoned all the knowledge that Atreau had given him, Fremy brought up the names and powers of fiends that she knew, and Rolonia drew from her scant knowledge of the Saints to consider their powers.

But they failed to reach a conclusion. They just rejected one possibility after another, unable to figure out why the Saint's poison had failed.

*   *   *

Hans and Goldof's battle with the fiends continued. They had shaved down the horde by about twenty under Mora's remote observation.

"Goldöf went to yöu!"

"Stinkíng Hans, die, die! Eat yöu up!"

As the fiends tried to surround Hans, Mora listened to their loud conversation and telegraphed her instructions with the power of the mountains. "Hans, at this rate, they'll have you surrounded. Head for the peak for now and then circle around to the western side."

"Yeah, *meow*! Run, Goldof! Follow me!" The two of them sprinted off, cutting down monsters as they went.

Hans was so powerful, simply watching him fight was enchanting. He had to be the most outstanding member of the party, excepting Chamo. And even more startling than his abilities was the accuracy of his situational analysis. Even with Mora's support, it should have been next to impossible to continue fighting without ending up surrounded. Plus, it was dark, and they weren't able to use lights.

Goldof was strong, too. He was following Hans's directions, in no danger as he fought. For this battle, at least, it seemed Mora had no need for concern.

"Goldof, if yer gettin' tired, ya tell me, *meow*. Can ya still fight?"

The knight didn't even shake his head. Still as sulky as ever.

"Hans, once the situation calms down, could you investigate the situation beyond the mountain? The reach of my powers is limited to this one alone," said Mora.

"*Meow.*" Hans and Goldof headed to the summit, and from the top, they looked down at the foot of their stronghold. "Don't see no lights, *meow*. Don't look like a big herd is comin', either."

"I see. Understood. Continue your battle." Mora was impatient. She still hadn't caught sight of Tgurneu. At this rate, she would be unable to use her barrier to trap the fiend. *What on earth are you doing?* Mora silently cursed Tgurneu. Why weren't the commander and the seventh making their move? And what had it meant when it said she only had two more days? Doubts kept popping up in her mind one after another, and the answers refused to show themselves.

"..."

Mora had one concern that had been on her mind ever since the party had been trapped inside the Phantasmal Barrier—did the seventh know about Mora and Tgurneu's secret agreement? Tgurneu had said that it wouldn't speak of their contract to anyone, but if someone had been eavesdropping on that conversation, that was another story. And though Mora's promise had been conditional, she had nevertheless promised to kill one of her allies. If this was found out, the Braves would surely suspect her. Fremy might try to kill her on the spot. Even if Mora wasn't immediately killed, the rest of the group would no longer believe anything she said. To make it worse, she had made grave mistakes during their battle within the Phantasmal Barrier and lost much of her allies' trust. This was the perfect opportunity for the seventh. But there was no sign that her contract with Tgurneu would be exposed, and aside from Fremy, none of the group strongly suspected Mora.

What was the impostor after—and what was Tgurneu after?

"Mora, which way should we go? Are ya sleepin'?" From the summit, Hans asked Mora what to do.

Flustered, she stopped mulling over her situation and scanned the area with her powers, giving them instructions. "Descend the mountain and circle around to the south side. The fiends' forces there are thin."

"*Meow*, ma'am."

That was when, in the back of Mora's mind, a tiny spark of an idea was born—but she quickly discarded the possibility.

It couldn't be. Mora *herself* couldn't possibly be the seventh.

They must have been discussing their situation for around two hours, and the trio was running out of things to say. They had run through every possible ability that could have stopped the Saint's poison after it permeated Tgurneu's body. They had also spent a long time considering what the creature may have been hiding from Fremy, but she had simply not been exposed to enough information to pin down its secret.

The air between them was heavy. Adlet, Rolonia, and Fremy looked at one another. "Maybe we should change tacks," Adlet said, unable to stand how circular the conversation had become.

"How?" asked Fremy.

"Instead of asking what kind of power could block the poison, we ask if there was anything odd about Tgurneu's behavior. Let's think about that."

Fremy and Rolonia did not react with enthusiasm. "Everything Tgurneu does is odd," said Rolonia. "It popped out from underground, talked about how greetings are the first step of something-or-other and complained about my 'foul language'…"

She was right. "Has Tgurneu always been like that, Fremy?" Adlet questioned.

"Oh, yes. 'Greetings are the first step toward living a bright life.' That's what it always said. If its vassals failed to greet it properly, Tgurneu would get mad."

What the hell is with that fiend? wondered Adlet. "And what was that mouth on its chest? Is that like its storage closet or something?"

"That's right. Tgurneu would put lots of different things in there."

"What was inside?" asked Rolonia.

"Tgurneu often kept memo books and writing tools in there, and a compass and a map…and candy and toys made by humans, too."

"It sounds like it's nothing but mundane things in there," said Rolonia.

That was when Adlet remembered—among Tgurneu's many bizarre actions, there was one thing in particular that had stuck out. "Hey…why did Tgurneu have a fig?"

"?"

"Fiends don't have to eat very often, right? So why was Tgurneu walking around with food?"

"It ate unusually frequently. It told me that it was just innately hungry more often than regular fiends."

"Is that true, Rolonia?"

"That its body made it eat more often? I couldn't really say…"

Adlet thought back to when Tgurneu had appeared in Adlet's village, eight years ago. Back then, it had taken a seat at a table to speak with the villagers—and for some reason, there had been a large volume of food on that table, too. "Maybe there's a secret behind that fig."

"The fig?" Fremy echoed dubiously.

"What did Tgurneu normally eat?"

"Anything. Humans, animals, fruits and vegetables—fruit in particular quite frequently. Tgurneu would make the captured humans grow it, which it then carried in the mouth in its chest."

"It ate fruit, huh?"

"I could tell that from tasting its blood before. Tgurneu really does eat anything," said Rolonia. "Like figs, and animal meat, too, and grass and things. And…" Partway through, Rolonia hesitated. "It also ate fiends."

Adlet was shocked, but Fremy seemed unfazed. "Yes, Tgurneu eats fiends," she said. "It would eat useless, low-level types, and also those it suspected of being loyal to Dozzu. Tgurneu said it made it stronger."

"It even eats its own kind… Sickening." A fiend that ate ravenously. That part stuck in Adlet's mind. But what did that imply? He couldn't say if it meant anything at all. But the thing had pulled a fig from the mouth on its chest and eaten it. That just didn't strike Adlet as an inconsequential act. "…Tgurneu wasn't described as a big eater in the old records, though," Adlet commented absently.

"Old records?" Fremy seemed curious.

"You don't know about *Barnah's Chronicle of War*? It's a historical document written by a survivor."

"I've never even heard of it. Does Tgurneu make an appearance in it?"

Adlet nodded. Anyone who aspired to be a Brave of the Six Flowers would have read *Barnah's Chronicle of War*.

"I've read it, too." Rolonia raised her hand.

"Heroic King Folmar was cool, wasn't he?" said Adlet. "Especially in that scene where he accepts Zophrair's challenge to fight one-on-one."

"My favorite was Pruka, Saint of Fire. Though she was the first of the six to die." Adlet and Rolonia began chatting away.

Fremy interrupted. "I'm curious. What does it say about Tgurneu?"

"Tgurneu's name isn't mentioned directly," said Adlet. "There's just a fiend among Archfiend Zophrair's underlings that was described as looking just like Tgurneu."

"Archfiend Zophrair?"

She doesn't know about that, either? Adlet was surprised. "Zophrair was in the first Battle of the Six Flowers. They say it used to rule over all the fiends, ranking second to the Evil God. The author of the *Chronicle*, Barnah, gave it the name *Archfiend*."

"Such a fiend existed? I had no idea," said Fremy.

"You know how the first generation of Braves came to the Howling Vilelands by boat, approaching from the western side?" Adlet began. "They distracted the fiends and disembarked at a vulnerable point where the enemy defenses were thin. Then they headed straight for the Weeping Hearth, taking them by surprise. The Archfiend Zophrair and its twenty-two underlings stood in their way.

"Apparently Zophrair looked quite bizarre," he continued. "It had the wings of a peacock, something like a cross between a bird and a cat. Barnah said that it was the most beautiful thing he'd ever seen in his whole life."

"You sound like you know all about it," said Fremy.

"I've read *Barnah's Chronicle of War* so many times, I've memorized it. Let me continue. Zophrair had unique powers. Barnah described it as a controller-type."

"What kind of powers did it have?"

"The power to control other fiends. When Zophrair's minions fought the Braves of the Six Flowers, they were *perfectly* coordinated. They didn't talk to each other or look at each other; they were just flawlessly in sync. And the *Chronicle* says that no matter how many times Zophrair's twenty-two minions were killed, they revived again. As long as Zophrair was alive, none of them would fall."

"What's a controller-type?"

"Zophrair didn't give orders. It apparently just assumed complete power over its minions. They forfeited their wills to become a part of their overlord. What we know is that Zophrair gave a portion of its own flesh to its minions. It was by giving them its flesh that it could command them. That's the 'controller-type' power. Though that last part was really just a hypothesis on the part of Barnah—the author of the *Chronicle*."

"Apparently, Zophrair also had the ability to strengthen its subordinates," Rolonia said, supplementing his explanation. "The moment Zophrair died, its minions were radically weakened."

"So then what happened?"

Adlet continued. "Three of the Six Braves held Zophrair in check while the rest of them went straight to the Weeping Hearth and defeated the Evil God. After that, Zophrair challenged Heroic King Folmar, the leader of the Braves, to single combat. Folmar accepted the challenge, and after a fierce struggle, they both died."

"..."

"Zophrair doesn't appear in the records left by the second generation of the Braves of the Six Flowers," he continued, "and neither do any fiends with the same ability. Zophrair was the only controller-type fiend, one worthy of being dubbed the Archfiend."

"Where does Tgurneu come into this?" asked Fremy.

"A fiend that resembled Tgurneu was among Zophrair's minions. Other Braves left a number of their own records aside from *Barnah's Chronicle of War*, but his is the only one that mentions Tgurneu."

"What did it do in this *Chronicle*?"

"Not much," Adlet replied. "Fought with the Six Braves, lost, and went down. That's all."

"I didn't know any of this. This is nothing like what I was told about the old Battles of the Six Flowers. I've never heard of the Archfiend Zophrair."

That's odd, thought Adlet. Zophrair was, unquestionably, the most powerful fiend that had ever lived. Judging from their earlier fight, Adlet didn't think Tgurneu was equally strong. Wouldn't stories of a creature that powerful have been passed down to later generations of fiends? "You didn't know about the old battles?"

"I've heard about them, but what I heard was entirely different from what you've just told me. I heard that in the first Battle of the Six Flowers, no one led the horde. Tgurneu said they attacked the Braves in disarray and were defeated."

"That's weird." Tgurneu had clearly been hiding from Fremy the fact that Zophrair had ever existed. But to what end? There were so many things that stuck out here. The food. The greetings. Concealing information about Zophrair. But how was that connected to the enigma of Tgurneu? It was all too obscure. Nothing came to him. "It looks like we just have to go back there." Adlet was referring to the hill where Tgurneu had attacked them. If they hurried, they could make it in about half an hour.

"That would be difficult," Fremy countered. "We're surrounded. And if there's actually some kind of clue there, Tgurneu would come try to stop us."

Since they still couldn't solve the mystery, Adlet wanted to avoid another altercation with Tgurneu. They might not be able to escape a second time. But they still had to think of a way to return to that hill—if any clues did exist, they'd find them there.

"I'll go. You two stay here," said Fremy as she got to her feet.

"You plan to go alone?" asked Adlet.

"It's easier that way. I won't have any distractions."

"You can't. I'll go, too. You come with us, Rolonia."

"Your injuries still haven't completely healed," argued Fremy. "And Rolonia is out of the question. I can't go with someone who could be an enemy."

But then—Mora's cry reached them from outside. "Tgurneu is here!"

Together, the three dashed out of the cave.

Chapter 4

A
Sudden
Turn

It was three years before the Evil God's awakening, and the day after Mora had made her agreement with Tgurneu.

"This is bullshit!" An angry cry echoed through Mora's quarters at All Heavens Temple. The Elder was sitting at her table, opposite another woman. Her guest stood up and punched the table. It instantly split in two, sending the teacups and flower vase flying. A moment later, the slabs of table transformed into slabs of salt and crumbled onto the carpet.

"Willone, don't break my furniture," said Mora.

The woman's name was Willone Court, the Saint of Salt. She was twenty-five years old at the time, with light brown skin; long, pitch-black hair; and a taut, muscular body. The sleeves had been cut off her vestments, and she wore leather gloves on her hands.

Salt had the power to purify evil. Past Saints of Salt had long been skilled at creating barriers to keep away fiends and nullifying the toxin that covered the Howling Vilelands, albeit temporarily. Willone also had the ability to turn her enemies into lumps of salt, which made her a capable fighter, rare for the Saint of Salt.

Mora had revealed the entirety of her contract with Tgurneu to Willone. When she heard the story, she was shocked and furious—not at Mora, who had made this unforgivable contract with a fiend, but at

Tgurneu, who had taken a hostage. "How can I be calm, boss?! Why didn't you just slaughter that jackass?!"

"It ran away. Besides, I couldn't have defeated it alone."

"...That shitstain!"

The maids cleaned up the mountain of salt and carried in a replacement table. After making sure they had left, Mora was about to continue the conversation when Willone suddenly tried to leave.

"Where are you going?"

"Where else?! I'm going out to go destroy that damned fiend! You come with me, boss!"

"Calm down. You don't even have an idea of Tgurneu's location."

"It's obviously gonna be in the Howling Vilelands, and with my powers, I can get in! We'll take Chamo and Athlay, and maybe the princess and Granny Leura or whoever. It'll be like a pre–Battle of the Six Flowers!"

"'Twould be reckless. Your abilities would give us two days in the Howling Vilelands, at most—not nearly enough."

"Damn it!" Willone withdrew reluctantly and sat down on the sofa again.

Mora trusted the other Saint deeply. She was a good person, the type to lay everything out on the surface. She was faithful and tight-lipped, and once she made a promise, she would never break it. Her one flaw was that she was simple and impulsive. But even so, she was the only Saint whom Mora could speak with concerning her contract with Tgurneu.

"So is Shenira okay?"

"You just saw her. She's the picture of health."

"Yeah, the maid was teaching her to read. She's a good kid. Does she know?"

"I've told her nothing. She believes her ailment has been cured." The pair sighed miserably.

"Isn't there something we can do for her? You can ask me anything, boss," Willone said emphatically. This was what Mora liked about her.

"From this point forward, I'll be focusing on training. I cannot kill Tgurneu as I am now. While I train, you will protect All Heavens Temple in my stead."

"You leave it to me. If that's all you want, you didn't even have to ask." She flexed an arm and slapped it with the other hand.

"Tgurneu may have also blackmailed other Saints. Tighten perimeter security and get Marmanna to help you investigate to see if any others had hostages taken as well. There is much to do."

"It'll be okay. Don't worry about it—just focus on your training."

Mora had also asked Ganna to advise Willone for her. Now there should be nothing else to concern herself over. But just as she began to relax, Willone spoke again, her tone dark. "Hey, boss. Can I just ask one thing?"

"What is it?"

"This isn't something I really wanna say, but…" Willone was being uncharacteristically evasive, choosing her words carefully, as though it was difficult for her to form the question. "If you can't kill Tgurneu by the deadline, and you have to kill a Brave of the Six Flowers, what'll you do then?"

"Don't think about that. I *will* kill Tgurneu."

"O-of course. Sorry for asking such a weird question."

"Don't try to back out of it. Ask what you want to ask. Nothing you might say would anger me," said Mora.

Willone summoned her resolve, and then she spoke. "Boss…if you can't finish it off in time…will you kill one of the Braves to protect Shenira?" She fixed Mora with a razor-sharp glare. "Because if that's your plan, then I have to take you down. To protect the world. I care about Shenira, too, but I can't give the world for her."

"Don't worry. That's not my intention," said Mora.

Willone breathed a sigh of relief. "Sorry. I shouldn't have asked."

"It's no trouble. That's an obvious question to ask."

"Please, boss. You're the only one we can count on. You've got to kill Tgurneu and save Shenira," Willone said, smiling. "I care about her—and you, too, Boss."

The Temple Elder smiled and gave her a small nod.

Mora figured it had been about three hours since Hans and Goldof had set out to battle. The night was deepening, and the moon was high in the sky. "Hans, return to the barrier for now. You may not have realized it yourself, but you're showing signs of exhaustion. You're slowing down." So the fiends wouldn't hear, Mora sent her directions echoing to Hans with the power of mountains.

"*Meow*, I s'pose so. I reckoned it was 'bout time, too."

Hans and Goldof were a fair distance away from the Bud of Eternity. Mora called on her clairvoyance to find a path for the two of them to follow back to the barrier. "Climb to the summit, and then rush straight down. There are fiends coming, but I'll have Chamo support you."

"*Mea-meow*. Roger. Goldof, c'mon." The pair began to make their way back.

To Chamo, intent on stuffing wild game into her mouth, Mora said, "Can you rouse your slave-fiends? If you can, dispose of the enemies above us."

"Sure," said Chamo, and she coughed up several slave-fiends to send up to the top of the mountain. Mora noticed their bodies gleamed with an uncanny luster—they looked a little different from before.

Bones of wild animals were strewn around Chamo. She had tucked nearly every creature on the mountain into her stomach. "*Ergh.* This is kinda making Chamo sick, though," she said with a great burp.

"What on earth have you been doing?"

"Gathering animal fat."

"Fat?" Mora questioned.

"That weird powder seems to get hot when it touches water, so if all Chamo's pets are covered in fat, the powder'll probably not work as good."

I see. It seemed the younger Saint was working things out in her own way.

"Who knows if it'll work all that great. There's not enough fat. But we'll probably manage somehow."

"Will you go fight Tgurneu?"

"No, we'll wait. Chamo's not a kid. Chamo can wait."

Mora smiled. She was slowly growing, after all. "Indeed. You're a good girl by nature. You just sometimes go astray."

"Chamo is *not* a kid." When Mora patted her head, Chamo brushed her hand off grumpily.

Even as she conversed, Mora surveyed the whole mountain vigilantly. Hans and Goldof were heading to the Bud of Eternity, the slave-fiends backing them up as they went. Though their foes were fewer now, there was no sign of coming reinforcements, or even any apparent intent to summon them.

Mora scanned the area to make sure nothing else was happening—and that's when she found an anomaly. Her entire body stiffened reflexively.

"What's wrong, Auntie?"

Tgurneu was strolling along the western side of the mountain at a leisurely pace, as if simply out for a stroll. Four other fiends accompanied it, two of them large-sized creatures over ten meters in length. One was shaped like a reptile with a gigantic mouth, and the other resembled a large, monstrous jellyfish. There were also a monkey-fiend with rainbow hair and another that looked like a human made of stone.

"Chamo Rosso sure was amazing, don't you think? Hearing about it and seeing it for yourself are entirely different things," came Tgurneu's voice.

"Indeed! I wonder just how that stomach of hers is structured!"

"A single look at that is enough to make one burst out laughing. Good grief, is that actually human?" Tgurneu chatted pleasantly with the monkey-fiend. Nothing about its manner suggested it was concerned about the situation at the Bud of Eternity or its fellows on the mountain.

"Once we kill Chamö, will the fiends she's controlling be freëd, then?"

"Who knows? Well, we don't have to worry about it. They're just Cargikk's minions, anyway." Tgurneu smiled and continued. "Has Mora killed someone for me yet?"

"There are no reports of incident at the Bud of Eternity. She must still be undécided."

Tgurneu shrugged. "Foolish as she may be, I think she understands that she has no time, though. How long does she plan to make me wait?"

As Mora listened in on them, rage turned her skin to gooseflesh. Just how deep was the creature's contempt for her?

"Will she reälly kill one?"

"She may need another push or two. Still, it's only a matter of time. Let's wait a little longer." After that, Tgurneu continued its stroll.

Beside Mora, Chamo said, "What's wrong, Auntie?"

"The time has finally come." From her packs, Mora pulled a stake. It was small, about the thickness of her thumb and thirty centimeters long, and packed with hieroglyphic patterns so fine they were invisible until closer inspection.

In the three years since Mora had made that contract with Tgurneu, she had done much in preparation to kill the fiend. She had summoned a number of Saints to the temple, and together, they had created a variety of weapons. This stake was one of those. She had made it with the help of Willone, master of barrier creation. The Saint of Salt had named this barrier the Saltpeak Barrier.

"Tgurneu has come!" cried Mora, and Adlet, Fremy, and Rolonia dashed out of the cave.

"...That's the current situation," finished Mora.

Hans and Goldof were back at the Bud of Eternity, and Mora had just informed the others of Tgurneu's activities. When Adlet had heard their foe was just ambling along in a casual chat, his eyes had filled with anger. The boy, too, carried deep resentment toward Tgurneu.

"I'm capable of entrapping Tgurneu immediately. Are you ready to kill it?" asked Mora.

Adlet glanced at Rolonia and Fremy and then shook his head in disappointment.

"*Still?* You had tons of time. Chamo's all ready." Chamo pouted.

Mora was disappointed, too. She had known that they were short on leads, but she had also expected Adlet would be able to pull it off anyway.

"Then we have no choice. We'll attack now, as a group." She raised the stake to thrust it into the ground, but Hans stopped her.

"Hey. How can we fight neow? Nothin's changed from last time."

Mora tried to push Hans's hand away. "We won't have many opportunities to kill Tgurneu. Do you intend to let this one slip from our grasp, too?"

"I love bein' in trouble, but I hate bein' reckless and crazy. And I think fightin' now is just plain reckless."

"Have you lost your nerve, Hans?!" Mora couldn't disguise her irritation.

Rolonia cut in. "Lady Mora, what's wrong?"

"Why are you so impatient about this?" Fremy joined her.

Mora's allies were giving her searching looks. If she continued to press the matter, it would only make her look suspicious. "I'm sorry. But this is unquestionably the best opportunity we will have. We cannot let this go."

"Don't raise my suspicions—it'll make me want to kill you," Fremy said coldly. Rolonia watched their exchange with fright.

"Mora, if you raise the barrier now, how long'll it last?" asked Adlet.

"It was made to last six hours. But it's an instantaneous force field—I know not if its strength will be as expected."

"Give me three hours. We'll solve the mystery of Tgurneu before that time is up. And if we can't do it in three hours, we'll give up and attack Tgurneu together."

"What's your plan?"

"I'm thinking we'll leave the mountain and go back to the hill where Tgurneu first attacked us. Most likely, that's the only place we'll be able to find a clue as to its weakness."

What Mora really wanted to do was to go end Tgurneu's life right that moment. It had said that she had only two more days. But she couldn't object to Adlet's plan. "Understood, Adlet. Be sure to find us a clue. Meanwhile, I will not let Tgurneu escape." Mora showed the others the stake she held. "This barrier prevents the passage of fiends only. You will be able to pass through freely. Once it is active, head straight to the hill."

"Wait—then I won't be able to get out," said Fremy.

"I'm sorry, Fremy," answered Mora. "You were not known to us when we made this barrier. You remain here."

"That's not good. There may be some clues that we can't find without Fremy there," said Adlet.

"Couldn't you just activate the barrier once Fremy has left it?" suggested Rolonia.

"Then she wouldn't be able to get back in after. We have no choice—Fremy stays here." As Rolonia and Adlet talked, Tgurneu remained under Mora's clairvoyant watch. It was still chatting, seeming entirely without caution.

"I'm about to create the barrier. Shall I?" Mora said, and Adlet nodded. For some reason, Hans's expression revealed mixed feelings. Fremy also seemed hesitant.

"What's wrong?"

"*Meow*, I have some bad memories when it comes to barriers, ya know?"

Mora was in complete agreement, but this was not the time to worry over that. She channeled power from the Spirit of Mountains, and the stake in her hands glowed.

It was fundamentally impossible to erect two barriers in the same location. But the Saint of the Single Flower's Bud of Eternity had different properties. Saints of past generations had already confirmed that a second force field would not clash with it.

The instant before Mora thrust the stake into the ground, she checked on their target one more time.

Tgurneu was strolling along the mountain as it had been before, still conversing with its minions. "Is Cargikk still doing nothing?" it asked.

"Apparently. Does Cargikk even want to win?"

"What can you do? The most simpletons can hope to accomplish is to barricade themselves in." It seemed they were just chatting, entirely unaware of the coming threat.

It can't be—is this creature nothing more than a fool? The thought crossed Mora's mind. "*Hnh!*" She thrust the stake into the ground. The engraved hieroglyphs glowed, and the earth trembled briefly. "O Mountain, release the power that you hide, and bequeath it upon Mora Chester." She addressed the mountain, and in turn it replied.

The technique of absorbing energy from nature and making it your own was an advanced one; only a limited few Saints were capable of it. Mora had called out to the salt that was within the earth of the mountain as she absorbed its power of purification and transformed it into a barrier to block fiends.

Vast power flowed from the earth into Mora. Her body filled with intense heat, showering sparks around her. She packed the energy into the stake, and the carvings on it formed it into a wall. "Saltpeak Barrier, activate!"

There was a thunderous roar. Invisible waves emanated from the stake. Instantly, the whole mountain was enveloped in a veil of light. "Did it work?!" Adlet yelled. No reply was needed. It was basically perfect.

This barrier could only have been made via the cooperation of the Saint of Salt and the Saint of Mountains. What's more, it would have been impossible had both of them not been particularly powerful. There was also the risk that Mora would be unable to control the large volumes of power that flowed into her—in that case, she would have been destroyed.

"...Oh?"

As Mora watched from afar, the fiend looked up at the veil of light spread above, smiling. Though Tgurneu was acting unconcerned, she could see clearly that it had been shaken.

"They've created a barrier! Concentrate the minions near the commander! Protect Commander Tgurneu!" yelled the monkey-fiend. Its subordinates immediately scattered about the mountain, summoning the rest to converge on this location. "If you stay here, Commander, you may come under attack by the Braves of the Six Flowers. Let us leave the mountain at once."

"True, but though I'd like to go, I don't think I can." Smiling stiffly, Tgurneu descended the mountain.

"I have Tgurneu trapped, Adlet," said Mora. "You and Rolonia, go to the hill now."

Adlet nodded. "Rolonia, let's go. And you come with us, too, Hans. All right?"

"*Meow*, of course it's all right. Yer comin' with us, too, Goldof. You wouldn't be useful if ya stayed here, anyway," Hans quipped and whacked the knight on the back. Goldof didn't react, but he appeared not to mind.

"So it's the four of us, then. Everyone hurry and get ready," Adlet said, and he dashed into the cave.

Meanwhile, Tgurneu had arrived at the foot of the mountain, the wall of the Saltpeak Barrier. One of the fiends body-slammed the light, but when it made contact, its body sizzled in a shower of sparks and smoke. The fiend slammed the barrier again and again, but it did not break. Ultimately, it died, its entire body scorched black.

"Oh, my. I expected as much." Tgurneu touched the corpse with one hand. "It's probably Mora, though I doubt she could make something like this on her own. Perhaps she had help from Willone." The subordinates scattered about the mountain came to concentrate around Tgurneu, and the fiend gave them their orders. "Being trapped in like this is rather a bother. Break the barrier for me."

The gigantic reptile-fiend headbutted the barrier, and the jellyfish sprayed acid on it, too. All at once, the large mass of fiends began to attack.

Mora fell to her knees, clenching the stake. With each impact against the barrier, the stake shuddered. She poured the power of the Spirit of Mountains into the stake, reinforcing her spell.

Tgurneu regarded the whole scene with disinterest.

What an utter buffoon, thought Mora. All she had to do now was wait for

Adlet to bring back his results. Until then, she had to keep protecting the barrier. *Please, Adlet.* Her beloved daughter's life was in his hands.

Adlet opened his iron box and packed every one of his tools that could possibly be useful in the investigation into the pouches at his waist. "I'm ready, Addy," Rolonia announced. He had told them all to hurry, but it turned out that Adlet was the only one who had preparing to do. He swiftly filled his belt.

"Adlet, take this with you." Fremy handed him two small firecrackers—the kind used for communication, like the ones she had given him back inside the Phantasmal Barrier. If he shot these off, it would alert her to his location. "I carved numbers into them. The first one is a call for help. If you detonate it, we'll take down the barrier immediately and head out to help you. The second is meant as a message. If you find any clues, use that one."

"Got it. I don't think I'll be using the first one, though." Adlet stood up and left the cave. He looked at Goldof, who was waiting. Still as sulky as ever. "What's going on with the fiends?" he asked Mora.

She was still clenching the stake, protecting the barrier. "The majority are gathered around Tgurneu, on the southwest side. There are some enemies on watch, but they are few. Their forces are thinnest on the northern side."

"I want to avoid the fiends noticing that we've left, if possible. Is there a way to get out without being seen?" Adlet inquired.

Behind him, Chamo piped up. "That's easy. You can just go while Chamo's pets are distracting the enemy." Adlet was a little surprised. He hadn't thought she would volunteer to cooperate.

Fremy drew her gun and scanned their surroundings as she said, "I'll finish off the enemies that are watching us now. No problem."

"Then let us begin," said Mora. "We have little time. We'll end this before Tgurneu makes a move."

They all got moving. Under Mora's direction, Fremy and Chamo

took out the fiends on recon, while Adlet's party waited until all the enemies around were gone and then ran off silently northward. They proceeded under cover of night, their bodies hunched low, until they received
instructions from Mora.

"Three fiends before you. I doubt you can evade them unnoticed as
you pass. Get rid of them." Adlet could faintly see the outlines within the
darkness—the fiends had not detected them yet. Adlet threw paralyzing
needles, and the moment the group heard their quiet moans, Hans and
Goldof darted over and silently finished them off.

"Next, run straight from the barrier," instructed Mora. "And stay on
guard."

"Roger," said Adlet.

I can't be careless, he thought as they ran. If he came too close to the
answers, the seventh would act to protect Tgurneu. If the seventh was
one of the three with him—Hans, Rolonia, and Goldof—then they would
most certainly try to take Adlet's life.

They came to the foot of the mountain, the massive, luminous shroud
before them. The four exchanged a glance before they left the Saltpeak
Barrier, racing off to the east.

Mora watched them go with her clairvoyant eye. Once they left the
barrier, they were beyond the range of her powers. "They've left the
mountain. They're heading to the hill without issue."

"So they pulled it off, huh? Though that much is sort of expected," said
Chamo. The hard part was the next step. All of this would be meaningless if
Adlet's party failed to get ahold of some clues and come back safe.

There was no sign of any fiends around, only silence. Fremy stood in
the quiet, still looking in the direction Adlet had gone.

"What's wrong, Fremy?" Mora asked. But she didn't reply. She averted
her eyes and moved to separate herself from the other two. Still gripping
the stake, she tried again. "Fremy, are you that concerned about Adlet?"

Fremy's silence continued for a bit, and then she muttered, "That
idiot doesn't understand anything."

"How can you say that? He's a reliable man."

"Right now, the only person we know for sure is really a Brave is Adlet. It's obvious which of us would be targeted by the seventh. So how can he act so careless and unguarded?"

"It may be that he wants to make himself a target. You haven't considered that he's *deliberately* inviting the seventh to attack him?"

"If that's what he's doing, then I'd like to punch his lights out." Fremy did not conceal her anger.

But Mora found that charming. "Are you attracted to him?"

"..."

Fremy fell silent again. The Elder chose not to press for a reply.

Chamo yawned as if to say she didn't care in the slightest.

"I hate him. He makes me so furious."

"Why?" asked Mora.

Still staring at the ground, Fremy explained, "When I show concern, he snubs me. He doesn't even try to understand my feelings."

"I see."

"Being with him is always unpleasant. When he gets hurt, I hurt. When we talk, I get angry. That redhead's given me nothing but bitterness, sorrow, and misery. Not a single good thing has happened since we met."

"It never does go well, at first."

"I want to get rid of these feelings. I want to forget him. I've even considered wishing he was dead—at least that'd be easier." Fremy looked up, eyes on the sky in the east, the direction Adlet had gone. "I'm sure Rolonia has never felt this way." Surely not. Rolonia was up front with her feelings, unlike Fremy. "I wonder what love is? Tgurneu occasionally talked to me about love."

"Really?"

"It said love is a very mysterious power that humans had, that it was the most important thing to them. It said in order to defeat the humans, first, you had to understand human love."

"Tgurneu said that?" asked Mora.

"I didn't know what it meant by that. I still don't." Fremy pressed her hand to her heart. "If this is what love is, then I'll never be able to understand humans. I have no idea how they can value something that makes them feel like this."

"You can never know the answer right away."

"What should I do? And what do I want from Adlet?" After that, Fremy fell silent for a long time. Mora was unable to say anything. "...I've talked a little too much," she said, and she went into the cave.

Mora was no longer using her clairvoyance at that point. She was tired. It would be a long battle, and she wanted to get what rest she could. That was why she didn't notice, didn't hear what Tgurneu said at the foot of the mountain.

"Hellooo! Good evening!" Tgurneu called quietly, cupping a hand around its mouth. "Mora! Good evening. Good evening!" The fiend repeated itself a few times and then tilted its head. "That's odd. You aren't sleeping, are you? I'll be rather lonely if you don't answer. I wanted to give you a hand killing one of the Braves." It made one more attempt. "You have to hurry up and kill one of the Braves of the Six Flowers! At this rate, Willone of Salt will kill Shenira!"

There was no reply. Tgurneu contemplated for a moment, then stopped trying to call Mora.

"Are you okay with the footing?" Adlet asked the three behind him as they made their way through the nighttime Howling Vilelands. In his hand was the gem Fremy had given him, still glowing faintly.

"Of course I'm fine. Also, that way's the cliff, so *you* watch out," said Hans.

"Um, where are we going?" asked Rolonia as they walked. They didn't make their way east directly. They went south, and then when they reached a spot with a decent view, Adlet lay down on the ground and looked back upon the mountain. He could faintly see the outlines of fiends illuminated by the light of the Saltpeak Barrier. The wind carried their chatter toward the Braves.

"What do you think, Hans?" asked Adlet.

"Doesn't look like Mora was lyin'. I think we can trust her for neow."

Mora had informed them of the fiends' activities, but without seeing it for themselves, they hadn't been able to trust her completely.

"What're they doin'?"

"Probably trying to break the barrier," said Adlet. The fiends were assaulting the wall of light, but whenever they touched it, sparks flew, and the screams as they died reached their ears. Most likely, quite a few were already gone.

"We can't be dawdlin'. Let's go," said Hans. The party headed east. Apparently most of the fiends in the area were gathering at the mountain. There was nothing to block their way.

Running at full speed, the party would make it to the hill in less than half an hour. It wasn't long before they were there, back on the slope where only half a day before had engaged in a mortal struggle with Tgurneu.

"Is this it?" Amidst the smell of fresh blood and carrion, Adlet shone the gem into an open hole in the ground.

The monstrous corpses lay everywhere. Hans and Goldof examined them carefully, but there were no live fiends to be seen. There was no sign of any enemies near the hill, either—it seemed it was completely undefended. Was that because Tgurneu was unsuspecting, or because there was no information to be found here, and thus no need to have it guarded?

"I found it. It's over here." Rolonia raised her hand. At her feet was the hole Tgurneu had made when it had burst out of the ground. The four gathered around the opening, peering down into it. Even with the light of the gems, they couldn't see what might await them at the bottom.

"It's pretty deep," Adlet commented.

"I can probe the inside." Rolonia took her whip in hand, extended it, and dropped the end into the hole. They heard it smack around for a bit. "There's no one inside."

"I guess I'm going in." Adlet grabbed on to her whip and slid down into the pit. He landed at the bottom and illuminated his surroundings with the light gem.

The hole was something that might be called a dirt cellar, or maybe just a burrow. The space was about five square meters, bare earth with no decorations on the walls. Wood supports on the ceiling prevented any cave-ins. It was completely plain. In the center of the space was a single crude table and chair, and on top of the table lay a cloth-bound book. Adlet timidly picked it up and gave it a look. "What the heck is this? That fiend reads stuff like this?" he said without thinking. It was a collection of stage plays. Being ignorant of the arts, the boy was not capable of appreciating its value.

He set the book down and looked around. Narrow tunnels extended to the north and south. They were incredibly tight, and as big as Tgurneu was, the fiend would probably have had to hunch down low to get through them. Adlet shone his gem into one of the passageways. It was deep—he couldn't see the end. "All right, let's investigate." Tgurneu had been there just twelve hours earlier—and, most likely, the one who had nullified the Saint's poison had been there, too. Adlet had to find out who that someone really was. Surprisingly, though, there was nothing else in the cellar, just the book, table, and chair.

Then Hans called down from above. "Should I come down, too?"

"No, it's okay. You keep watch," said Adlet. Perhaps the tunnel itself was the trap, and it was rigged to bury him alive. With the other three aboveground, they would be able to save him. He would've liked to have had Chamo around with her power to search through the earth.

As Adlet pondered, he went to search the northern tunnel. He went about ten minutes in. The tunnel branched off multiple times, and farther down were even more branches. Adlet didn't have the slightest idea how far he'd have to go in order to reach the exit.

"I see."

He understood now that the fiends had been preparing for that surprise attack for quite some time. Tgurneu must have had tunnels dug throughout the hill and moved around between them. Then, once the Six Braves were above with their guard down, he could attack them immediately. That had been the plan.

"So?" Hans called to him, once he'd returned to the original hole.

"There's way too many passages for us to search all of them. It'd take until morning. How are things outside?"

"All peaceful-like," said Hans, and then suddenly something huge fell down into the cellar from above. Goldof had crouched his massive frame and nimbly hopped into the hole.

Adlet reflexively dropped into a guard stance, thinking that Goldof was coming to attack him. But the other boy just looked him in the eye, not doing anything. "Wh-what is it?"

"Addy! Are you okay?" Rolonia yelled, peering into the hole.

After a long silence, Goldof spoke. "It's dangerous...being alone."

"Oh! He talked!" Rolonia cried from above.

Adlet was also more than a little surprised. "What, you can talk now? Don't make us all worry like that."

"...Sorry." Goldof was still not entirely back to normal, after all. It took him some time to reply. "...I've...been...thinking. I still don't have the answers, but...I think I will soon."

"Thinking about what? What answers?"

"I'll tell you...eventually." Goldof walked off to the other tunnel, the southern one. "I'll go look. If I...find something...I'll let you know. Leave it to me," he said, and he disappeared inside. The dim light of his gem eventually diminished from sight.

Adlet pressed his chest. *The stuff this guy does is bad for my heart*, he thought.

"What will we do about him, Addy?" Rolonia called down.

"For now, let's just leave him be," he answered. Goldof was strong. Even if he did encounter the enemy, he could probably resolve it on his own in all but the most extreme cases. At this point, Adlet just had to focus on solving the puzzle. "Rolonia, Hans, you stay where you are. If something happens to me, come save me," he said, then he pulled out from under his cloak the bottled substance for inspecting fiend traces. It was the same one he had used within the Phantasmal Barrier. When this solution was sprayed on an object, any part a fiend had touched would change color. Adlet sprayed it on the table, chair, and then floor of the tunnel in turn. He had to hurry. Mora's technique would not hold forever.

At the Bud of Eternity, Mora stood, arms folded and eyes closed. She focused her mind, continuing to send power into the barrier. The veil of light that covered the mountain was continually trembling. The fiends were using all their strength in an attempt to break the barrier, and maintaining it was tougher than she had anticipated. But this was no time for complaints. If this barrier broke, she would lose her best shot at killing Tgurneu. "Is Adlet not back yet?" she asked.

Fremy replied, "No, and he hasn't sent me notice that he's found a clue, either. Hold on for one more hour."

"I shall. I can manage that well enough," said Mora, and sent more power into the barrier. In order to pour all her energy into maintaining the barrier, she was no longer scanning the mountain. She only checked on Tgurneu briefly once every five minutes.

Masses of fiends were crowding near the Saltpeak Barrier from both within and without. They summoned all their effort to attack the barricade. Chamo's slave-fiends tried to stop the fiends attacking the barrier, but they hadn't yet recovered completely, so their assaults were sporadic. Tgurneu sat on a rock, protected by its minions as it gazed absentmindedly at the barrier. The fiend did not give any orders or conspire any tricks. To Mora, it looked as if it was waiting for something.

Suddenly, Tgurneu raised a hand, and all the fiends stopped their barrage. "All right. I've ascertained its strength now." The veil of light was still.

What is its plan? she wondered, watching Tgurneu.

Suddenly, it looked up at the mountain, directly at the Bud of Eternity. "Will you reply to me now, Mora? I've been calling you and calling you."

Mora swallowed.

"You can hear my voice, can't you? I know you have the ability to talk to me. Why won't you say anything? Are you scared to converse? I swore I wouldn't lie to you."

"Mora, what is going on?" asked Fremy, beside her.

The Elder's heart hammered. "I know not. The fiends suddenly stopped attacking the barrier. Don't speak to me right now. I wish to focus on observing Tgurneu."

The half fiend observed Mora with sharp eyes. If Mora did anything to make Fremy suspect her, the Saint of Gunpowder would kill her. But still, Mora couldn't ignore Tgurneu's call. "What do you want, Tgurneu?" she asked, using her power of mountain echo. She did so without speaking out loud so as to avoid Fremy's suspicion.

"Finally, a reply. Now then, as I've said over and over—you have no time. If you don't kill one of the Six Braves within the next two days, Shenira is probably going to die." Mora shivered, goose bumps standing out on her whole body. "Did you perhaps kill one already? Was it Adlet, after all? Or perhaps Rolonia? Those two seem easy to kill. If it was Hans or Chamo, I'd jump for joy. Those are the two I'm *really* scared of, after all."

"I've killed no one."

"I thought not." Tgurneu shrugged. "You really are a cruel mother. I thought a mother's love was supposed to surpass everything. Do you know just how many opportunities to save her you've let get away from you?"

"Be silent. What would a fiend understand? You're a monster that knows neither love nor justice," said Mora.

For the first time, a faint swell of anger seeped into Tgurneu's expression. "I will ignore that discourtesy—I'm a generous fiend."

"I want to ask you something. What do you mean, I 'have no time'?"

"Oh, I *do* wonder what I meant there. Do I really need to be telling you that? What you should know is that you have only two more days. That's all," Tgurneu said, and it smiled unpleasantly. "This barrier did surprise me, but your efforts are useless. Your party can't kill me. I'm going to leave this barrier, and I won't appear to you again for the following two days. This is your warning. If you want to save your daughter, then hurry up and kill a Brave."

Mora was speechless.

"If all of you came and attacked me right now," Tgurneu continued, "then you might be able to defeat me. But you still aren't ready to pull that off, are you? If you were, you'd come straight for me."

Then Fremy, standing beside Mora, grew tired of waiting and said, "What's going on, Mora? Explain."

"I know not. Nothing has happened, so there's nothing for me to say."

"This is getting nowhere. I'm going to go see what's going on with Tgurneu." Clenching her gun, Fremy ran off. Chamo followed after her.

Mora did not pursue them, resuming her exchange with Tgurneu instead. "Who is the seventh? Tell me, and I'll kill one of the Six Braves at once."

"Are you trying to negotiate with me? I can't comply." Tgurneu shook its head. "If you kill Hans Humpty, Chamo Rosso, Fremy Speeddraw, Rolonia Manchetta, Goldof Auora, or Adlet Mayer, then I will release your daughter. Which of them is the seventh has nothing to do with it."

"So you don't care if I kill the seventh?" Mora muttered. What was Tgurneu thinking? Using her clairvoyance, Mora checked the situation halfway down the slope. Fremy and Chamo, on their way to see what was going on with Tgurneu, were currently held up by a dozen-odd fiends.

"Come on, Mora," said Tgurneu, "there's someone fighting up there. If you go and punch them from behind, your beloved daughter will be saved. Don't you love her?"

"Why?! Why is it only two more days?! The deadline was supposed to be twenty-two days after the Evil God's awakening!" Mora burst out. It was a good thing Fremy had left. At her outburst, the fiend pressed a hand over its mouth and exploded into laughter.

"What's so funny?!"

"Oh, pardon me. I was just remembering something amusing. When I remember how you were three years ago, I just can't stop laughing." Tgurneu's mouth warped into an uncanny sneer. Up until now, no matter how uncanny the creature had looked, there had also been something humanlike about it. But this smile was entirely monstrous. "Twenty-two days after the awakening of the Evil God? You really are dim-witted. That time limit is utterly meaningless."

"What did you say?"

"You made one mistake—if not for that, you may have had another seven days to spare."

"What are you talking about?"

"You brought Willone, Saint of Salt, into this. That was your mistake."

Mora's legs suddenly felt unsteady beneath her. Willone's face and her hearty smile came to her mind. *It couldn't be. Impossible. Willone would never betray me.* She never denied those in need, never condoned any wickedness or unfairness. She was a close friend, one Mora had known for a very long time, and she had been fond of Shenira. Mora had chosen her because she had trusted her most of all the Saints.

"Willone hasn't done anything wrong," said Tgurneu. "She's a truly praiseworthy human. But you know, she is a little dim." Suddenly, it pulled from the mouth on its chest a charcoal pen and a piece of wood. "I showed you this once, didn't I? I can forge any sample of handwriting, just having seen it once. I think I deserve a compliment for that. I practiced that skill diligently every single day over the course of fifty years."

Mora remembered—three years previously, Tgurneu had sent her a letter written in the handwriting of Torleau, Saint of Medicine.

"I sent a letter to Willone in your handwriting," continued Tgurneu. "The letter surely reached her some time ago. Simply put, it said this:

Dear Willone,

Show this letter to no one. Once you have read this letter, burn it forthwith. Ganna is a soft-hearted man. If he were shown this letter, he might go mad."

As the fiend spoke, it transcribed the words on the wood scrap. It was very clearly Mora's handwriting. Mora herself might have mistaken it for her own.

"Tgurneu has deceived me. It may no longer be possible to save Shenira. Fifteen days after the Evil God's awakening, the parasite in her chest will excrete a particular

poison. When that poison takes effect, Shenira will be transformed, still alive, into a fiend. Once that happens, any attempt to kill her will be in vain, and it will be physically impossible for her to die. It would be a living hell for her. Tgurneu swore to me that Shenira would not be attacked. But to Tgurneu, that is no attack, but rather a grand act of benevolence, granting her rebirth as a noble fiend."

Tgurneu tossed away the scrap of wood, but continued speaking.

"Even Torleau cannot save her. She would, doubtless, not even be capable of grasping that such poison has entered her system. I swear I will kill Tgurneu before fifteen days have passed after the awakening. But if that cannot be…"

"You…vile…" Mora's legs trembled.

"Once midnight on the fifteenth day has passed, if the mark on Shenira's chest yet remains, kill her."

Tgurneu raised both hands up high like a melodramatic actor. "What do you think of that? Not bad, huh? The letter then goes on about how sorry you are and how much you loved Shenira, but I'll spare you that." With a cruel smile, it continued, "If your husband were to see this letter, he might realize that it's a forgery. But would Willone ignore the first line? I'm sorry, but Willone Court is rather simple, and she's loyal and honest. I doubt she will realize this letter is a fake, and I believe she will follow your orders. Of course, Willone or your husband might figure out the letter is a counterfeit, or even if they don't, they might hesitate to kill Shenira. But this is enough to threaten you, isn't it?"

Tgurneu had promised that it wouldn't lie to Mora. The fiend really had sent that letter. "What I promised to you is that I would not lie to *you*," Tgurneu emphasized. "I can lie to Willone. And I promised that no fiend would touch Shenira. But a *human* killing her wouldn't be in violation of my oath."

Mora was speechless. She was seeing it all in her head. Willone reading the letter and agonizing over it. Shenira cheerfully awaiting Mora's return. Willone's hand on her daughter.

"Incidentally, I'll let you know that the traitor is the clerk you hired five years ago, Kiannan. He was easily bought and told me a variety of things. He even helped me implant the parasite in your girl. He didn't realize his employer was a fiend until the moment before he went down my throat. Well, not that anyone cares about that."

Mora couldn't even hear him.

"You're a bit of a simpleton, but you must have grasped what's going on by now," continued Tgurneu. "You have only two more days, and in order to save your daughter, you have no choice but to kill one of the Braves of the Six Flowers."

"Tgurneu…"

"I'll say it one more time. Trying to kill me is futile. I have a plan—a plan to escape your barrier, and I'm gradually nearing success."

Mora looked to the east for Adlet. *Come back soon*, she pleaded silently.

"How was it, Addy?" Rolonia called down.

Adlet didn't reply as he intently focused on the ground and the walls. The cellar was red all over from the solution that reacted to evidence of fiends. When this substance came in contact with an object, any part that had been touched by a fiend would change color, and each fiend would make it turn a different color. Adlet sprayed the solution on his own armor to compare. The places Tgurneu had touched became a dark red.

The boy covered the cellar with the solution. There were more traces here than he could count, but they all turned the same color, the same dark red. There had been no other fiend but Tgurneu in this hole. Adlet investigated the tunnels, too but got the same results. "The only fiend that was here…was Tgurneu."

"So does that mean a Saint is cooperating with Tgurneu?" Rolonia supposed. However, that couldn't be right. Adlet had meticulously searched the floor of the tunnel. There was no sign that any human had been underground here, not a single footprint in the soft earth. There were also no signs that any prints had been erased. Where on earth could the fiend—or Saint—that had blocked the poison have been?

"…" At this point, Adlet was forced to consider that his initial assumptions were simply incorrect. Either Rolonia's analysis was wrong or the assumption that the Saint's poison would work on every fiend was wrong. "No…that's not it." He was overlooking something. He examined the cellar one more time.

That was when the table caught his eye—just one small part of it. The table was splotched dark red all over from the spray, but there was one little spot, just the size of a fingertip, that had turned orange.

Adlet immediately sprayed more solution there. That one part of the table turned orange, a circle of less than three centimeters in diameter. It was so small he had missed it. Had a different fiend carried the table? That couldn't be. The color change was on top of the table, near the middle.

One other fiend aside from Tgurneu had been there—probably one so small Tgurneu could pluck it in its fingers. Adlet had never heard of any fiend that size. What was this tiny creature? And what had it been up to all this time? Where had it gone? Recalling their fight with Tgurneu, Adlet arrived at just one conclusion.

It couldn't be. If so, then how the heck…?

"Addy. Addy!"

Adlet had been so lost in thought, he hadn't noticed Rolonia calling him. "What is it?"

"Where did Goldof go?"

Adlet looked around. He considered for a moment, and then dashed into the tunnel Goldof had disappeared into.

A single minute felt like an hour—or a day. Mora poured power into the barrier, desperately awaiting the return of Adlet's party. She checked on Tgurneu through her second sight. The fiend was calmly sitting on a rock, looking up toward the Bud of Eternity. Its minions had ceased their assault on the barrier.

Mora didn't know how long she could keep Tgurneu trapped. The barricade was holding, but she couldn't anticipate Tgurneu's next move. The fiend had declared that it had already come up with a way to break out.

Mora gently placed her hand on her stomach, thinking about the trump card she kept within. She'd had a red gem surgically implanted there—her ultimate weapon, one that she and Liennril, Saint of Fire, had worked together to create. Stored within it was the power of volcanic eruption. If Mora recited the incantation written in the hieroglyphs, the gem would draw immense power from the magma within the earth. She would not need to control the power it would absorb. It would cause a massive explosion, blowing apart Mora and everything around her. When Mora had first fought Tgurneu, she had hesitated to use this weapon because at that time, she had thought she would still have more opportunities to kill it. Now she was starting to regret that.

Moments later, Fremy and Chamo, who had been out doing reconnaissance, returned to the Bud of Eternity. "Just as you said, Tgurneu isn't doing a thing," said Fremy. "What's going on here?"

"Is Adlet yet to return, Fremy?" inquired Mora.

The Saint of Gunpowder scrutinized Mora's expression, deemed it unusual, and turned suspicious. "Not yet. He also hasn't contacted me to say that he's found anything, either."

Mora despaired at no word from her companion. How long did she have to wait for him to fulfill her hopes? She had no more time. She picked up the iron gauntlets that lay on the ground, put them on, and then walked out of the Bud of Eternity.

"Where are you going?" asked Chamo.

"I'm going to go fight Tgurneu. I can wait for Adlet no longer."

"What's wrong, Auntie? Calm down. Tgurneu's trapped in here, right?"

"Just concentrate on maintaining the barrier," said Fremy. "Let's wait for Adlet."

"No. I must kill Tgurneu now," Mora insisted.

"There's no need to rush. Even if we do let Tgurneu get away, it's not such a big deal. This won't be our only chance to kill it. We'll fight Tgurneu once we've made sure we can win."

"That's right," Chamo agreed. "What're you going on about?"

Indeed, from their position, maybe that was the best choice. But Mora had no more time. She ignored them both and kept walking.

"Mora, stop." That was when Fremy drew her gun, thrusting it toward Mora's ear. "I'm sure of it now. You're hiding something. I'm not putting my gun down unless you explain to me why you're in such a hurry."

"What're you doing, Fremy?" Chamo demanded angrily. She vomited up a few fiends, sending them to surround Fremy.

"Think about it, Chamo. Mora is not acting normally."

"Neither are you. You've never acted normal."

Fremy and Chamo locked eyes, glaring at each other. Mora was facing away from them, so she couldn't see them, but she could perceive what was going on behind her using her clairvoyant sight. The moment Fremy's gun turned to Chamo, Mora sped away in a straight line.

"Mora!" Fremy yelled.

The Elder could not rely on Adlet any longer, and she couldn't expect help from Fremy or Chamo, either. She had no choice but to kill Tgurneu with her own hands. She would use the ultimate weapon implanted into her stomach to destroy that beast and save her daughter. She had no other options left. Tgurneu said it had a plan to escape the barrier. She would not give the fiend the time to put its scheme into motion.

About a minute's run away from the Bud of Eternity, fiends set upon her. She didn't stop, even for an instant, body-slamming into one of her attackers. She didn't have the time to waste on small fry.

Tgurneu, perhaps noticing the distant sound, spoke. "Hmm? Something's happened. Hellooo, Mora? What's going on?"

Of course Mora was not going to reply. She punched a fiend that blocked her way and stomped on it. Tgurneu wouldn't yet have realized she had an eruption gem. If she could just get near it, she could take Tgurneu down. It was expecting her to kill one of the Six Braves. That meant it would want to avoid killing Mora. She would be sure to find an opportunity to get close. No...she had to *make* the opportunity.

Fremy was behind her in pursuit. "Mora! Stop right there!"

"If you're going to shoot me, then shoot!" Mora ignored Fremy, grabbing a fiend. The muzzle of Fremy's gun spewed fire, and a bullet skimmed Mora's arm, a scrap of her sleeve dancing in the air.

"Fremy! If you kill Auntie, I'll kill you!" Chamo cried from behind them. She was chasing them with her slave-fiends in tow.

"It looks like the Braves are attacking. Half of you, go slow them down," Tgurneu ordered. Its subordinates inside the barrier obeyed and moved out. Mora tracked them with her powers, and when she scattered the fiends, Chamo's slave-fiends finished them off. More and more of them came to stand in her way. The Saint of Mountains punched down a gigantic dog-fiend and then forced down a lion-fiend until its neck snapped. She plunged forward—ever forward.

"Mora! Go back to the Bud of Eternity!" Fremy's bullet skimmed her shoulder.

Mora ignored it and kept on running. As long as Chamo was there, Fremy couldn't kill her, and there were fiends attacking the gun-toting Saint, too.

"Auntie! This is so sudden! What's going on?! Chamo won't understand if you don't explain!" The fiends came after Chamo, too, though she fought them off as she desperately chased after Mora.

The situation was chaos. Mora kept pressing forward, while behind her, Fremy attempted to stop her. Chamo was preventing Fremy from killing Mora while also trying to stop her charge. The fiends attacked all three of them indiscriminately. From the outside, the entire scene must have looked like a comedy.

As Mora fought, she employed her abilities to watch Tgurneu and its minions from afar. They were moving into formation. The one that seemed to be the highest-ranking among Tgurneu's minions, the monkey-fiend, was giving orders. The commander was sitting on the tail of a reptile-fiend, hand on chin, observing. There were now eighty or more fiends standing in Mora's way. These were not the sort of numbers she could handle on her own—but she couldn't stop. She couldn't let Tgurneu get away.

"Go back, Mora! What are you trying to do?!" Fremy surged forward to stand in front of Mora, blocking her way.

"What else? I'm going to kill Tgurneu!" Mora screamed.

Fremy hesitated. If she had been certain that Mora was the seventh, she probably would have shot her, heedless of Chamo's presence. But Mora was not attacking her allies—she was trying to attack Tgurneu. "Are you the enemy? Or are you just a hopeless idiot?"

"You're in my way! Move!" Mora ordered, and quickly slipped by Fremy, blocking the shot that followed with one of her gauntlets. When her companion threw a bomb at her, Mora did not flinch.

"Just *what* is Mora trying to do?!" Fremy asked Chamo.

"Chamo doesn't know, either!"

Mora yelled, "You two, help me out! Cut a path before me!" Fremy and Chamo were confused. *But I won't let that trouble me*, she thought. She would not rely on anyone else now. She'd always known that she was the only one who could save Shenira.

At the foot of the mountain, by the barrier, Tgurneu turned toward the battlefield and smirked. "Mora, I can hear your voice from all the way over here. I think you should try not to get so worked up." Only half of its forces were fighting. The rest were simply in formation, waiting patiently. Even as Mora approached, Tgurneu did not appear the least bit anxious.

"Auntie! What're you trying to do, charging in all by yourself?! Do you want to die?!" Chamo yelled.

That was exactly what Mora intended to do—she would die if it meant her daughter's life would be saved. Mora had regrets. Her own naive ideas—that if they all just worked together, they could kill Tgurneu and that she still had time before Shenira would die—had invited this situation. She would hesitate no longer. She would accept death, for her daughter's sake.

How much time had passed? Mora's sense of time was shot.

A massive fiend shaped like a reptile stood in her way, one of the higher-order fiends previously accompanying Tgurneu. She had been fighting it for a long time. She punched it over and over again, but it never went down. "Move!"

She would kill Tgurneu. That singular thought had consumed Mora for the past three years. She had trained her body, refined her techniques, and sparred with the strongest warriors in the world to compensate for her lack of experience in real battle. Together with Willone, Saint of Salt, she had created a barrier to entrap Tgurneu. With Liennril, Saint of Fire, she had created the ultimate weapon to defeat Tgurneu. But all of that did not diminish the anxiety in her heart.

Mora had told Willone that she didn't plan to kill one of the Braves of the Six Flowers in order to save her daughter's life. However, Mora had known all along that no matter what happened to her, she couldn't abandon her daughter. If Tgurneu escaped now, she *would* slay one of the Braves.

"Chamo, retreat! We should give up on Mora!" Fremy yelled. She lobbed bombs at the approaching fiends, running from the attacks. "Mora is going to kill herself! If that's what she wants, then let her do it!"

"No! Chamo's taking Auntie back! You just run away by yourself!"

Fremy had already given up trying to shoot Mora. She had her hands full with the enemies swarming toward her.

"You're in my way! Silence! Don't bar my path!" Was Mora yelling at the fiends or at Chamo?

She plunged her hand into the mouth of the reptile-fiend that loomed before her, seizing its tongue. She dug her feet into the ground and let out an earth-shattering shriek, hurling the fiend over her shoulder. Another hundred meters to go until she reached Tgurneu—so close that if it were day, she would be able to see it directly. Tgurneu was looking her way, guarded by its formation of minions.

The reptile-fiend she had flung away stood up again and sprang upon her. Mora caught the blow and in the instant before she would be crushed, she just barely turned the creature away to the side. The fiend immediately rose again to attack her.

Then Tgurneu shouted out. Mora didn't have to use her powers—she could hear it directly. "You can leave Fremy and Chamo alone! Don't let Mora get close to me!"

Instantly, Mora understood. Tgurneu had figured out what she was trying to do. It probably didn't know about the eruption gem, but it had realized that Mora was on a suicide mission. "Tgurneu! Have you lost your nerve?! Come at me!" she yelled as she fought the reptile.

"No, I can't do that. I can tell quite clearly what you're going to do."

"I'm telling you to come at me!"

But Tgurneu did not move, and Adlet did not return.

As the red-haired boy ran through the tunnel, he heard a queer sound, like someone far away was screaming. It echoed manifold within the broad tunnel, and Adlet couldn't tell which direction the scream was coming from. "What's that idiot doing?" He sprinted like mad through the complex web of tunnels, though he also stopped along the way to carve signs in the wall so he wouldn't forget where he had come from. It would be no joke if one of the Braves of the Six Flowers ended up lost. "Goldof is just nothing but damn trouble." He muttered his frank opinion.

There was no guarantee Mora could keep Tgurneu trapped indefinitely. Their foe might have done something, and Fremy and the rest of them could be in danger. There was no time to waste. It had probably been around two hours. At this rate, they'd be forced to go back with no results to show for it.

"But what is that screaming?" The noise from the depths of the tunnel was a cry of agony. It wasn't Goldof, but a fiend's voice. Soon, the cries became weaker, and then they were gone. After that, the sound of something snapping echoed faintly through the tunnel. "Over there, huh?"

The sounds were finally getting closer. As Adlet reached a corner, he raised his sword. He had no idea what might come leaping out at him.

"What...?" When Adlet turned the corner, there was Goldof—and the corpse of a steel-skinned human-type fiend. His stomach roiled. He had seen the bodies of many fiends, but this sight was particularly cruel. "What are you doing?"

Both of the fiend's arms had been broken, both legs wrenched off at the knee, and the part Adlet assumed was the face was smeared in rust-colored blood. Goldof had his hand on the dead fiend's neck, constricting it as tight as he could. When he saw Adlet, he responded quietly, "I'm...fighting a fiend."

·"I can tell that much." The other boy's spear was still slung on his back, and there was not a single drop of blood on it. *No way. Did he demolish that fiend with his bare hands?*

"I tried...torturing it, but...it didn't...go well. It was my first time... so I...didn't really know how."

"Look, Goldof—"

"Oh yeah...someone said before...torture...doesn't work...on fiends," Goldof muttered as he crushed the fiend's face. Seeing the power of his grip, Adlet gulped. He was every bit as superhuman as Hans.

"How dumb are you? Did you think a fiend would talk? We've got to head back now." Adlet set off the way he had come, and Goldof obediently trailed behind him.

"Fiends...are...chattier...than I thought they were."

"Yeah."

"They have no problem...sacrificing themselves...under orders... but...they also...want to keep living. That one kept saying...*I'm not gonna die here...I'm gonna kill you*...over and over. It was strange."

"Oh? I'm glad it was a learning experience for you. Run faster." Perhaps it was Adlet's annoyance that turned his tone rude.

"Apparently...it was...one of Tgurneu's. It didn't say...what it was... here for. It didn't say anything about...who the seventh is...or where Her Highness went, either."

Adlet could think of nothing but the mystery at hand. Who was that tiny fiend? And why hadn't the Saint's poison worked on Tgurneu?

"That fiend was so...frustrated...that it couldn't kill me. It said...over and over...it wanted to kill me." Adlet was just about to tell Goldof that he was allowed to shut up. "It said... *If I had Commander Tgurneu's power...you trash would be nothing.*"

When Adlet heard that, he stopped in his tracks, and Goldof bumped into him from behind, knocking him forward. Adlet collided with the ground face-first.

"Are you okay?"

Goldof tried to help him up, but Adlet didn't take the hand he offered. He just lay facedown. His intuition was speaking to him, telling him that what Goldof had said was important. Sprawled on the ground, Adlet chewed over the oddness of that statement. "Say that one more time—that exact thing."

"*If I had Commander Tgurneu's power...you trash would be nothing.*"

"Was that exactly what it said? You're sure?"

"Yeah...that's just what it said. *If I had...Commander Tgurneu's...power.* Come on, get up."

That remark led to one single deduction—that Tgurneu had the ability to bestow power upon other fiends. But Rolonia had said that Tgurneu didn't have any special powers. All that had happened spun around in Adlet's head—their first fight with Tgurneu, Rolonia's analysis, what they'd discussed with Fremy, Archfiend Zophrair, the fact that Tgurneu had once been Zophrair's minion, the odd fiend traces in the cellar, that fiend's seemingly ordinary remark. And finally, that the Saint's poison had not worked on Tgurneu. Adlet arrived at one conclusion. All the facts were pointing to it.

"Goldof, you may have just accomplished more than any of us have managed so far," Adlet said, getting to his feet. They urgently raced back to the cellar, grabbed hold of Rolonia's dangling whip and clambered up to the surface.

"Yer finally back. I was gettin' pretty sick of waitin' for ya, *meow.*"

"Did you find anything?" asked Rolonia. "What should we do now?"

"I've found a possibility—but no positive proof."

"Are we headin' back? I'm worried about Mora," said Hans.

Adlet shook his head, looked out over the dark hill and said, "No, we're gonna look for proof. If memory serves me, we should find some on this hill."

"Proof?"

Adlet told them what they were going to search for, and Rolonia and Hans's jaws dropped. Understandable—this idea was pretty damn out there. But if he was right, then this would resolve every one of the mysteries.

The reptile-fiend finally fell, and Tgurneu had still not fled. Just fifty meters more. Mora would get right close to Tgurneu and trigger the eruption gem, and then it would all be over.

"You guys just can't hack it, can you?" Tgurneu said to its minions as it watched Mora draw nearer. "I gave you one order: Don't let Mora come near me. You can't even manage that much?"

About fifteen underlings charged recklessly toward Mora. She drove her fist into one, trying to mow a path through, but it clung to her with its face smashed in, pinning her arm.

"Good, good! You can do it if you try!"

The fiends grabbed at Mora one after the other, slowing her down for a few seconds each at the cost of their own lives. Tgurneu observed with satisfaction.

"Auntie! Chamo can't watch this anymore! Your arms better be ready for this!" Chamo's slave-fiends began to attack both the fiends and Mora.

The Saint of Mountains roared and thrust the slave-fiends aside. Tgurneu's fiends surged toward Mora, and Chamo's tried to restrain her while also killing the enemy. She shoved them aside as she desperately struggled forward. Fremy had her gun trained on Tgurneu as she readied her bombs.

The situation was now completely out of control, Tgurneu alone laughing among the chaos. "*Ah-ha-ha-ha!* This is so much fun! Quite the spectacle."

No matter how many slave-fiends Mora shoved aside and hurled away, they quickly swarmed upon her once more. A gigantic slug curved around Mora and caught her feet in its sticky mucus, pulling her backward. "Let me go! Release me, Chamo!" Mora tried to shake the slug off, but the slave-fiend could not be peeled off with strength alone. She fell to the ground and frantically struggled to drag herself forward with her arms, but another slave-fiend pressed her back to hold her down. Still glaring at Tgurneu where it sat just a little farther away, Mora could move no more.

That was when she wondered—why had her target not tried to flee yet? It had said that it had a plan to break through the barrier, so why had it not yet done so?

"That's for the best, Chamo. Hold Mora down for me," Tgurneu said as it stood. Instantly, everything fell silent. The surviving fiends stopped fighting and gathered around their master.

That's when Mora figured out Tgurneu's plan and just how terribly she had fallen for its deception. Tgurneu didn't have any way to destroy the barrier—not aside from its plan of exhausting its creator, to drain her of the strength she needed to maintain it. Tgurneu had toyed with her and made her come charging in to try to kill it.

How much power remained in her now? Did she have enough to uphold the wall?

"Mora, it was only two hundred years ago that I acquired the seventh crest," said Tgurneu. "The seventh crest is, in a way, not a fake. The Saint of the Single Flower herself created it—for a different purpose than the crests the Six Braves bear."

"Why...are you suddenly talking about this?" Fremy's weapon was raised as she listened.

"I searched for a long time for a creature worthy of bearing the seventh crest. I kept thinking about this for a long time—what sort of person would be appropriate to bear it? When the time came, the crest would be given to the one who was worthy, on the body of the seventh that I chose." Mora crawled along desperately, listening to Tgurneu.

"Auntie! You're supposed to stay still!" Chamo yelled, but Tgurneu disregarded her and continued.

"You're truly magnificent, Mora. A true villain. You're so good at pretending to be virtuous, and yet you still believe that you're not evil. No one knows the truth in your heart. No one but me. I'm thankful it was my fate to have encountered a human like you. Your love will surely destroy the world for me." A moment later, the surviving hundred-odd fiends dashed at the barrier, and as they did, the fifty other fiends on the other side body-slammed it. When the horde crashed into the barrier, their bodies burned up, turning into filthy mud. But they didn't care—one after another they charged to their deaths. They were all ready to give up their lives.

When Mora had created the barrier, she had not anticipated this—that a hundred and fifty fiends would choose death in order to break the barrier. The veil of light flickered wildly. Mora sent her remaining power to it, but the wavering only grew worse, and it wouldn't stop. "Wait... Wait, Tgurneu!" she cried.

At last, there remained the gigantic, jellyfish-like fiend. Tgurneu gave its body to the fiend, and the jellyfish swallowed the leader up inside itself. "I'll tell you one last thing, Mora. The seventh...is you!" Tgurneu's body was sucked all the way into the jellyfish, completely out of sight. The fiend leaped at the barrier, and the sound of it roasting rang out together with an agonizing scream. But as scorched as it was, it passed through the barrier. Leaking fluids, dragging along its burned body, it ran off westward.

"Tgurneu! Wait! Wait, you!" Mora screamed. She screamed and screamed and screamed. But Tgurneu gave her no further reply. Inside the jellyfish-fiend, it disappeared into the darkness.

The few subordinates that remained followed Tgurneu into the west. In a heartbeat, the mountain was quiet. Mora, having expended all her powers, slowly faded from consciousness.

"...Auntie! Come on, Auntie!"

How much time had passed? Mora was in Chamo's arms, and the small girl was calling her name repeatedly.

"Tgurneu?" When Mora opened her eyes, that was the first word out of her mouth.

"It ran away. It's a shame, but there's nothing to be done. We'll have many more chances to kill it."

Fremy's gun was trained on Mora. Mora had no intention of resisting.

"I want to kill you right this moment, but for now, I'll have you explain yourself." Fremy's finger moved to the trigger.

The slave-fiends blocked her shot. "Chamo won't let you kill her."

"Move."

"Auntie isn't the seventh. She's doing stuff that doesn't make sense, but she hasn't attacked any of us. You're the suspicious one." The two glared at each other.

Mora muttered, "Tgurneu said that I'm the seventh, didn't it?"

"Chamo's smart," said Chamo, "so it makes sense enough. That was obviously just a lie to try to fool everyone. Fremy's stupid, so she's letting Tgurneu trick her."

"Obviously, anything Tgurneu says is a lie of some sort. I have other reasons to suspect Mora."

But Mora knew that Tgurneu had been telling the truth, because it could never lie to her. *I see...so I was the seventh.* That would explain the various inconsistencies, like how none of them had cooperated with Nashetania within the Phantasmal Barrier and why the seventh had not done anything in their initial battle with Tgurneu. Now both those things made sense.

"Move, Chamo," said Fremy.

"Then lower your gun."

Mora interrupted them. "Have Adlet decide whether I will live or die. I'll abide by his decision."

"Are you okay with that, Auntie? Adlet's a dummy."

"I trust Adlet. He'll not fail to recognize the truth. Is he yet to return?"

"Not yet," Fremy replied. "He hasn't contacted me to say he's found any proof yet, either."

"I see."

To Chamo, Fremy instructed, "Go and bring back Adlet. Tgurneu might be after them. You back them up."

"And you're not just gonna kill Auntie here?"

"I will, this one time, listen to what Adlet has to say. I won't kill her until then. Of course, that's only if Mora doesn't do anything."

"You watch out, Auntie," Chamo said before she ran off eastward. She didn't seem to be in a hurry, as she ran no faster than usual.

Fremy took about five steps backward, putting some distance between herself and Mora. She kept her crosshairs trained on the back of the Temple Elder's head.

Without looking back, Mora said, "Fremy, allow me to treat my wounds."

"Don't move. Heal yourself with the energy of the mountain or whatever."

"The energy of the mountain is not so all-powerful. Without poultices and sutures, the wounds will not heal."

"...Fine, then," Fremy said, gun still in hand.

Mora kept some first-aid medicine tucked away in her boots. Adlet wasn't the only one who fitted tools into his gear. Under Fremy's watch, she removed her vestments and armor and treated her wounds.

"..."

For three years, Mora had been tormented by nightmares of what would happen if she was unable to defeat Tgurneu, unable to save Shenira. Whenever she saw that possible future in her dreams, she would leap out of bed. Some nights, she couldn't sleep at all without her husband, Ganna, by her side. With each nightmare that tormented her, Mora thought, *I never should have become a Saint. I never should have become a warrior.* Beloved Shenira had been targeted because her mother had become powerful enough to be chosen as one of the Braves of the Six Flowers.

Those nightmares had now become her reality.

As Mora treated her wounds, her thoughts turned to the past. It must have been about two years before when Mora and Ganna had been face-to-face in their bedroom. They had asked a maid to handle Shenira so the two of them could talk alone about the management of the temple, which she had left to Ganna; the leadership of the Saints, which she had entrusted to Willone; and the looming battle.

Once they finished the discussion, Ganna had suddenly said, "Mora… if it turns out that Shenira can no longer be saved…"

Mora was startled. Voicing that possibility had become a taboo between them. She would save Shenira, save the world, and return. That was what they had promised each other. "Don't speak of that. Did I not say I would save her?"

"I'm no keener than you to discuss it. I don't even want to think about it. But we must."

Mora didn't want to hear it. "You don't trust me?"

"It's precisely because I trust you that we must talk about it." Ganna fixed his eyes on Mora's. "If you cannot defeat Tgurneu by the promised day…if you must weigh the life of a Brave of the Six Flowers against Shenira's…" He faltered, his expression heartbroken. "If that comes to pass, please, let Shenira go. You mustn't kill one of the Braves of the Six Flowers."

His wife couldn't reply.

"I know just how much you love Shenira, and that's why it frightens me that you may invite disaster in order to protect her."

"They won't lose. The Braves of the Six Flowers will not lose." Mora averted her eyes.

Ganna gently embraced her and said, "Even if you were to kill one of the Six Braves, they still might be able to defeat the Evil God. But then what would become of Shenira after that? She would spend the rest of her life with a debt on her shoulders—the debt of being the daughter of a Brave-killer."

"…"

"Shenira is a good girl. I know she'll grow up to be a wonderful woman, like you. If she discovered someone she'd never met had died for her to live, it would surely bring her sorrow as an adult. It would wound her in a way that would never heal. I don't wish that for her."

"Stop it, Ganna. I can't take it anymore." Mora pushed her husband away and buried her face in a pillow.

"I'm sorry. I know this brings you more pain than me… I'm sorry." He gently put his hand on her shoulder. "I'm a cruel father."

"No…you're not. Not…ever." Mora buried her face in the pillow and sobbed.

It had been approximately one month ago, around the time Mora had finished the surgery to implant the eruption gem inside her body. She hadn't even waited for the incision to heal to return to combat training with Willone. Exhausted, her stomach empty, she fell into bed. Right as she was about to fall asleep on the spot, Mora noticed her daughter standing beside her bed. "What's wrong, Shenira?"

The little girl seemed different from usual. She was usually so cheerful and babyish, but now her lips were pressed tight together, and she held back tears.

"Mommy…are you going to die?" asked Shenira.

Without hesitation, Mora embraced Shenira and the stuffed animal the little girl held in her arms. Shenira already knew about the Evil God, and she probably also knew that Mora would likely be chosen as a Brave of the Six Flowers. "You have nothing to worry about. Mommy is going to win. The Evil God is nothing to fear." Mora petted her back to calm her down.

But then Shenira said something that her mother couldn't have expected. "Are you gonna die 'cause of me?"

"Huh?"

"Are you gonna die 'cause I'm sick? I don't…want that…"

Mora had been most emphatic with both Ganna and Willone that they were not to tell Shenira anything. She should have believed that she was cured. But this meant that Shenira had figured out the truth quite some time ago. Sometimes, children could be mysteriously intuitive at picking out when adults were lying. Her daughter sobbed and sobbed for a long time. No matter how much Mora tried to soothe her, she didn't stop. Ganna scooped her into his arms and sang her songs until she finally fell asleep.

After that, Mora found out—for a few months now, Shenira had been praying every day before a certain statue of the Spirit of Fate in All Heavens Temple. *I'll always eat my vegetables, so please save Mommy. I'll never do anything bad my whole life, so please save Mommy*, she had prayed before the Spirit's image. *I'll die instead, so please save Mommy*, Shenira had said to it.

Mora had known all along—no matter how much she fought it, she couldn't abandon Shenira. She knew it wasn't out of love but due to her own weakness. "Fremy," she said as she treated her own wounds. In her hand, she clenched a metal tube about the size of her index finger. She crushed it in her fist and sprinkled the medicine inside on her body. "If Tgurneu dies, will you know?"

"Why are you asking me that?"

"I'm concerned that even if we do kill Tgurneu, another might assume command in its place."

Fremy observed Mora steadily as she gave the matter careful consideration. "If Tgurneu dies, every fiend that follows it will know immediately. They would all grieve and moan and begin to panic."

"I see." Then that meant Tgurneu was still alive, and everything it had told Mora was true. If that was the case, then it must also be true that Mora was the seventh. Oddly enough, finding out that she herself was the seventh was a relief. The mystery was solved. Now she need no longer fear the seventh. "What sort of relationship does Tgurneu have with its minions?" she asked.

"Tgurneu commands absolute loyalty. Their allegiance to Tgurneu is equal to their allegiance to the Evil God." Their idle chat was beginning to make Fremy suspicious. "Mora, what are you hiding? What is your plot, here?"

"I *am* hiding something. But there's no plot."

"Talk. What's your plot? If you won't tell me, I'll shoot you."

"I shall tell you everything, and leave nothing out—after Chamo returns with Adlet."

"You—" Fremy hesitated for just a moment, and when she did, Mora whipped around and attacked her. It was not the kind of attack Fremy could block. Normally, she probably would have shot Mora in the head on the spot. But when she fired, the bullet only skimmed past her ear.

"!"

Mora had not dodged. Fremy had missed. Her typically precise aim was off, having failed to hit a target only five steps away. Mora didn't give her the time to jump back and get away. She grabbed the hem of Fremy's cloak, pulled as hard as she could, then wrapped her arms around Fremy's slender body, circling her hands about the girl's neck.

"Mo—" With the artery in her neck cut off, she fell unconscious only moments later.

"..."

Mora released her grip, and Fremy dropped to the ground.

Tgurneu had said that Mora was a true villain. Was it right? Mora doubted that many in the world were as evil as her. She had sworn to her husband that she would not kill any of the Braves of the Six Flowers. She had sworn to her daughter that she would save the world. But in the shadows, she had been preparing to kill one of the Six Braves—meticulously, deftly, and secretly.

Mora picked up her iron gauntlets, heaved Fremy over her shoulder, and ran off toward the Bud of Eternity. "I'm sorry, Shenira." She apologized not to the Saint slung over her shoulder but to her beloved daughter far away. "I'm sorry this is the kind of mother I am."

The unconscious Fremy breathed quietly on her shoulder. It would be easy for Mora to snap her neck. But she couldn't kill Fremy—not here, not yet. She had put a lot of time and effort into working out her plan, and she was not yet ready to kill one of the Six Braves. The plan required the help of a certain someone, someone she had reared and trained for the purpose of implementing her plan to kill a Brave.

Rolonia Manchetta, Saint of Blood. Mora had kept the child prodigy close at hand, taking on the role of her teacher and training her personally.

She had raised her for the purpose of killing one of the Braves of the Six Flowers.

Chapter 5

The
Traitor's
Truth

When Mora had first met Rolonia, the girl had had nothing.

Six months after making her agreement with Tgurneu, Mora received troublesome news. She learned that someone unworthy of Sainthood received the power of the Spirit at the Temple of Spilled Blood. The new Saint was apparently an orphan who had been working at the temple as a servant. She was stupid, lacked any redeeming features, and seemed entirely unfit for the responsibility. Apparently, the girl did not want to be a Saint. Mora would have preferred to leave such miscellaneous matters to Willone, if possible, but custom dictated that the Temple Elder's approval was required for a Saint to resign, so Mora had no choice but to head to the Temple of Spilled Blood.

When she arrived, she found the new Saint doing laundry at the back of the temple by the well. Mora had been told that this was her only job. The maid's uniform she wore was dirty, and her hands were cracked all over. The miserable expression deeply etched into her face illustrated she was entirely used to being on the receiving end of ire.

I don't have time to be dealing with this, Mora thought before she addressed the girl. "Are you the newly chosen Saint of Spilled Blood?"

When the girl realized she was being spoken to, she stood up and turned around. The moment Mora saw the girl's eyes, a faint current ran through her body. It was a sign detectable only by those who knew battle—a sign that this girl was powerful. Mora sensed this timid-looking girl was already in the possession of abilities that were not to be underestimated.

"I-I'm sorry. I'm the one who frayed the undergarments so badly. I'm sorry!" The girl seemed mistaken about why Mora had come as she bowed her head over and over.

"I want to ask you something." Mora gently took her hands. "Could you manipulate your blood to heal these cracks?"

"Huh? What? Um…I was just chosen as a Saint by mistake, I can't…"

"I asked whether you can do it or not. Just try."

"Yes, ma'am. I'm sorry, um…" The girl stared hard at her fingertips, then sent her power into them. Red enveloped her hands as they warmed. Before their eyes, the skin of the girl's hands grew healthy once more.

Those elected by the Spirits are not generally able to use their powers immediately. Saints trained in order to control their power, communing many times with their Spirit in order to finally become a fully fledged Saint. Mora knew this girl had unique talents. "I am Mora, Saint of Mountains. What's your name?"

"It's Rolonia Manchetta. I'm just a servant." The girl bowed again and again.

As Mora watched, her thoughts were elsewhere. A while back, an idea had come to her, but she'd written it off as impossible. Perhaps, with this girl, she might be able to actually make it happen. It was a disgraceful idea—and a disgraceful plan.

Mora immediately took Rolonia into the custody of All Heavens Temple and determined that she would be given special Saints' education. She also announced that she would train the newest of their number to be one of the Braves of the Six Flowers within the next three years. Many of the Saints were against this. They all said that although Rolonia might have the qualities necessary to be a Saint, she didn't have what it took to be a warrior. And they were right—clearly, Rolonia was not suited for fighting. But Mora faced down the opposition and took her into All Heavens Temple.

Rolonia was constantly flustered, frightened, panicked, and crying.

First, Mora taught her the skills that the Saint of Spilled Blood would need: how to heal wounds, how to manipulate her whip by controlling the blood within it, how to analyze blood by taste, and how to control her opponent's blood so as to wound them fatally. Just as Mora had expected, Rolonia had unbelievable talent. It took practically no effort for her to absorb these skills.

Next, Mora instructed Rolonia to learn from powerful warriors from all over the world. She'd had the old hero Stradd Camus teach her the mindset of the warrior and the legendary strategist Tomaso Halderoy drive the fundamentals of strategy into her head. She'd had the fiend specialist Atreau Spiker instruct her on the creatures she would encounter.

But, as Mora had predicted, Rolonia wasn't warrior material. When she met an enemy, she was immediately frightened. But worse, she was afraid of hurting her foes. No matter how many Saints' techniques she learned, there was no sign that she would overcome these things. A warrior had to be arrogant. You had to believe in your own strength before you could defeat your enemies. But Rolonia was completely incapable of doing that.

She had been bullied by the acolytes for a long time. Throughout her childhood, she had been told that she was clumsy and forgetful and would always be useless. She was convinced that she couldn't do anything. Someone who doesn't believe they can get stronger never will.

"Hey, boss," said Willone one day, helping Mora train Rolonia. "You need to give up already. That kid isn't gonna be a Brave. She isn't cut out for a fighting role. She's suited to being a healer."

"No, Willone. I can tell—she will be a great warrior," said Mora, but she wasn't confident about it, either.

"Rolonia is a good girl. Healing and recovery techniques are more her style. It'd be better for her to go around helping the sick and the injured, like Torleau does. Why can't you get that?"

Willone was right, and Mora knew it. But Mora needed Rolonia for her plan, no matter what. Her protégé had to grow to become one of the strongest warriors in the world and be chosen as one of the Braves of the Six Flowers. Mora couldn't tell Willone or Rolonia about her plan. There was no way she could tell anyone in the world that she intended to use this girl to kill one of the Six Braves. "Trust me, Willone. I will turn her into a fine warrior."

When Rolonia had returned from the mountain where fiend specialist Atreau Spiker lived, Mora summoned her to her quarters and offered her wine. Confused, the girl brought the cup of alcohol—the first she'd ever had in her life—to her lips.

"Rolonia, have you ever felt the desire to become a warrior?"

Eyes on the ground, Rolonia replied, "I felt that way…a little bit, just once." Mora was surprised. "I…made a friend. At Master Atreau's place. He was training to be one of the Braves of the Six Flowers…and he was trying really hard."

What happened while she was with Atreau? Mora wondered.

"I thought if I could become a warrior and be chosen as one of the Braves of the Six Flowers, maybe I could be useful to him." Rolonia flailed. "S-someone like me shouldn't be thinking of that sort of thing, though, right? Like being one of the Braves of the Six Flowers, that would be crazy. I mean, there's so many other powerful warriors out there, like you and Willone—"

"Rolonia." Mora stood from her chair, took her guest's hand, and bowed her head.

"Lady Mora…wh…wh-wh-why are you…?"

"I regret what I'm doing to you."

"Um…"

"Please. Be a warrior, for me. Battle the fiends by my side. I need you, whatever it takes."

"Me? But…but…"

"It must be you!" Mora yelled. Rolonia trembled.

"I cannot say why. All I can do is bow my head and beg of you. Tell me you will be my warrior with no complaints. I need you."

Rolonia shook her head, her voice frightened as she spoke. "I'm afraid, Lady Mora. I don't know what I should do. I mean…this is the first time…anyone's ever needed me."

"Everyone has a first time."

"…But…"

Mora knew that there was virtue in Rolonia more powerful than anyone else's. More than anyone Mora knew, Rolonia was glad to be useful to others.

"What should I do if I just can't? It's not going to work out, anyway."

"…Do your very best. That's enough. I ask for nothing else."

"…I understand. I'll do everything I can. If I just have to try my hardest, I think I can manage that." Then Rolonia gave her the faintest smile. In her smile was the joy of having someone rely on her for the very first time, the gladness of being useful for the very first time. That was the first time that Mora ever saw Rolonia smile.

After that, her student changed—just a little. She became less frightened. She apologized for no reason less often. And she had become serious about gaining strength.

It must have been about one year earlier that Mora had found Rolonia in the arena at All Heavens Temple doing something strange. In the center of the arena, there was a doll made of bundled straw. The words *Fiend! Really bad guy!* were inked on its chest. Rolonia was standing in front of the doll, screaming, "You jerk! I hate you! You're my enemy! A bad guy!"

Willone stood behind her. "No, no! More anger! One more time!"

"I-I'll…beat you up! I'll clobburb you!" Seemingly not used to yelling, Rolonia occasionally garbled her words.

"That's a little better. Do it like that."

"I-I'll slaughter you! You putrid monster! Go to hell! I'll make sure your heart never beats again!"

Willone patted Rolonia on the shoulder. "That's it! You've got it, Rolonia!"

"I did it, Willone!" The pair embraced in the middle of the arena.

Impatient, Mora cut in. "Now can I ask just what it is you're doing?"

Scratching her head, Willone explained. "Well...Rolonia just doesn't want to fight bad enough. Like, she lacks that aggressive spirit, you know? So I've been thinking that maybe she could make up for that by practicing venting her anger at an enemy, like this." That didn't lessen Mora's exasperation at all.

"Um, Lady Mora, I think this is really good. I think maybe doing this could make me stronger."

"If it works, then that's fine, I suppose." Mora was nonplussed.

"It sounds like you don't really know much in the way of insults, Rolonia," said Willone. "You have to expand your vocabulary, too."

"Yes, ma'am. I'm sorry."

"It's okay, I'll teach you. Listen, Rolonia. There are probably more than a hundred different ways out there to tell someone to go to hell."

"Really? Please teach me, Willone!"

When the two of them were about to leave the arena together, Mora called out to them. "Have you forgotten, Rolonia? Today you're studying healing techniques with myself and Torleau."

"Oh...that's right. I'm sorry, Willone."

"Oh, it's fine," Willone replied. "See you tomorrow."

Mora took Rolonia with her, and they headed out to the infirmary, where Torleau was waiting for them. "Today's class will be tough," said Mora. "You'll be taking part in Torleau's surgery. While she's excising the affected part, keep the blood circulating and the heart moving. Curtail any bleeding to prevent the patient's death by blood loss. You will also be using techniques to increase blood volume. Stay sharp."

"Yes, ma'am!"

Rolonia's progress had been remarkable. She had learned the healing arts and enthusiastically studied human anatomy. Her healing abilities were now no less than Mora's. And, though progress was slow, she was also learning combat. Mora knew that Rolonia possessed one other virtue, too—when she tried in earnest, she did so to an impressive degree. She was extremely dedicated.

Just as Mora had planned, Rolonia improved. One year later, she progressed to the level where it wouldn't be unexpected for her to be chosen as a Brave of the Six Flowers.

Mora could not tell Rolonia of her true intentions—that the real reason she had nurtured her thus far was for the sake of killing one of the Braves. It would be a lie to say Mora had no pangs of conscience. But she had no choice but to do it—for her beloved daughter and for herself.

"The time for you to be useful to me has come, Rolonia," Mora murmured as she ran to the Bud of Eternity, eyes to the east, toward the girl.

Adlet's party of four crawled on their hands and knees along the hill in the dark. They illuminated the ground with their light gems, searching for the evidence their leader had instructed them to find.

There were many remnants of their battle on this hill. The bodies of a number of fiends. The poison needles that Adlet had thrown. The bullets Fremy had fired. The footprints where Mora's feet had plunged deep into the ground. The lashes of Rolonia's whip. Adlet examined these as he searched his memory, going out to try to locate the place where this evidence should be. He pushed aside the sparsely growing grass and smoothed the dry sand, carefully searching. He had to keep an eye on where he was stepping, too. The thing they were searching for was very small. If one of them kicked it by accident, it would probably fly off somewhere, and if they stepped on it, it might be crushed.

It was nearly the time they had promised Mora and the others they would return. Adlet lifted his head and looked to the west. Were they safe? And was Tgurneu still inside the barrier?

"*Meow!*" After about ten minutes of looking, Hans had already admitted defeat.

"Don't be so loud," said Adlet. "You'll attract enemies."

"I can't take no more of this. There's nothin' I hate meowr than rummagin' through a haystack to find a needle," complained Hans, sprawled out on the ground.

Adlet paid him no mind and continued his search.

"What're ya thinkin', Adlet? How does findin' somethin' like that prove anything?"

"I don't have time to explain."

"You've figured it out, right? The answer to Tgurneu's mystery? That's all ya need."

It didn't work like that. Adlet's idea was far too fantastical. He himself would not believe it until he saw the proof with his own eyes.

"Let's stop lookin' for this thing and hurry back. I'm worried about the others," said Hans.

"Th-they'll be okay," said Rolonia. "Lady Mora is at the Bud of Eternity. If anything happens, she should be able to manage things, somehow."

"Rolonia, why do ya trust Mora so much?" asked Hans. "She's pretty suspicious."

"She's a great woman. I can't even imagine she could be our enemy." Hans didn't reply. Still sprawled on the ground, he scratched his neck.

Mora's clairvoyance alerted her to something unusual. Seven fiends were nearing the Bud of Eternity. They stopped right at the edge of the barrier, where the repulsion force didn't reach.

"What do you want?" she asked.

"Commander Tgurneu has ordered us to help you kill one of the Braves of the Six Flowers." The one that spoke was one of the commander's companions from before, the stone man-fiend.

Just how well prepared is Tgurneu? The thought made Mora shiver.

"It seems there was no need for us to come. You're just the kind of person Commander Tgürneu knew you were. We saw you a moment agö with Fremy over your shoulder."

Mora raised her fists and answered coldly, "Leave this place. Now. Go to the southern edge of the mountain and feign death. Stay there and await my direction."

"You still haven't killed her? Why not?"

"I have no need to tell you."

"Don't you wänt to save your daughter?"

"If you do anything at all contrary to my orders, then this plan to kill a Brave stops immediately. I will reveal that I'm the seventh and surrender myself. This is no bluff."

The fiend looked Mora in the eyes for a moment, pondering. At this fiend's level of intellect, it should not catch on to what she was trying to do. "We häve been told to follow your orders," said the fiend.

"Then go now. Or would you die here?"

The fiends immediately moved out.

Now Chamo would soon return, having heard the gunshot. Mora had to hurry and prepare. It was two more days until Tgurneu's deadline. Her only chance was that night. Adlet's party was busy with figuring out Tgurneu's mystery, and Chamo did not yet suspect her. That night would be her only chance. There was much to do. She had to incapacitate Fremy and Chamo, then lure the other four back and split them into two groups. She would then create a situation where she, her target, and Rolonia were the only ones present. Then she would fight the target and win. Every step of this plan had to work, or it would fail.

Mora caught sight of Chamo with her clairvoyant eye. She was astride a gigantic slug fiend, accompanied by five other slave-fiends. "Fremy! You killed Auntie, didn't you?!" She was making a beeline for the location where Tgurneu had been moments ago. When she found that no one was there, she was confused. "Auntie! Where did you go?! Are you dead?!" Scurrying about on the giant slug, she ordered her fiends to search the area.

Meanwhile, Mora went into the cave, Fremy slung over her shoulder. Once inside, she pulled a metal tube from her packs and stomped on it. The fluid inside splattered, and Mora kicked it around to disperse it with her feet.

"Auntie! Are you really dead?! You dummy! Why'd you have to die?!" When Mora checked with her powers, she found that Chamo was still searching for her. "You numbskull! Piece of poop! Weakling! Useless lump! You're so stupid, Auntie!" Mora couldn't tell if Chamo was cursing her or worried about her. Despite the seriousness of the situation, she chuckled.

Then Chamo seemed to realize something and rolled up the hem of her skirt to look at the Crest of the Six Flowers on her thigh. "Oh! She's still alive." Apparently Chamo had finally remembered that every time a Brave died, a petal disappeared from the crest.

Mora began to drip with cold sweat. Next, she had to incapacitate the most powerful Saint alive. If her luck was poor, she would be dead before long. With her mountain echoes, she shouted, **"ADLET! CHAMO! COME BACK! IT'S A TRAP!"**

"Auntie?"

Mora had modulated her cry so it would only reach Chamo. Adlet and the others, on the distant hill, would not be able to hear.

"Where are you? Where are you, Auntie?!"

"THE BUD—" Mora cut off before she finished the sentence. That would be enough for Chamo to get it.

As Mora had expected, Chamo headed back to the Bud of Eternity, all her slave-fiends behind her. The Saint covered the flower that shone inside the cave with a cloth and recited an incantation to snuff out the light gem.

"Auntie! What happened?!" Chamo burst into the barrier of the Bud of Eternity. When she found no one there, she headed to the cave.

"Stay away, Chamo!" Mora yelled.

Chamo stopped at the cave entrance. "What's wrong, Auntie? Why's it all dark in there?"

"Don't come in. And no lights. *No* lights."

"What happened?"

Mora didn't reply. Right now, she was playing for time. Chamo hadn't noticed that Mora had scattered a certain drug around the dark cave, a drug she'd had Torleau, Saint of Medicine, make for her. Ostensibly, the medicine was for pain and to prevent infection. Technically, it could be used as medicine; Mora had used it earlier to treat Adlet's wounds after Nashetania had cut him. When Mora had ordered Torleau to make large quantities of this medicine, the doctor had been puzzled. This medicine was potent—too potent, in fact. A solution of half a drop dissolved in water was sufficient. The undiluted solution, when applied directly, would inevitably be harmful. The drug relaxed the body, making the affected person feel intoxicated, as if drunk. It was so potent, a mere sniff would cause a person to stagger. Mora had told Torleau that while the medicine was good, it was not something she could take with her to the Howling Vilelands—but in truth, she had secretly filled a metal tube with the dangerous undiluted solution and carried it with her.

"What do you mean, no lights?" asked Chamo.

"Don't come in. You can do nothing for me."

"That's why I'm asking! What happened?!"

Mora was being deliberately vague in order to make Chamo stay where she was and inhale the powerful drug. Mora had used the medicine herself many times, building up her resistance to it in order to avoid intoxicating herself—all for this moment. She had done it in preparation for killing a Brave of the Six Flowers.

"I'll keep it under control, so stay away."

"Sorry, Auntie, but Chamo can't just do nothing," Chamo said, slowly entering the cave. Mora was crouched in the back of the cave, watching the other Saint from the darkness. "Keep what under control? Where did Fremy go?"

"Fremy…ran away."

Then Chamo stopped. She looked at Mora. "Hey…you're acting kinda weird, Auntie." She'd figured it out, but it was too late. Mora surged to her feet and savagely rushed Chamo. The younger Brave tried to dodge, but she stumbled and fell over.

"!" The slave-fiends descended upon Mora. The slug spat acid, while the protozoan shot a tentacle at her. Body burning and one arm bound, Mora grabbed Chamo by the neck.

There were two reasons Mora had been lying in wait inside this cave. First, to ensure the drug would be as effective as possible, and second, to prevent the slave-fiends from attacking all at once.

Mora wrapped her fingers over Chamo's carotid artery and squeezed, just enough to avoid crushing it. It was only moments before the drugged girl passed out. When she lost consciousness, the fiends were sucked back into her mouth.

"Ugh…" Mora groaned. She, too, had been quite affected by the drug. But this was only the middle stage of the battle, and the real fight—the plan to kill one of the Braves of the Six Flowers—was yet to come.

Still searching the hill, Rolonia lifted her head. Her neck and eyes must have been tired. The four have them had been searching for the evidence for a long time. "I just can't find it, Addy," she said tiredly.

Adlet put a hand on a hand on his forehead, thinking. Perhaps Tgurneu had already destroyed what they were looking for. Maybe it would be better to give up on trying to find it and withdraw. Most of their allotted time was gone.

"Can I go back neow?" Hans was lying in a sprawl, scratching his butt.

"Please," said Rolonia, "um…please put a little more effort into it."

"I might put in a li'l effort—if ya pay me fer it, *meow*. In advance."

"I'm sorry. I…don't have any money at all."

Adlet looked toward the mountain, where the Bud of Eternity lay. There had been no contact from Mora. In this case, was no news good news, or did it mean disaster had come to pass?

That was when Goldof reached out toward Hans's feet. He picked up something stuck in the ground and showed it to the leader of the party. "Is this it?"

Adlet examined the dirt-covered thing, then pulled out the solution that reacted to fiend traces and sprayed the item. He watched it turn orange and gulped.

"Does this thing…tell you…something?" asked Goldof.

"*Meow?* Did ya find somethin'?" Hans finally sat up.

Adlet didn't even hear the two men speak. Elation welled up from deep in his stomach, making him tremble. "I've caught it," he said. "I've finally caught Tgurneu." Adlet tucked the thing away at his waist and prompted Hans to stand. "We're going back," he said before dashing off. The other three, flustered, followed after him.

"I've figured out what Tgurneu really is. Now we just have to come up with a way to kill it," Adlet said, gloating. "Listen up. Tgurneu is actually—"

"Wait." Rolonia cut off his explanation as they ran.

"...ISHED..."

Adlet had been so excited that he hadn't noticed the voice. From the direction of the mountain, he could hear something—Mora's mountain echo. When Adlet heard her voice, in a flash, the glee in his heart turned to ice.

"I guess we're goin' to have to wait to hear what Tgurneu really is, *meow*," said Hans, and he drew his swords.

Mora forced Fremy and Chamo, both still unconscious, to swallow the sedative. They wouldn't awaken for a while now.

She left the cave and sat down on a rock, covering her face as she curled up. She did so not out of exhaustion or dizziness. "You still hesitate?" she said to herself. *Pathetic*, came the self-loathing whisper. Mora had thought she'd already made up her mind to do anything for her daughter, but even so, she was still irresolute. The faces of her allies flashed through her mind one after another. Sometimes, they had made her anxious, and she had thought them unreliable. They had also angered her at times. But they were all fine young people. They would surely defeat the Evil God and protect the world.

Once it was all over, there was no question in Mora's mind that she would be killed. Knowing she would never see them again, the faces of her husband and daughter rose in her mind. *Forget about it*, she told herself. She didn't deserve to see them anymore. From this point on, Mora would fall to the depths of villainy. No—she had been a villain already, for quite some time now.

The elder Saint stood. Then she used her power of mountain echo and yelled, **"ADLET! THE SALTPEAK BARRIER HAS BEEN EXTINGUISHED!"** She paused a moment, and then called again, **"COME BACK! THE BARRIER HAS BEEN EXTINGUISHED!"**

Their four lights swayed as the group made their way through the Ravine of Spitten Blood. Adlet, Rolonia, Goldof, and Hans were sprinting full speed toward the Bud of Eternity.

The Saltpeak Barrier had been extinguished. Mora had said just that one thing, and afterward, there was no further contact. Adlet's heart pounded with anxiety as he wondered why she wasn't communicating.

When they emerged from the ravine, the pitch-black shape of the mountain rose in the distance. Adlet noticed the Saltpeak Barrier, which had been covering the whole mountain, was indeed gone.

"*Meow*. She didn't say it was *broken*. She said it was *extinguished*. What's that mean?" asked Hans.

The barrier had not been broken or breached—but extinguished. Adlet couldn't imagine what had happened. The mountain was quiet. He could hear no fiends' voices, no sounds of battle, no nothing.

Mora stood on the mountain, a little ways up from the Bud of Eternity, as she watched the east. She could faintly see four lights. It looked like it would be a few minutes before they would reach the mountain. She shouted one more time, **"ADLET! YOU'RE NOT HERE YET?!"** The four lights stopped for a moment and then started running again. They had heard Mora's mountain echo. **"TGURNEU RAN AWAY, AND THE OTHER FIENDS FOLLOWED IT. BUT…AGHH!"** She cut her message off there and paused again. It would probably seem unnatural if she sounded too calm about what was going on. **"BUT A FIEND I'VE NEVER SEEN BEFORE…HAS ATTACKED THE BUD OF ETERNITY! DAMN IT!"** Mora pretended to be gathering her words once more. **"HURRY! THE FIEND IS ATTEMPTING TO BREAK THE BUD OF ETERNITY!"** she yelled, and then she made a lot of noise, smashing a boulder and punching the ground. The noise would suggest a fight going on there. It was a quiet, dark night. Silence would make them suspicious.

After hitting the ground a few more times, Mora turned to look behind her. Two of the seven fiends Tgurneu had sent were still there, waiting. Both of them seemed to be superior and intelligent beasts.

"You two pretend to fight here. Yell as if you're attacking. Understood?" The fiends nodded. "After about five minutes of fighting, kill yourselves. If you break your word, know that your efforts will have come to nothing." As Mora punched the ground again, she thought anxiously, *Will this deception really work?*

The four lights neared the mountain. A little closer, and they would be within reach of her clairvoyant eye. Mora breathed out a long breath and calmed her heart. Then she began the final stage of her ploy to split up Adlet's party. **"FREMY! WHERE ARE YOU GOING?! COME BACK! WHAT IS YOUR INTENTION?!"** she yelled. Of course, Fremy hadn't gone anywhere. She was sleeping inside the barrier of the Bud of Eternity. **"FREMY! WHERE ARE YOU GOING?! ... ADLET! HURRY BACK! FREMY HAS FLED!"**

"Where'd Tgurneu disappear off to?" Hans muttered as they scrambled up the incline. Adlet was wondering the same thing. The Saltpeak Barrier's disappearance was not the only peculiar thing here. There had been so many fiends, but they were now all gone. Adlet could faintly hear the sound of fighting—but it only sounded like there were a few. Why had the enemy made their move all of a sudden? In just thirty-odd minutes, during the time the four of them had run from the hill to the mountain, the situation had changed dizzyingly fast. Unnaturally fast.

Unnatural. The word ran through Adlet's mind. It couldn't be that all of this was a lie, could it? But now was not the time to be thinking about that. Whether this was real or fake, they still had to get back as quickly as possible.

"FREMY! WHERE ARE YOU GOING?!"

Something had happened again. Adlet wanted to say, *What is it this time?* as Mora's call to Fremy reverberated through the mountains.

"ADLET! HURRY BACK! FREMY HAS FLED!"

When Adlet heard that yell, he stopped automatically. "What?" *Fremy has fled.* For a moment, he didn't even understand what those words meant.

"Addy, you can't stop. We have to hurry." Rolonia tugged Adlet's hand. But he didn't move. Hans and Goldof were forced to stop as well.

"FREMY HAS GONE TO THE SOUTHWEST, THE DIREC-TION TGURNEU FLED! I DON'T KNOW WHY!"

"*Meow!* What in the heck is she doin'?" Hans said carelessly. Goldof said nothing. He seemed like he was thinking of something, but then again, maybe not.

"HANS! GOLDOF! HEAD SOUTHWEST AND FOLLOW FREMY! ROLONIA AND ADLET, COME TO MY AID NOW!" Mora's mountain echo cut off.

"Fremy…it couldn't be," Rolonia muttered as she gazed toward the Bud of Eternity.

"*Meow…*so is she the seventh, after all? That answer just don't seem clean to me."

"No way she's the seventh," Adlet shot back. Fremy must have had some kind of idea, or if she didn't, maybe Tgurneu was controlling her. "Hans, Goldof. Can I ask you two to take care of Fremy?"

Goldof nodded. But Hans shook his head. "Naw, Fremy hates me. I think it'd be better for you to go." Adlet got the feeling Hans was trying to hint at something else, but before he could ask, Hans grabbed Rolonia's hand and ran off. "*Mya-meow!* C'mon, Rolonia!"

"W-wait, please!" Rolonia stuttered. In a flash, Hans was gone.

"Let's go, Adlet," Goldof said, and Adlet came to his senses. He set out to the southwest, as per Mora's instructions.

The four lights split into two groups, one heading southwest and the other running up toward the Bud of Eternity. *Now the most difficult part is done,* thought Mora. Splitting Adlet's party into two separate pairs had been the biggest hurdle. If all four of them were acting in accord, or if they had split into a group of three and one person alone, then the plan would have failed utterly.

"Fiends, Adlet and Goldof are headed straight for your location." Through her echoes, Mora transmitted orders to the remaining accomplices Tgurneu had sent her. "Hold them in position as long as you live. Once that is done—all of you, die."

The fiends stood. Adlet and Goldof didn't notice anything as they raced along.

"It's time to go." Mora hastened down the mountain at full speed toward Rolonia.

She had made one miscalculation. The one with Rolonia was Hans.

The original plan was to kill Adlet. He was weaker than her—one-on-one, she could beat him easily. And the young Brave was the trusting type. If she could catch him off guard, she could probably kill him. Even if she were forced to fight Goldof, she'd have a chance of winning. He was stronger than Adlet, but he still had his weaknesses. But her opponent was Hans. He was cautious and alert, so she probably wouldn't be able to get him by surprise. Plus, there was no question that he was superior to Mora in terms of combat abilities.

Oddly enough, Mora wasn't afraid. Now that she had thrown away everything, she had nothing more to fear. She had only two options: to save Shenira and die, or to fail to save her and die.

Fists clenched, she raced down the slope. She didn't have to use her clairvoyance anymore—she could see both of their lights. *This contest will be decided the moment we meet*, thought Mora. *I have to kill him before he draws his swords.*

"Lady Mora?" she heard Rolonia say.

But right when Mora clenched her fists, about to swing at Hans, he hurled his light gem at her. The tiny lantern flared in her sight for an instant, burning her eyes. "*Ungh!*"

The concentrated light was especially bright to her eyes, accustomed to the darkness. She pressed a hand to her face and stumbled backward.

"Hans! What are you doing?" Rolonia cried, and in that instant, Mora rolled to the side. She heard the tips of her hair being sliced off, informing her that death had missed her by mere centimeters.

"*Meow-hee-hee.* I bungled that one."

Mora managed to just crack her eyes open to a squint. Hans was spinning his blades in his hands.

"Hans! What on earth are you doing?! And Lady Mora, your wounds—" Rolonia pulled out her whip and readied it. When she saw Mora covered in blood, she lost her voice. The suddenness of the situation made her legs tremble, her eyes dart about. She hadn't grasped what was going on.

"Adlet woulda been fooled, *meow*. He's a dyed-in-the-wool sucker. *Agh*, dealin' with such a hardcore bleedin' heart is a trial, I tell ya."

As Mora fought back the pain in her eyes, she raised her fists. "I've finally succeeded in luring you out. Give yourself up. Your true identity has already come to light." This was all to deceive Rolonia. If she could get her protégé on her side, she could turn this battle into a two-on-one.

"*Mya-meow?* For the spur of the moment, that's a pretty good lie. I thought you'd been raised like a lady, but you ain't half-bad." Hans was not ruffled.

"Just what are you talking about? What is going on?!" Rolonia demanded, sounding like she was about to cry.

"The seventh is Mora, and she's gonna try to kill me."

"The seventh is Hans! He was planning to kill you!"

Hans and Mora exclaimed at the same time.

Rolonia just looked back and forth between the two of them, unable to move. She must have understood that there was something wrong with the situation, too, and she may even have noticed that Mora had been lying. But she had only met Hans just that morning, and she had spent the past two and a half years together with Mora. Even if she suspected her mentor, Rolonia wouldn't be able to fight her.

"*Meow.* You just sit tight and watch, Rolonia. If you get in the way, I'll end up cuttin' ya both up." Hans slowly went into action. He approached, shifting in an enigmatic manner that included a lot of seemingly pointless dancing. Rolonia retreated a step, and Mora judged that she would not be able to win her over.

"Rolonia, don't interfere," Mora said, eyes locked on the girl. "Believe in me."

Hans immediately dove toward her with blinding speed. Mora blocked the slice aimed at her feet with the iron plate of her boot. The single strike numbed her leg up to the thigh.

"*Hrmya-mya-mya-mya-meow!*" Unrelenting, Hans slashed at Mora. He moved like a cat chasing a toy on a string and smiled like a frolicking kitten.

"Did you hear that, Goldof?" As they ran, Adlet glanced back behind them. He could just faintly hear the sound of something like an argument, far away. Human voices traveled a long way on the quiet mountain.

Goldof was looking in the same direction. He'd noticed something was off, too. They hadn't heard Mora's echo for a while now, and no matter how Adlet called for Fremy, they didn't get a single reply back. They hadn't seen any trace of Tgurneu or other fiends, either.

Jogging along, they came upon the body of a leopard-fiend, Fremy's bullet lodged in its head. When Adlet touched the body, he found it was cold.

"This really is weird. What Mora's been saying doesn't make sense." The boy made up his mind. He would capture Mora and question her. She'd probably been lying about Fremy running away. "I wonder if Fremy and Chamo are safe?" When he checked the back of his right hand, all the petals were present on the crest. They were both definitely still alive.

Then Goldof drew his spear. "Fiends," he said. Five enemies had surrounded them, unawares. The two Braves stood back-to-back, and Adlet readied his poison needles and his sword.

The fiends didn't attack. They just stayed in a circle, gradually inching in closer. Adlet took advantage of a momentary opening to fire off a needle. The wolf-fiend flinched when the poison dart hit its mark, but as Adlet followed up with a blade, a stone man-fiend's fist struck at him from the side. After the two exchanged three blows, the stone man withdrew, putting some distance between them to hold Adlet in check.

When the fiends did not pursue them, Adlet realized they were trying to slow them down, and he figured out Mora's goal in all of this, too. She was in cahoots with these creatures, luring in the Braves of the Six Flowers and trying to separate them.

A beast ran silently through the darkness. Without a light, Mora couldn't see it clearly. The brute was only faintly illuminated by Rolonia's gem.

"*Hrmeow!*" Hans cried. Crouched low enough to skim the ground, he rushed for Mora with fearsome speed. His swords swept together, scissoring toward Mora's leg.

Unable to block the attack, she jumped to dodge his blades. Hans thrust one weapon into the ground to abruptly halt his movement and stabbed at Mora while she was still midair. The assassin's body was frighteningly flexible, snapping from an unbelievable stance to an unbelievable strike.

"*Gah!*" In the air, Mora crossed her arms, blocking the sword with her iron gauntlets. She may have been a woman, but she was not by any means lightweight in her iron armor. Nevertheless, the thrust effortlessly sent her flying backward.

Hans scampered like a cat, mercilessly positioning for a follow-up offensive. Still in the air, Mora struck her iron gauntlets together as hard as she could. The shock wave–like sound made Hans flinch slightly. Rolonia, watching from the side, covered her ears reflexively. And the next attack from Hans was ever so slightly slower. "*Mya-ha!*"

When Mora landed, she turned away from her opponent and ran. She had to put some distance between them and get a better position somehow. She was trapped on defense. Hans's fierce strikes gave her no time to counterattack. She had not anticipated he would be so much stronger than her. Despite her shortcomings, she was still a Saint, one who called upon the power of a Spirit for battle. Her physical speed and strength far surpassed that of a normal human. Hans, on the other hand, was nothing more than his own flesh and blood.

"Yer not gettin' away!"

Mora somehow managed to block the blow with her metal gauntlet. Hans was not even going to let her retreat.

"*Hrmeow!*"

"Ah…oh…wh-what should I…?" Rolonia chased the pair as they ran around wildly to the west and to the east.

Mora couldn't use the drug that had taken out Fremy and Chamo, either. If she used it here, Rolonia would be affected, too, and the girl needed to stay safe until the fight was over.

As Mora blocked Hans's sword, she unleashed a desperate kick. Hans blocked her leg with a blade and leaped way back. Once there was some space them, Rolonia raised her whip and cut between the pair. "Wait, please, Lady Mora, Hans!"

"*Meow.* I told ya to stay away. Didn't ya hear me?" Hans gave her a cat-like, shiver-inducing grin. A bloodthirsty aura emanated from his body, as if to say he'd kill her, too.

"Let's talk. Let's wait until Addy's here, and then we'll talk."

A very Rolonia-like idea, thought Mora. She felt bad for her, but she couldn't allow Adlet to come. The only way to save Shenira was to kill Hans right there, right then.

"Yer bein' pretty quiet," Hans said to Rolonia. "You ain't gonna come at me with yer crazy wailin' like this afterneown?"

"I-I…"

Mora knew, though—all that shouting was just a ritual she used to will herself to fight. Rolonia was, by nature, cowardly. It was only through such an extreme habit that she was able to fight at all.

"But who cares 'bout that. Neow the fun's gettin' started. Don't get in the way."

"Fun…?" repeated Rolonia.

"When I see a powerful warrior, I just get this natural urge to kill 'em. Bein' all buddy-buddy ain't bad, either, but killin' is what I love meowst, after all."

Rolonia took a step back. She was afraid of him.

"Get back, Rolonia. This one is only a petty monster." Mora raised her fists. Rolonia didn't say anything. There was not trust in her eyes, but suspicion. "Come, Hans!"

"*Meow-ha-ha-ha!* I wouldn't stop even if ya asked!" Hans jumped high. Mora squatted down, drew in her arms, and protected her face. Keeping her body balled up, she focused on enduring the assault.

The five fiends were all powerful foes. Adlet killed one, while Goldof killed four, including the stone man. When they were sure that all of their enemies were still, Goldof asked, "What do we do, Adlet?"

From the eastern side of the mountain, he could just faintly hear the clash of metal. That wasn't the sound of fighting with fiends. Mora and Hans were fighting each other. It was now clear to him that the Elder had deceived them. *Should we go save Hans and Rolonia?* Adlet considered it, but he quickly changed his mind. "They'll be fine. Hans is sure to make it through. He's not quite as powerful as the strongest man in the world, but he's still pretty good."

"Then..."

With no time to reply, Adlet set off at a sprint. What he was worried about right then was Fremy and Chamo, of whom they had seen no trace. He glanced at the crest on his hand. Still no petals missing. All six Braves were alive.

Their destination was the Bud of Eternity. He didn't know what had happened, but any clues as to whatever it was would probably be there.

"...The seventh is...Mora. But why make her move now?"

As Adlet ran, he thought back on Mora's behavior. There had been some suspicious things about her. But if she really was the enemy, then her actions up until this point made no sense.

They made their way at a steady clip, and it wasn't long before they'd reached the Bud of Eternity. When Adlet stepped into the cave, he immediately discovered Fremy and Chamo. "Are you okay?!" he cried, raising Fremy into a sitting position.

She moaned quietly, her eyes opening a crack. Apparently she had just been put to sleep. "Don't worry. I'm fine." Once she was standing, she picked up her gun.

"What happened?" asked Adlet.

"Mora attacked me. I passed out, and when I woke up, I was here. Other than that, I have no idea—not why she attacked me, or why she didn't kill me, either."

"...Chamo is...all right, too," remarked Goldof as he checked on the girl. It looked like she'd just been sleeping, too, and she didn't seem to be injured badly.

"Goldof, let's worry about the treatment later!" said Adlet. "We're going to go capture Mora!" Adlet and Fremy ran off, and the knight followed, Chamo in his arms.

In a mere three minutes of battle, it had become painfully clear to Mora that she had no chance of winning. Before she had been chosen as one of the Braves of the Six Flowers, she had studied various techniques and worked together with other Saints to develop new weapons. But she had never anticipated an enemy like this, one who moved so fast in such a bizarre way.

Mora's body had been sliced to ribbons. Blood gushed from the artery in her upper arm. She'd been kicked in the side, and she sported a broken rib. There were also deep wounds in both her legs, and she wasn't even sure if she would be able to run. Blood streamed down her forehead, obscuring her vision, and it was hard to see Hans properly.

"Lady Mora, please, stop this fight! You can't win," Rolonia pleaded.

Hans prevented her from coming near. "*Meow-hee.* Yer still on her side?"

"Are you the seventh, Lady Mora? You're not, right? This is some kind of mistake, right? Please, stop this!"

"Not gonna happen. I'm killin' her neow."

"Hans..."

Vision blurred, Mora glared at Rolonia. And then, in a murderous tone, she said, "Get back. Our battle is not yet done."

"There ya go," said Hans. "Let's do this." He darted in.

Mora raised both of her gauntlets before her face, glued both elbows to her sides, and then curled her body with her knees in front of her. In that extreme, balled-up stance, she jumped backward. She held her body like a turtle to shield herself.

"I'm not lettin' ya get away!" Hans sliced at the cracks in her defense, unleashing one strike after another.

Mora weathered his attacks with only the smallest possible movements. She just had to block any fatal wounds, whatever it took. "*Ngh!*" As she fought back the pain, she hopped backward some more, frantically maneuvering in order that he not get around behind her. She was already wounded all over. She had no strength left to fight back.

"*Ngh...ah...*" Unable to act, Rolonia stood still, sobbing as she watched them fight.

Hans was cautious and patient. He didn't rush; he just waited for Mora to wear herself out. He was fully aware of what she was trying to do. She would wait for him to attack and open himself up, and then she would strike back. That was the only way that Mora would be able to win at this point.

"*Hmeow.* Givin' up yet?" Hans twirled his blades. "Sorry, *meow*, it's too late. I'm havin' a blast, here. This ain't gonna end till yer dead," he said, and then recommenced his attack. Mora tucked her body inward again, doing all she could to withstand the assault.

She was impatient. Adlet and Goldof would be there soon, and surely they'd already figured out that she'd lied to them. They would capture Mora and kill her. But if she attacked now, she would lose. If she made any move at all, it would open her up, and Hans would never miss that. There was nothing she could do but continue guarding. She hadn't given up. She was going to save Shenira. Mora had lost everything, and all that remained was this one desire. If she were to give up on that, too, then all she had would be gone.

"Saints sure are tough, *meow*. If ya don't hurry up and die soon, I'm gonna lose confidence in myself!" Hans's strikes became even more powerful. Mora was certain he intended to end this. His sword skimmed past her head, and a sliver of her scalp flew away, hair attached. He cut her legs, and she collapsed to her knees. He circled around behind her.

Mora's eyes were closed, but with her power of clairvoyance, she watched everything around her so that she wouldn't miss the moment Hans came to attack her from behind. *"Urmya-meow!"* Hans aimed for her midback, just under her ribs. It was one of the vital spots of the human body—the kidney. When an assassin wanted to make a sure kill from behind, they would always aim for the kidney.

The instant before the tip of the blade stabbed into her back, Mora twisted just a bit, and the blade missed its mark slightly. Mustering her remaining strength, she tensed her back. *"AAAAARGH!"* she roared, and slammed her own body onto Hans's sword.

The sword impaled her torso. The cold sensation of the blade slicing her organs rushed through her. Tensing the muscles of her back with all her strength, she held it fast within her body. As she did, she stretched out her legs and pushed back on the blade as hard as she could, with force equal to running full-speed. Any regular human would simply be skewered and die.

"Meowgh!"

Mora could hear a popping sound behind her. Using her powers to see, she could tell that was the sound of Hans's left wrist dislocating. The sword had plunged to its hilt within her. It slipped from Hans's grasp, and as it did, Mora whipped around to kick him in the face. He threw his upper body backward, and her kick just barely skimmed his forehead. Instantly, he stumbled. Just by grazing him, Mora's full-power kick had thrown him off balance. Hans rolled away and ran, and she immediately tossed off her iron gauntlets, going after him. She grabbed the hem of his clothes with her fingers and yanked him toward her as hard as she could.

"Lady Mora!" Rolonia cried.

Mora hit Hans in the chest with an open palm and heard his ribs crack. She flung his body to the ground hard enough for it to bounce. She had struck the left side of his chest, which would make a person's heart stop for a moment and knock them out. No amount of training could enable a human to prevent that.

Mora drew the sword out of her torso and leaned over Hans. Then she pressed the blade to his carotid artery and thrust.

"Hans! Rolonia! Where are you?!" Adlet ran through the night across the mountain. Fremy, Goldof, and the now-conscious Chamo followed behind him. The earlier sound of metal clashing against itself was now gone. Hans had been fighting until a moment ago. Then it was over.

They ran over the mountain, their light gems held high as they searched for Hans. Then Fremy yelled, "Adlet! Look at the back of your hand!"

"!" That was when Adlet noticed the Crest of the Six Flowers that marked his hand—one of the petals was gone. His legs went weak with fear. One of the Braves of the Six Flowers had lost their life. Someone had died—Hans, Rolonia, or Mora. "Hans! Rolonia! Are you dead?!" he yelled, even louder.

Her victory had been by a narrow margin. If Mora had failed to evade his strike at the vital point on her back, she would have been the one to fall. If they had fought ten fights, Hans would have probably won nine of them. He was that much more powerful than her.

The battle was over. Blood spurted from Hans's neck. Then its flow quickly reduced until it ceased completely. Mora put her hand on his chest. She felt no heartbeat.

"*Ahh...ahhh...*" Rolonia was moaning.

Mora stood. Her pierced organs screamed as blood dripped from her lips.

Rolonia approached Hans. Hands shaking, she touched his neck.

"Listen, Rolonia. Do just as I taught you," Mora said, staggering away from the two of them. She meant to leave them, but her feet got tangled up and she fell. She could hear Adlet's yells coming close. "Listen to me, Rolonia! Do just as I've taught you!" she repeated, rising to her feet again.

Then Adlet appeared, having climbed up the cliff. Mora, her back turned to him, said quietly, "You're too late, Adlet." Now it was all over. Mora's whole fight was over. The parasite should now be gone from Shenira's chest. Tgurneu would not break its promise, because there was no reason for it to.

Mora told them all that she had killed Hans. She also told them that she was the seventh. As she spoke, she kept her eyes steady on Rolonia as the girl treated Hans. Rolonia was so focused on healing him, it was as if she didn't even see what was going on around her.

"What's the meaning of this, Rolonia?" Adlet demanded. "Hans is dead, and you're not even scratched."

"You were with him. What were you doing?" Fremy demanded immediately after.

Rolonia didn't reply to either of them.

Good, thought Mora. She and Torleau, Saint of Medicine, had told Rolonia over and over to concentrate only on her work when using healing techniques.

Chamo approached Mora where she knelt and hit her with her tiny fists, yelling and punching, faint tears welling in her eyes. Mora was surprised that Chamo would get so upset over Hans. She hadn't realized the young Saint had been fond of him.

They'll kill me. Everything in front of her seemed very far away. Was this what it felt like to be on death's door? "This was not my desire. I did not wish to kill Hans. Not him, not anyone," she said. She meant it to be her final testament.

"What did you say?"

"There was nothing for me to do but kill him. Every avenue aside from his murder was closed to me." A single tear fell from her eye. "I wanted to protect the world. I wanted to defeat the fiends together with you, to stop the revival of the Evil God."

"Who could believe that?" snapped Chamo.

"Up until just yesterday—no, up until one hour ago—I had every intention of doing just that," Mora said, and instantly, Chamo grabbed her by the collar.

"Don't you lie!" she shouted, her eyes burning.

But Mora wasn't looking at her. She was focused only on Rolonia treating Hans. "You cannot just circulate his blood, Rolonia. It will quickly become impure. Return the blood that's drained from him."

"What're you talking about? Look at me, Auntie!" Chamo hit Mora's face, but the woman's eyes did not leave Rolonia.

"What are you doing, Rolonia? There isn't enough blood. Do you not understand? I thought I taught you this!"

The timid Saint finally reacted. "Y-yes, ma'am. The blood...Hans's blood..." Rolonia put one hand on the ground, and then focused her nerves.

"It's difficult to use two techniques simultaneously. But you, Rolonia—you should be capable of it now!"

With her hand on the blood-soaked earth, the healer took a few deep breaths.

"What're you doing, Rolonia? Look at me. I've got questions for you, too," demanded Chamo.

Fremy, watching beside her, spoke as well. "It's no use. His heart has stopped, and he's lost most of his blood."

"...I can't...do the wrist..." Rolonia muttered. As she focused all her concern on the techniques, the mumbled words sounded like delirious babbling.

"His wrist?" said Fremy. "What are you talking about?"

"His wrist is dislocated...and his ribs are broken...I can't heal that."

"What?"

Eyes still on the ground, Rolonia cried, "But the rest, I can heal!"

"Heal him? Don't be ridiculous!"

"I can! I know I can! I mean, it's just that his heart has stopped and he's bled too much!" As the girl spoke, her hands shone, sucking up the blood that had seeped into the earth. It pooled into a red sphere that enveloped Rolonia's hand.

"Don't return it like that!" Mora ordered. "Remove all the foreign matter!"

"Yes, ma'am!" The sphere undulated and spat out a dirty mixture of wet sand and mud. "Hans! Please, come back to us!" Rolonia cried. As the blood disappeared back into the wound at Hans's neck, his body, which had been deathly pale, began to be tinged with color. All the while, Rolonia was manipulating the small amount of blood that remained inside Hans's body. She circulated it between his lungs and brain while also managing the work of the cells themselves so that even with his heart stopped, his brain would not die.

Rolonia had assisted Torleau, Saint of Medicine with her surgeries many times. Through much practice, she had learned and perfected the technique of returning drained blood to the body. Mora had helped Rolonia with this by submitting herself as a subject for experiment.

"Next...if his heart can start again..." As Rolonia pressed her left hand on his wounded neck, she set her right hand on his heart. She was trying to move his stopped heart by controlling his blood. To train this skill, Mora had requested the help of an elderly person with only a few days left to live, working on them in the moments before death.

"It can't be... He's coming back?" Fremy gasped.

Once Hans's heart had stopped, the Spirit of Words would have ordered Tgurneu to make the parasite within Shenira die—and they could also tell by how the petal on the Crest had disappeared. The spirits had determined that Hans was dead, and Tgurneu had probably already released his hostage, as promised.

Mora had indeed promised that she would kill a Brave of the Six Flowers—but not that she wouldn't bring the Brave back to life.

The very moment Mora had met Rolonia, she'd thought this girl, with her rare talent, would perhaps be capable of even techniques to revive the dead. The most difficult part of this plan had been to kill Hans in such a way that he could still be revived afterward. Rolonia's power was only to control blood. If his neck or any bones in his head had been broken, or if his organs had been badly damaged, it wouldn't have been possible to revive him.

"Is there any way I can help, Rolonia?" Adlet understood now what she was doing. He sat down next to Hans.

"His breathing… I have to get him breathing again…"

"Leave it to me. Artificial respiration, right? I know some medical stuff." Sitting down beside Hans, Adlet blew air into his mouth. Rolonia maintained regular circulation as she stopped the gash in his neck from bleeding.

"No way," said Chamo. "He's coming back to life?" It was no wonder she couldn't believe it. Rolonia had to be the first Saint in history who had successfully brought the dead back to life. Even Torleau wasn't capable of this.

"*Guhhaaaa!*" Hans gasped. Blood spewed from his mouth. He clutched his chest and coughed over and over. Adlet wiped the blood from around his lips while Rolonia rubbed his back. When the coughing stopped, Hans put his hands over his neck and wailed. "*Meeeow! Meeeeeooooow! Hrmeoooow!*" He was panicking. No surprise there—he had been dead until just a moment ago.

"Adlet, show me your crest," said Mora.

He first checked it himself, then showed it to Mora. There were very clearly six petals on the flower.

So it was a success. Mora was relieved. She had walked a long tightrope of a battle. She couldn't have killed Fremy or Chamo. Fremy was half fiend, so she would differ biologically from a normal human. A resurrection almost certainly would not work on her. Dying and then coming back would also place great strain on the body, and Chamo's small frame probably wouldn't have been able to withstand it. Mora had been forced to kill Adlet, Hans, or Goldof.

"You planned to do this all along, didn't you?" Adlet said. "You needed to kill Hans for some reason, but at the same time, you couldn't have him die. Isn't that right?"

She nodded.

"What on earth happened to you?" he asked.

*   *   *

Mora informed them it would be a long story, so the whole group returned to the Bud of Eternity. Hans leaned on Adlet's shoulder, while Goldof kept Mora restrained.

"This doesn't make sense," Chamo muttered as she trailed behind the group. Adlet felt the same way.

Once they were at the Bud of Eternity, they tended to Hans first. Adlet snapped his dislocated wrist back in and set his broken ribs, and Rolonia encouraged his circulation to prevent any aftereffects. At the boy's instruction, Fremy treated Mora, though she seemed to have mixed feelings as she stitched her wounds and daubed medicine on her.

"Are you okay, Hans?" Adlet asked.

His expression bitter, Hans replied, "My whole body feels numb, and I can't meowve right."

Once Mora's wounds had been treated, she knelt on the ground, hands together behind her back.

Adlet said, "So, talk."

"Of course. There's no need to hide a thing now." Surrounded by the whole group, Mora dispassionately told them the truth—about her secret contract with Tgurneu, the reason she had trained Rolonia, and how it had come to be that she had to kill one of the Braves of the Six Flowers within the next two days—and finally, that she was the seventh.

Adlet quietly listened to Mora's story, and then he pulled from a pouch at his waist the thing that he had discovered at the hill, looking at it intently. *I see…so that was it*, he said to himself silently.

"…and that's all I know. I am prepared. Be done with it quickly." And with that, Mora concluded her long confession. For a while, nobody said anything.

Goldof was the first one to speak. "You…don't know anything about…the princess?"

Mora shook her head. "Tgurneu told me nothing of Nashetania. For my part, I had other concerns."

"I see. So Her Highness…" Goldof started to say something and then stopped. Then he fell silent again.

"I dunno about this now. I was gonna kill you, but now I kinda feel sorry for you," said Chamo.

"Are you going to kill Lady Mora?" Rolonia asked. "But she didn't have a choice. Her daughter was taken hostage, and Hans did get properly revived."

"*Meow...*I've kinda got mixed feelin's about this." Hans, unusually for him, seemed angry.

"You made your own decision to fight alone, and you lost. You reap what you sow," Fremy said coldly.

Then Mora said, "Rolonia. 'Twould be naive not to kill me."

"Lady Mora..."

"There was no guarantee that he would return after his death. And even if the revival was a success, he could have been severely disabled. I killed Hans, even knowing that."

Rolonia was silent.

"No matter the result, I betrayed you. I must take responsibility. Moreover...I have no wish to live on so shamelessly as the traitor to the world."

"Well, I guess we hafta, then. Though it's too bad." Chamo scratched her head.

"We can't trust everything Mora's said," said Fremy. "We really should kill her."

"But...," Rolonia protested.

As the discussion persisted, Adlet opened his mouth. "Hmm... I wonder where I should start?"

"What's wrong? Actually, you've hardly done anything tonight, have you?" Chamo scoffed.

Adlet ignored her. "I guess I'll just start by getting to the point. Guys, calm down and listen."

"...?" The present crowd seemed puzzled.

Quietly, but also with conviction, Adlet said, "Mora is not the seventh."

*   *   *

As he'd expected, all six of them gaped in speechless astonishment.

The first to counter him was Mora. "What are you talking about, Adlet? The evidence that I'm the seventh is all there. Tgurneu threatened me into killing one of your allies."

"Weren't you listening?" said Fremy. "Mora admitted that she's the seventh."

"Addy… I'm sorry, but that's just ridiculous." Even Rolonia agreed. The others didn't believe him at all.

Explaining this is gonna be rough, he thought. "First of all, Mora hasn't betrayed us, has she? She did her utmost to make sure none of us would have to die. She did everything she could to try to kill Tgurneu. She wants to defeat the Evil God and save the world. There's no way she could be a traitor."

"True," said Fremy. "She's not a traitor—but she is the seventh."

"You have no proof," Adlet insisted. Fremy's eyes widened. "How was the seventh crest created? How was the seventh chosen? We don't have any of the facts. Calm down and think about it. In the end, the only evidence we have that Mora is the seventh is that Tgurneu said so. That's all."

"But that evidence is everything," said Mora. "Tgurneu will never lie to me."

Adlet said, "The very idea that Tgurneu won't lie to you is the trap."

"What do you mean?" asked Mora.

"Tgurneu's goal was clearly to make you kill a Brave. It was positive you'd never abandon your daughter. But beneath that, it laid another trap—one to make you believe that you were the seventh."

What he was saying made Mora hold her breath.

"All of us already considered the idea of falsely accusing a real Brave to make everyone else think they're the seventh. But what we didn't even think to consider was that you could trick a real Brave into thinking that *they themselves* had the fake Crest. Nobody would doubt someone calling themselves the seventh, right? Tgurneu's a real piece of work. I almost wanna compliment that fiend for it. Nice job." Adlet smiled. "Mora, from what you've said, though Tgurneu swore to the Saint of Words, it's not like it can't lie at all anymore, right? And all the Saint of Words can do is make any liar pay the predetermined price."

Mora nodded.

"It's so simple, it's ridiculous. Three years ago, Tgurneu swore to the Saint of Words that it wouldn't lie. On the surface, that was to get you to be willing to sit down and negotiate. But the other goal was to make you think it couldn't lie."

"..."

"You believed that Tgurneu wouldn't lie under any circumstances. And then it told you, falsely, that you're the seventh. So you mistakenly believed it—just like Tgurneu wanted. Simple, huh?"

"Wait. Do you think that I didn't doubt Tgurneu? I also considered that Tgurneu could be lying. But the power of the Saint of Words is absolute. None can escape from it. Even the Saint of Words herself cannot nullify the contract."

"Are you saying that even the power of the Saint of Words doesn't work on Tgurneu?" said Fremy. "That's impossible. If that were true, it would mean that Tgurneu really is immortal."

"There's no such thing as immortality," countered Adlet, "and if there is, then it's only the Evil God. I don't know much about the Saint's power, but it's probably impossible to cancel out the Saint of Words."

"So what is it, then? You can't mean to say that Tgurneu died in order to tell that lie?"

"..." Adlet considered a bit, thinking about how he should explain things. "You said that after Tgurneu declared that Mora was the seventh, a jellyfish-fiend sucked it up. That wasn't in order to escape—that was in order to hide that Tgurneu had died. It died in exchange for that lie, just as it had promised the Saint of Words."

"That's impossible," said Mora. "Tgurneu is one of the commanders of the fiends. If it died, then all its minions would lose their chain of command and turn into a disorderly mob. Such a creature wouldn't die for the sake of a single lie."

"Tgurneu isn't dead," agreed Fremy. "Its death would cause chaos among its subordinates. I know it is alive."

"Calm down. I'll explain in full," said Adlet, and then he paused. He organized everything in his head, wondering where to start. "The three-winged lizard-fiend we fought—the fiend that we recognized to be Tgurneu—was not Tgurneu."

"What do you mean?" asked Fremy.

"When we were on that hill, I figured out what Tgurneu really is. Let me explain. We—me, you, and Rolonia—spent the whole day talking about Tgurneu's mystery."

"We did."

"We used all the brains and powers we had at our disposal to try to figure out why the Saint's Spike didn't work. The conclusion we reached was that Tgurneu couldn't have blocked the Saint's poison with its own power." Adlet outlined Rolonia's analysis and how Tgurneu lacked anything to make it immune. "So that means that another fiend, or a Saint, was helping Tgurneu. But then, what kind of power could nullify the Saint's poison? Some detoxification power? The power to die in his place? Even though I've inherited all of Atreau Spiker's knowledge, and Fremy was one of the fiends herself, no matter how much we racked our brains, we couldn't come up with any fiends that had powers like that."

"So then...?"

"Then a Saint? Couldn't be that, either. We went to the hill where Tgurneu first attacked us and searched underground, but there was no trace of any humans. No Saint helped. At this point, I was at the end of my rope. For a minute, I was about to give up."

"We don't need to hear ya gibber on about *meow* hard it was. Just get to the point," said Hans.

"It was what Goldof did, just by chance, that gave me the big hint." Adlet told them about how Goldof had tortured the fiend in the tunnel.

"There was one thing it said that bothered me: *If I had Commander Tgurneu's power, you trash would be nothing.*"

"What's so odd about that?" asked Fremy.

"Don't you think that's a weird way to put it? Shouldn't it be, 'If Commander Tgurneu were here'? Why did that fiend choose to say, 'If I had'? What it said led me to a hypothesis—that Tgurneu has the ability to give other fiends power."

"I've never heard of an ability like that," Fremy replied.

"We know of one other fiend that had the ability to give power to other fiends—the strongest fiend that ever lived, the one that was there at the Battle of the Six Flowers seven hundred years ago: Archfiend Zophrair. You've all heard of it, at least." All of them, excepting Fremy, nodded. "Zophrair was called a controller-type fiend. Its ability was to amplify the powers of other fiends by giving them a part of its flesh. By doing that, it could take complete control of the fiend and make its body do whatever Zophrair wanted."

"Yes, I do seem to remember reading something like that, but...," said Mora.

"That's when I realized the controller-type power could negate the Saints' blood."

"Wh-what do you mean?" asked Rolonia.

"Recall how the Saint's poison affects a fiend's body. First, it becomes deranged and overcome with pain. A fiend that's been affected will writhe in agony, unable to think straight. Next, it'll lose its sense of balance. Then it won't be able to move. Finally, it begins to experience visual and auditory hallucinations, and then memory loss, and within five to ten days, it's dead. In other words, the effects are like nerve toxin on a human. The poison destroys the brain and the motor center."

Fremy lifted her head as if she'd just realized something.

Adlet continued. "But what if the poisoned fiend was under a controller-type fiend? What if it wasn't moving under its own will, but was in fact a puppet? On the surface, it'd look like the Saint's poison hadn't worked, right?"

"You can't mean…" Fremy trailed off.

"Tgurneu—or the three-winged fiend we thought was Tgurneu—was being used by a controller-type fiend. Tgurneu is the one manipulating the body of the three-winged fiend."

"This so sudden, it's hard to believe, though, *meow*." Hans tilted his head.

"Wait," said Fremy. "Do you even have any proof of that? If that three-winged fiend isn't actually Tgurneu, then where was the real one? I've believed that was Tgurneu all this time. And when I think back, I just can't believe that there was another fiend behind that one."

"Of course you wouldn't have realized," said Adlet. "Tgurneu was always planning to get rid of you, so it made sure you wouldn't know what it really was."

"What is it, then? What is the real Tgurneu?" she pressed.

Adlet scanned the faces around him. It seemed the three who'd gone to the hill with him—Hans, Rolonia and Goldof—already understood. "Look at this." He pulled a tiny, sand-covered object from a pouch at his waist. This was what the four of them had been searching for on the hill where they'd been attacked, the thing Goldof had stumbled upon.

"What's that piece of trash?" asked Fremy.

"*Meow*, so that's what it was. I can't believe it. When ya told us to look fer this thing, I thought you'd gone crazy," said Hans.

"This is a piece of the fig that Tgurneu was eating." Adlet recalled when they had been fighting Tgurneu, and suddenly, the fiend had pulled out this fig and eaten it. At the time, he had seen a tiny piece fall from the corner of its mouth. "Fremy, do you remember when we explained what the controller does to take over other fiends?"

"I do."

"This kind of fiend exercises its power by giving a part of its flesh to another. Basically, it makes the other eat part of its body."

"No…"

"This isn't just a fig. It's a fiend," said Adlet, and from a pouch at his waist, he pulled out the solution that reacted to fiend excretions. When he sprayed the fragment, it turned orange. "The fig that three-winged fiend had—*that* was the real Tgurneu."

"This is unbelievable," said Mora.

"Do you remember, Mora," said Adlet, "when you were negotiating with Tgurneu, was it eating a fig like this?"

"I'm sorry. I truly cannot recall. I get the feeling it was, though."

"Fremy," Adlet said, addressing her next, "the times you spoke with Tgurneu, did it ever eat figs like this?"

"I remember quite clearly that it often ate them, but I'd never taken notice of it."

Satisfied by her response, he nodded. "Tgurneu made sure to hide its true nature from you. It pretended to just naturally have a big appetite in order to avoid drawing attention to all those figs. And Tgurneu didn't tell you about the Archfiend Zophrair so that you wouldn't know that such an ability existed."

"…That would explain it, but…" Fremy trailed off.

"Those of you who fought Tgurneu with me must remember," said Adlet. "It randomly pulled a fig out of the mouth on its chest and ate it, right? Then after that, it suddenly became more powerful. That wasn't because it stopped going easy on us. That was because of the power of the controller-type to strengthen other fiends." He examined the sand-covered piece of fig in his hand. "I was surprised, too. I thought all fiends were big—at least as big as humans—and scary. But fundamentally speaking, they can take any shape. It shouldn't be surprising at all that there's such a thing as a fig-fiend."

"Is that really the answer, then?" asked Fremy.

"I can't guarantee for sure that I'm right. And I can't deny the possibility that there's some fiend out there we don't know about with powers we've never heard of. But based off all the clues we've gathered so far, this conclusion seems to fit." Adlet turned his attention to Mora. "Now that I've explained all this, you get just how Tgurneu tricked you, I hope?"

"I do." Three years ago, Tgurneu had sworn to Mora, *If I lie, then may this core be shattered.* But that core had not been Tgurneu's—it had been the core of the three-winged fiend.

"The lizard was just a tool being controlled by the real Tgurneu, who saw it as a disposable pawn. From the moment it swore that oath to the Saint of Words, it planned to break its promise."

Mora was struck dumb. Apparently she could hardly keep up with the swift turn of events.

Adlet said to the group, "Do I have to explain the rest of why Mora is not the seventh? Tgurneu lied to Mora to make her believe she's the seventh. He tried to trick her. So there's no way she could be the seventh."

"Okay, okay, we get it, you don't have to spell out every little thing," Chamo pouted.

"I'm…not the seventh?" Mora was still on her knees, dazed. "I'm…I…am a real Brave of the Six Flowers? It…wasn't a lie? I cannot believe it."

"Whether you believe it or not, I'm sure you are," said Adlet, and he extended a hand to her. "Come on, pull yourself together. It's not just your daughter you have to save—you've gotta save the world."

Mora took his hand.

It had been half coincidence that had enabled Adlet to figure out Tgurneu's trap. If he had failed to notice that Tgurneu's body concealed a secret, or had given up trying to solve the mystery, then he probably wouldn't have figured out the truth. He wouldn't have realized that Mora was a real Brave, and he probably would have let her die. But even if it was only by sheer coincidence, a win was a win.

Meanwhile, a crowd was gathering in the infirmary of All Heavens Temple. It included Mora's husband, Ganna Chester; Mora's elderly mother and father; Willone, Saint of Salt; Marmanna, Saint of Words; Liennril, Saint of Fire; administrators who worked at All Heavens Temple; acolytes who had rushed there from the Temple of Mountains; and Mora's personal maids. The too-small waiting room of the infirmary couldn't contain them, and they filled the hallway as well.

"Not yet? Damn it!" Willone, Saint of Salt, muttered in irritation.

"Mora…I believe in you." In one corner of the room, Ganna was looking down, arms folded.

About thirty minutes earlier, Shenira had complained of slight pain in her chest. When her father had taken a look, he found that the centipede-like mark had disappeared from her skin. Had the parasite died, or was this a portent of strange things to come? Since Ganna didn't know, he had immediately summoned Torleau. Willone and the people of All Heavens Temple had all rushed over at once.

Torleau emerged from the examination room. All eyes gathered on her. She strode straight to Ganna—then took his hand and gave it a firm shake. "The parasite is gone. Shenira is saved."

"You did it, boss!" Willone cried, and she raised a fist high. She ran up to Torleau and squeezed her tightly.

The array of people crowded around them cheered, all shaking hands and embracing one another. Some of them even hopped onto the tables, whipped off their jackets, and whirled them around.

"How do you like that, you stinking fiend?! This is what our boss is made of!" Willone pulled away from Torleau to hug anyone and everyone available, her inhuman strength raising a few yelps here and there.

"Are things really okay? She couldn't have killed one of the Braves, I'm sure," Marmanna said in an indifferent tone.

"No way!" Willone retorted. "The boss obviously slaughtered that big stupid bastard!"

Torleau's assistant emerged from the examination room, bringing out Shenira. The tiny girl was frightened of the uproar going on in the waiting room, but Ganna went to her and scooped her into his arms, and then, as if everything he had been holding back now overflowed, he wept.

"All right, time for some booze! If this isn't a drink-worthy night, what is?! I'll break out my secret stash!" Willone wrapped an arm around Marmanna's shoulders.

"You're jumping the gun," replied the Saint of Words. "It's not like they've defeated the Evil God yet."

"We're just having an advance celebration, come on! Fortune be to the Braves of the Six Flowers! Fortune in battle to all of them! Boss,

Rolonia, Chamo, Princess, Goldof, and...um...what was his name? Oh yeah, the Cowardly Warrior Adlet!"

There was no way for any of them to know that Shenira had been saved not because Tgurneu had been killed. It was because Tgurneu had promised to free her if it lied.

They didn't know about the battle raging in the Howling Vilelands, either. Hans had only told a limited few that he had been chosen as a Brave of the Six Flowers, and Fremy was a name totally unknown to all of them.

The eastern sky slowly became tinged with red. It was their first morning in the Howling Vilelands. Adlet, on watch, lost himself for a moment in the glow of the sunrise. They had decided to stay at the Bud of Eternity until Hans and Mora had healed. The two would probably be able to move around again by evening. It was a good thing they had two Saints with healing abilities in their party—they wouldn't have to be concerned over most injuries.

The Bud of Eternity and the mountain around it were quiet. There was no sight of any fiends or of Tgurneu. Aside from the lookout, all of them were resting in their preferred ways.

"Listen, Adlet...," began Mora. "Should I really be continuing this journey with you?"

He didn't reply.

Mora brooded. She wasn't particularly glad to have survived, and now her happiness at having saved her daughter's life was forgotten. The enemy had tricked her into killing one of their allies, with full knowledge of the possibility that he could not be saved afterward.

"Auntie, I thought for sure that this time, I couldn't forgive you." The one who replied instead was Chamo. "Just how many times do you gotta get tricked? Are you serious about this? Do you *like* getting tricked?"

She's really letting Mora have it, the boy mused.

Mora looked at the ground, downcast.

"Hans, I want to hear what you think," said Adlet. He was the one they should be prioritizing, given he was the greatest victim.

"Well...I get that she's still got to come with us...but I ain't all that happy about it."

No surprise there, thought Adlet.

"Once this battle is over," said Mora, "kill me. You can be certain I'll pay for what I've done."

"Neow what good'd that do me?" Hans put a hand to his mouth and gave her a nasty smile. "What else could I want? Cash. All Heavens Temple is rich, right? I'll clean yer treasure house out all the way to the back. *Meow-hee-hee-hee-hee!*"

"And that's all you want?" Adlet asked him, without thinking.

"Meowney is important. I was born to have a fun, exciting life. None of that happens if you ain't got the coin."

Mora nodded. *Well, if that's enough for him.*

Then the look on Hans's face suddenly turned serious, and he said, "Mora, I ain't gonna let ya blow this again. You gotta take out the Evil God—even if it means yer life. You better understand that's the only reason yer head's still on yer shoulders."

"Understood," said Mora. "We will win. I'll protect the world, even if it means my life."

Hans seemed to be done saying what it was he wanted to say.

Adlet looked at Rolonia. In a way, she had also been a victim.

"Lady Mora..." She hesitated. Rolonia had surely trusted Mora. Adlet couldn't imagine how she must have felt upon finding out the real reason that Mora had raised her—purely for the sake of her plot to kill one of the Six Braves. "I don't feel like I can forgive you, but I also feel like you had no choice for Shenira's sake...I don't know what do to."

Mora didn't respond. She just kept her head lowered.

"Just one thing...," Rolonia said finally. "Thank you very much for training me."

"I'm sorry, Rolonia. And thank you. Truly, thank you." Their eyes never met. They still hadn't sorted out their feelings.

"This is a sudden change of topic, but ya don't mind, do ya, *meow*?"

"What is it, Hans?" asked Adlet.

Completely ignoring the heavy atmosphere, the assassin brightly asked, "When I died, what happened to the crests?"

"Oh!" The youngest piped up. "Chamo saw it. A petal disappeared from Adlet's crest."

"Ain't that proof that I'm the real deal?" said Hans. "I mean, if a Brave of the Six Flowers dies, then one of the petals disappears, right?"

"S'pose so. So can we say that you're the real thing, then, catboy?" Chamo tilted her head.

"That doesn't prove anything," said Fremy. "A petal might disappear when the seventh dies, just as it does with a real Brave. We don't know anything about the extra crest."

"*Meow...*"

"If one of us dies and no petals disappear," Fremy continued, "then we can be sure that person was the seventh. But a petal disappearing when someone dies doesn't prove that person is the real thing. Sorry, but we can't state with certainty that you're a real Brave."

"*Meow.* This is difficult. It's makin' my head all itchy."

"The seventh, huh?" Adlet muttered. He gave his allies, who were chatting to one another, a hard look. In his head, a doubt was forming.

Tgurneu had made Mora, a real Brave, believe that she was the seventh. Perhaps the opposite was also possible—to make the seventh believe that they were a Brave. That could be a part of Tgurneu's machinations. The impostor had done nothing in either the battle of the Phantasmal Barrier or their battle in the Ravine of Spitten Blood despite numerous chances to kill the Braves of the Six Flowers. Maybe they didn't even know that they were the impostor.

So then, what on earth was the seventh? The battle was over, but they had still found no clues as to the greatest enigma: the question of the false Brave's identity. The situation had grown even more chaotic while the mystery had deepened further.

In the west, beyond the mountain, there was an expanse of deep forest. This was the land where the Saint of the Single Flower had once lost a finger on her left hand, giving this area the name the Cut-Finger Forest. There were about thirty fiends gathered there, and in the center of the group a fiend read a book. It had a massive yeti body and a crow's neck.

"This body is hard to move around. I'll search for something better soon," it muttered. On the creature's lap, there was a fig. "Hey. Morning," the yeti called to the sky.

A bird-shaped fiend flew down from the sky, landed on the yeti's shoulder, and told it something. The yeti closed its book and seemed to think for a while. "Your report is difficult to believe. All seven of them are still alive?" it said, picking up the fig in its lap and biting into it. "So did Mora fail? She didn't kill anyone?"

"No, Commander Tgurneu. Mora killed Hans. But then afterward, Rolonia brought him back to life."

"She got me!" The yeti-fiend—Tgurneu's new body—smacked its knee. "I see. So this was the reason she took in Rolonia. To kill him once and then revive him…what an idea. At the very last moment, Mora got me." Tgurneu stood and began to walk around.

"It seems they've also realized that Mora is not the seventh."

"I wonder who figured that out. Fremy? No…probably Adlet." The fiend Tgurneu looked deep into the forest. A few of its subordinates were burying something deep in the ground—the body of the three-winged fiend that Adlet's party had fought. "Total failure," it said. "Such utter defeat in both stages of my scheme could be called nothing else. I shall graciously praise their efforts." The fiend didn't seem anxious in the least, and neither was it angry nor behaving with any sense of urgency, now that its plan had been foiled. On the contrary, it seemed as if it was pleased at the victory of the Braves. "Oh, well. Let's begin the next game. It's best to forget what's done."

"Your orders, Commander Tgurneu?" asked the bird-fiend.

Smiling, Tgurneu said, "Tell the seventh not to do anything at the moment. The identity of our impostor should remain concealed." The bird-fiend spread its wings and disappeared into the east. As the devious commander watched the bird go, it muttered, "Now then, how will I play with them next? The Braves of the Six Flowers will entertain me yet."

Epilogue

Those
Who Lead

Along the northwestern fringe of the Howling Vilelands, there was a fort. The building was crude and primitive, a simple stack of unhewn rock. But it was as large and sturdy as any of the forts on the continent. Atop the rampart there stood a lion. This fiend walked on two legs, wore silver armor, and sported a silver mane. It leaned on a crude sword, a simple slab of obsidian, jabbed into the rock beneath it.

"Commànder Cargikk." A human-sized butterfly-fiend swooped down to land, speaking to the lion—Cargikk, one of the three commanders and the fiend famed as the most powerful alive. "The Braves of the Six Flowers had an éncounter with Tgurneu. This first battle was a victory for the Braves. Tgurneu lost over two hündred followers and fled."

"Your report is needless," said Cargikk. "Only report to me if Tgurneu dies or manages to kill any of the Braves."

"Ünderstood." Lacking a neck, the messenger bowed its antenna.

Cargikk looked toward the eastern sky, where the morning sun was rising, with an expression of displeasure. "I expect nothing from Tgurneu. Failure is inevitable."

"...Indeëd so."

"Battle is a clash of souls. You squander your life, carry death by your side as a matter of course, and challenge your foes with a mind void of any other thoughts. *That* is how victory is won." As Cargikk gazed up at the eastern sky, there was anger in its eyes. Red-black steam spurted from its mouth, and a faint haze rose from its entire body. "Tgurneu schemes away in order to ensure only his own survival as he attempts to scrape together the tiniest of victories. His acts are no different from those of a common sneak!" The scattering sparks singed the scales of the butterfly-fiend. Still looking to the east, Cargikk continued. "No—Tgurneu holds his own life so very dear, but he calmly tosses away the lives of his brethren. He's an ignoble sort even lower than a sneak! I should have killed him on that day two hundred years ago!" The commander's anger was not directed at the Braves of the Six Flowers—but at Tgurneu, who fought on the same side as Cargikk.

"We are the ones who will kill the Braves of the Six Flowers—I and my beloved children. It will not be Tgurneu," Cargikk said and continued to watch the eastern sky.

On the northern edge of the Howling Vilelands, a few fiends surveyed the sea.

Rocks as sharp as spears jutted out from the shoals everywhere, spewing steam at several-hundred-degree temperatures. This was the protective bulwark the fiends had built over the course of centuries. It would be impossible for even a swimming human to draw near, never mind an entire boat.

The fiends were searching for something in that sea through the shroud of hot steam.

"Over there!" One of the fiends picked out something that looked like a human drifting in the water. The creature was extremely small, about the size of a small dog. It had a soft coat, round eyes, big ears and a big tail. It was a curious creature, neither quite squirrel nor rat nor dog. The horn that grew from its head was less frightening than it was adorable.

This little creature called out to the shape on the water. "Nashetania! Over here! Please go on about fifteen meters to the right, and then come in straight to land!"

The shape—Nashetania—sluggishly moved her arms and legs and

began to swim. She had thrown away her armor, sword, and shoes, and was swimming slowly in her underclothes. A part of one of the stone pillars vented not searing steam but just warm vapor. The girl weaved in through that gap and made it to shore.

"Are you all right, Nashetania?" The cute fiend ran up to the half-naked Nashetania, and its companions wrapped her in a blanket.

"Dozzu." Nashetania called the fiend's name. That adorable fiend was, in fact, one of the three commanders: the rebel, Dozzu. "I'm sorry, I lost. Forget killing them all—I couldn't even take out one."

"I know," said Dozzu. "But let's leave that aside. Please, dry yourself off now. Once you're settled, we'll head to my hideout. This area is dangerous—Cargikk's followers have their eyes here."

The fiends lifted Nashetania in their arms and headed away from the coast and to the forest. Dozzu took the lead, alert to their surroundings as they proceeded.

She coughed violently, and her chilled body was trembling. "How did things go with you?"

"The negotiations failed. Cargikk didn't even listen to what I had to say."

"…" Nashetania looked down. "Is this the end for us?"

When Dozzu heard that, it stopped. It planted its short legs firmly in front of Nashetania. "What are you talking about? Say that one more time, please?"

"But Dozzu—"

Pale sparks flew from Dozzu's whole body. The electrical discharge fried the grass around the fiend. "You're going to give up now? Are you forgetting the hopes of all of our comrades who have sacrificed themselves for our ideals? What are your excuses for our fallen comrades on the other side?!"

"…I'm sorry. You're right. We're not done yet."

Dozzu closed its eyes, and then as if to say, *Good*, it nodded. "You've got it. Let's hurry to my hideout. I've prepared a hot meal and clothing for you."

The group made their way through the forest carefully, so as not to make a sound.

"Tgurneu is sure to hatch some scheme," said Nashetania. "And I doubt the Six Braves will go down easy, either. If we can take advantage of their fights and find the right opportunity, the path will open."

"That's the spirit. Come on, have some hope," Dozzu said with determination as they moved along. "Cargikk's faction will not be the winners—and of course, neither will the Six Braves. We will win. The world is wishing for our victory," said Dozzu, and Nashetania nodded quietly. "Our hands will be the ones to remake this world."

Dozzu, Nashetania, and the fiends that escorted them disappeared into the forest.

Good night.

AFTERWORD

It's been a long time since the last book. Ishio Yamagata speaking. How was *Rokka: Braves of the Six Flowers*, Volume 2? I hope you enjoyed it.

Right now, the *Rokka* manga adaptation is being serialized in the newly launched bimonthly magazine, *Super Dash & Go!* The artist is Kei Toru-san. His artwork is so beautiful, and I always look forward to seeing his drafts. I hope you all enjoy it, too. Toru-san, I'm looking forward to continuing to work with you in the future, as well.

I suppose I'll report on my current state of affairs. Not that I have anything in particular to write about, though.

I've noticed something recently. I have the habit of clenching my teeth whenever I write fight scenes, so by the time I'm nearing the latter half of the story, my jaw always starts to hurt. When I was writing the last volume of my previous series, *Tatakau Shisho* ("Fighting Librarians"), it got really bad. The dentist taught me some jaw exercises, though, so it's gotten a little better. I think, moving forward, Adlet and the team will be doing quite a lot of fighting, so I'm worried that I'm going to be stuck with this. I've been considering buying a mouthguard or something, but would that even work?

I went to visit my grandparents' graves. I was surprised to see that graveyards these days are so bright and pretty. There was also a considerable variety of unique gravestones. The place didn't feel eerie at all—it was baffling. I was like, *Is this a real graveyard?* Having it be so fancy must make it difficult for the ghosts to come haunting and transforming. If you saw a ghost orb, it'd just look like a part of the light display. Maybe we should be a bit more considerate of those who have to use the graveyard.

The other day, I bought a flask online for warming sake in the microwave. It was a great buy. The whole thing is rounded, and there's a shield in the upper part of the flask that blocks microwave radiation. This makes convection occur when you're heating, so you don't get sake that's hot on top while the bottom is still cold. And not only does it make the process easy, the taste of warm sake from this exceptional item is almost indistinguishable from sake heated from a flask in hot water.

In winter, there's nothing I look forward to more than mixing some grated daikon with shredded Japanese pickled plum, sprinkling on some shredded seaweed and bonito flakes, and then drizzling some soy sauce on top for a snack while I slowly sip away at my hot sake.

That concludes my report on my current state of affairs.

And finally, the acknowledgments.

To my illustrator, Miyagi-san, thank you for your wonderful illustrations in this volume, too. It was also very helpful of you to point out those unclear items.

To my editor, T-san, thank you very much for all the various ways you've cooperated with me. To everyone in the editorial department, thank you for all your support.

And finally, to all my readers, I hope to see you again.

Best,

ISHIO YAMAGATA